BLOOD SUBSTITUTE

Previous Titles in this series by Margaret Duffy

A HANGING MATTER
DEAD TROUBLE
SO HORRIBLE A PLACE
TAINTED GROUND *
COBWEB *

* *available from Severn House*

BLOOD SUBSTITUTE

A Patrick Gillard and Ingrid Langley Mystery

Margaret Duffy

This first world edition published 2008
in Great Britain and the USA by
SEVERN HOUSE PUBLISHERS LTD of
9–15 High Street, Sutton, Surrey, England, SM1 1DF.

Copyright © 2008 by Margaret Duffy.

British Library Cataloguing in Publication Data

Duffy, Margaret
  Blood substitute
  1. Gillard, Patrick (Fictitious character) - Fiction
  2. Langley, Ingrid (Fictitious character) - Fiction
  3. Women novelists - Fiction 4. Detective and mystery
  stories
  I. Title
  823.9'14[F]

ISBN-13: 978-0-7278-6688-2   (cased)

All Severn House titles are printed on acid-free paper.

Printed and bound in Great Britain by
MPG Books Ltd., Bodmin, Cornwall.

One

Detective Chief Inspector James Carrick stood in the driving rain, hands on his knees, blood dripping from his mouth on to the wet grass. The cut to his lip, not the reason for his stillness, would require several stitches, an assessment I had just made after looking at him through my binoculars. Having scored a try a few minutes previously – his police team, the Ferrets, were winning by some margin and the game was well into the second half – he had nothing to be ashamed of by coming off to have the injury attended to. But he appeared reluctant to give up nevertheless, even though also slightly stunned from the crashing, illegal tackle he had just endured, resulting in his head colliding with someone's boot. But the substitute was already running on to the field and the spectators cheered as the casualty, a little unsteady on his feet, was escorted off. A penalty was awarded to his team.

'I never thought he'd get back to the standard of fitness required to play again,' said the person on my right: Patrick, my husband. 'Or fully recover from being shot, for that matter.'

I thought that Carrick, a friend of ours, could well have been inspired by Patrick himself, who was badly injured when he was an army officer with Special Services. Having subsequently worked for D12, a department of MI5 where we both worked, he then resigned his commission and is now, as he puts it, 'helping SOCA with their enquiries', with his wife acting as 'consultant'. It appeared, when I first agreed to assist, that this novelist acquiring valuable material and ideas for her books, as a by-product, so to speak, would merely be on the end of a phone to offer advice and support. In reality my role is usually more along the lines of passing the ordnance.

SOCA, the Serious and Organized Crime Agency, is an amalgamation of the National Crime Squad, the National Criminal Intelligence Service and the investigations divisions of H.M. Customs and the Immigration Service. The organization appears to value Patrick's experience and expertise garnered during his army and MI5 days, although someone did once remark that his main value lay in an ability 'to get the opposition shit-scared'.

Right now though we were in Somerset on holiday – or at least visiting Patrick's parents over an extended weekend.

The wind increased, the rain battered down harder and began to seep through the hood and shoulders of my anorak, but we stuck it out. Carrick, his lip neatly hemmed, returned to the field for the final ten minutes of the game and then it was all over, his team winning by twenty-three points to ten.

'A pub; beer,' Patrick said succinctly as we made our way out of the Bath ground.

I had been rather hoping for a hot cup of tea and something home-made, squidgy and loaded with calories in Sally Lunn's.

'We *are* going out to eat tonight,' I was reminded when I had voiced this wish.

'I shall be dead of cold and starvation long before then,' I promised mulishly.

In the end we compromised and went to a city-centre hotel where it was possible to accommodate both preferences. Patrick gave James time to have his bath, sing rude songs with his team-mates – or whatever rugby players do these days – before he rang him with our congratulations on his performance and commiserations for the cut lip, this being the first time the DCI had taken the field since stopping a bullet in the chest during an investigation the previous year. James had almost died.

'He would like to have a chat with us about something when we're not on holiday,' Patrick reported when he had rung off.

'But if he wants to talk face to face then it's easier while we're here than for anyone to have to make special trips,' I pointed out. We live on Dartmoor; Patrick works mostly in London.

'Yes, I know. It's just that he's aware that we're here this weekend because it's our wedding anniversary today and we're going out to dinner with Mum and Dad.'

'Why don't you ask him and Joanna to have a meal with us somewhere on Monday?'

'I rather got the impression this problem of his doesn't involve Joanna.'

'So it's work?'

'And private – I *think*. He didn't go into details, probably because he wasn't alone.'

Patrick and I have been married twice – to each other, that is – the first time when we were in our early twenties after falling in love when we were in our teens. Although I did not disgrace myself at school I am sure that if I am remembered at all it is not for anything of a scholarly or sporting nature but that I nabbed the Head Boy. Patrick was pretty heady stuff even then and the main reason the marriage failed was that neither of us had had time to find out what the other was really like, being too busy – with our careers, having a good time and, frankly, in bed. When I recollect the household climate at the time it seems a miracle that we remained together for so long. But perhaps 'together' is the wrong word, for Patrick was away a lot with his regiment; too much to do, too many places to see, the whole world waiting to be explored. Eventual difficulties between us meant he cultivated an insufferably superior manner when we were in one another's company while the up-and-coming writer secretly went on the pill because she did not yet want children. He did, he found out and there was one terrible last row during which I threw his classical guitar down the stairs, smashing it. Then I threw him out too: it was our first home but paid for entirely with money my father had left me in his will and royalties from my books. Eventually we were divorced.

Patrick, then the second-youngest major in the British

Army, was in the Falklands when the divorce papers came through and, leading a small undercover unit, was involved in an accident with a grenade that seriously injured his legs. Now, the lower part of his right leg is of man-made construction, just about the best in the world, thereby costing a small fortune and I was glad to atone for my previous bad temper by helping him pay for it. Before then, however, he had arrived on my doorstep, limping heavily, with an offer of a job working with him for MI5 – a strictly platonic arrangement, he had stressed – this his own idea because there had been other serious injuries that meant he had completely lost confidence where women were concerned. He thought I was the last female on the planet who would want to sleep with him. What I had known, even as he spoke, was that here was a man making a silent plea to me to take him back. Perhaps I had day-dreamed of him eventually turning up on my doorstep like a whipped cur and of sending him away again, but as with lost kittens, dogs with thorns in their paws – even worms drowning in puddles – I could not just walk away. Feminist friends' lips curled when I lamely explained the situation by saying that he needed me. Very lonely, feeling dreadfully guilty about the way I had treated him and not very good at wrestling with things like cars going wrong and coping with Dartmoor in winter, in truth I probably needed him far more.

Human nature being what it is we soon tossed the platonic stipulation out of the window. But I had found myself back with a man vastly changed. Gone was the supercilious manner, and here again was the boy I had met at school, but now someone who had discovered that he was not immortal. Probably a lot more mature myself by this time – and having to be after accepting the job offer and thus putting my name down for nightmarish MI5 training sessions – I did not hesitate when he proposed to me a second time. I suppose I had fallen in love all over again. The date of that ceremony in an insufferably hot registrar's office somewhere in a back street of Kensington was not the one we would be celebrating this evening but rather the first, a church wedding at Hinton Littlemoor in Somerset where Patrick's father John is still rector. For, as John himself once said, 'Divorce is only a piece of paper.'

Despite Patrick's injuries, which had led him to be told that he probably could not father children, we went on to have Justin, who is now six, and then Victoria, a toddler. Then, when Patrick's brother Larry was killed we adopted his two; Matthew, now thirteen, and Katie, who is ten. That meant converting the barn on the other side of the court-yard at our Lydtor home into living accommodation for Patrick and me and building a large conservatory on the rear of the cottage which is for everyone, but, as far as the older children are concerned, is limited strictly to peace and quiet, reading and homework.

'When do you want your present?' Patrick asked suddenly, breaking into my reverie.

I had already given him his present: some new tack for his horse, George.

'Silly question,' I said, with a big smile. He smiled back, sparks of laughter in those wonderful grey eyes, and took a tiny package from his jacket pocket.

Moments later I gazed, dumbstruck, at the solitaire diamond ring it contained.

'I never got round to buying you another engagement ring.'

He knew that I had genuinely lost the first. But I had kept my wedding ring, not thrown it at him as some women might have done. Why? *Why?* A subconscious wish that the break between us was not final, or merely the action of a practical person who would never discard anything she could sell if she was ever stony-broke?

'It's fantastic,' I whispered, leaning over to kiss him. 'Thank you.' I slipped it on.

'What do you think we ought to do about James?' Patrick asked.

I had forgotten all about it. 'Why not call him back and ask when it would be convenient for us to call at the nick? You're not going back to work and I'm not going home until Wednesday.'

Patrick looked at his watch. 'We've an hour and a bit

before we have to set off back to the rectory to get changed. He could join us for an ale now and we can arrange it.'

I rather thought this was more to do with extra beer than anything else but felt all warm and soppy towards him after the wonderful present so agreed readily. James, it transpired, was on his way home but nearby (are policeman allowed to use mobile phones while driving?) and said he would be with us shortly.

When he arrived I saw that the bruising was beginning to emerge on his face and his mouth was a little swollen but he appeared content enough and I knew he must be very pleased with the match result.

'Och, I heal well,' he said in response to my query. 'Your good health,' he went on after thanking Patrick for the pint. 'And where are you off to tonight?'

'Toby's in Royal Crescent,' Patrick replied.

'Man, you'll need to take out a mortgage on your house. Folk tend to get all dressed up when they go there, don't they?'

'Black tie suggested but not mandatory. Ingrid reckoned it was about time I frightened the moths out of mine.'

'Joanna's always on at me about the place when it comes round to birthdays and anniversaries,' the DCI mused gloomily.

'I'll report back to her,' I promised gleefully.

'When d'you want this chat then?' Patrick asked.

Carrick's good-looking features darkened. 'Not now, that's for sure. Not on your special day.'

'I can't believe whatever you might say would prove to be that much of a dampener.'

'Nevertheless, I've absolutely no intention of burdening you with my private worries now. Shall we make it Monday morning?'

Patrick leaned forward and spoke quietly. 'James, old son, by not sharing a wee piece of it with us now we'll be thinking of you all solitary with your worries when we're drinking our bubbly tonight. I had an idea something was really bothering you when we spoke earlier.'

'Please,' I added. 'And then you and Joanna come out to eat with us on Monday evening.'

'I've said nothing to her about this,' Carrick admitted. 'But if what I've been told is true then she'll have to know eventually.' He was silent for a few moments and then said, 'You remember when I was on a trip to Scotland a couple of years ago and met Lord Muirshire?'

Patrick said, 'Of course. You just happened upon the Case of the Buried Opera Singer. Only she wasn't dead. And that led into the Case of the Secretly Imported Crooks for Cash. An Italian by the name of Capelli – I seem to remember shooting his murderous minder – was behind most of it and he was using weekend bashes at a castle belonging to Lord Muirshire as a front for his little business but without his lordship knowing what was really going on.'

I'd only had a brief walk-on part right at the end of that one but had been told by the pair of them about most of it afterwards. Other details had emerged at a later date – for instance how Carrick had at one stage thought Patrick had been too heavy-handed in questioning the aforementioned opera singer, had lost his temper and taken a broadsword to the inquisitor in the castle hall. Patrick had grabbed another similar weapon and the brief but electrifying duel is, I understand, still being talked about. The lady had actually been a little sloshed and shut her own hand in a drawer. Oh, and Patrick had won.

'That's right,' Carrick said. 'I don't think I mentioned to you at the time that Ross, Lord Muirshire, had been a good friend of my father.'

'Who was drowned at sea, I understand,' Patrick said.

'Ross was there, on the yacht, when it happened.'

This came as a surprise to me, for none of the circumstances had been discussed with us before and I had assumed that the accident had been on board some kind of fishing boat. I knew that Carrick wore a Kennedy tartan kilt but had not questioned before how a Lowland fisherman – both names are connected with Ayrshire – would have clan connections.

Patrick, also apparently a little puzzled, said, 'It was a private yacht then?'

'Yes, a racing yacht belonging to the then Earl of Carrick.

My father was a distant cousin but nevertheless close to the family.'

'So you're blue-blooded,' I said.

He gave me a twisted grin. 'I'm *told* he fully intended to divorce his wife and marry my mother – who was four months' pregnant with me and only seventeen years old at the time – but he was knocked overboard by the boom, the sea was freezing cold as it is off Scotland for most of the year, and that was that. The rest of the tale, in a nutshell, is that my mother had me, my pillar-of-the-Kirk grandad endeavoured to thrash the sin out of me as soon as I was old enough to tell him I hated him, and Mother and I upped from her parents' house to an aunt in Crieff where she changed her name to Carrick. That was the story as I understood it – until last week.'

We waited.

'He's not dead,' Carrick whispered. 'Robert Kennedy is still alive, although not very well, and has just been released from prison where he served six months for his part in a bank robbery where two security guards were shot and injured. He was driving the getaway car.'

Patrick broke the ensuing silence by asking, 'Where did this happen?'

'London. He's been banged up in the Scrubs.'

'Are you quite sure?' I asked. 'Couldn't it be a man with the same name – I mean, it's not an uncommon one.'

'I've requested the CRO to double-check in case there's been an IT error, but otherwise I'm pretty sure,' Carrick answered. 'I was doing my weekly trawl through convicts released throughout the UK – it helps to know which villains are back in circulation – when the name jumped out at me. I went into his records; right date of birth, next of kin listed as someone I'd once heard Ross mention. I rang him – Ross that is – and told him what I'd found out. We couldn't really discuss it over the phone as he had dinner guests that evening and would only say that he'd heard nothing that would confirm what I'd told him but would contact people. He himself was on the boat and they'd looked for the man overboard for over an hour. He wasn't wearing a life-jacket

– I'm not sure people did back then – and the sea was like liquid ice. He's insisting it must be someone else or, more likely, a man who's stolen his identity.'

'That sounds much more likely to me too,' Patrick murmured.

'I can hardly devote police resources to investigate this,' James went on as though Patrick had not spoken. 'But, obviously, I must get to the truth.'

'Aren't there photos of this man?' I enquired.

'Yes, and I've seen them.' Carrick shrugged, obviously having difficulty keeping his emotions under control. 'But he was in his early twenties when he got my mother into trouble and that was thirty-seven years ago.' Then, his voice breaking a little, he added, 'Just an unhealthy thuggish-looking man in his late fifties.'

'How can we help?' I asked.

'You can't really. I just wanted to share it with you.' After a pause he said, 'But I wonder if . . .'

'Yes?' I encouraged.

'Perhaps when you're not busy you'd cast your gaze over this character who's been listed as next of kin. According to the records he lives in your neck of the woods. I simply can't take time off right now to look into it.'

'A pleasure,' Patrick said. 'Where does he live?'

'On Dartmoor, somewhere near Princetown. His name's Archie Kennedy and the address is a farm but I've no idea whether he is a farmer.'

'I'll do it,' I offered. 'I'm always looking for excuses to head for the high moor.' Not only that, I was, belatedly, planning my next novel and had only got as far as deciding that it would be Sherlockian, dark, and bog-ridden.

Carrick looked dubious. 'You'll be careful, won't you, Ingrid? This man might be a distant relation of mine but I ken that side of the family are a wild bunch.'

'I'll be birdwatching,' I told him. 'That means you can carry binoculars and point them absolutely everywhere.'

Strictly speaking the farm wasn't near home at all but quite a journey to the centre of the moor. After driving through

Tavistock and then on to Princetown I had turned off on to a single-track road and, according to the compass, was now heading roughly south. Passing a few cottages and a barn I clanged over a cattle-grid and the road immediately deteriorated into a rough track with rudimentary passing places. Before me the moor stretched into apparent infinity: great russet and olive rolling downs, some of them crowned with granite tors. Overnight persistent rain had ceased, the wind direction now north-westerly bringing heavy showers with hail in dark grey and white curtains that blotted out some of the distant hills. Far to the south the sky looked brighter over Plymouth and the sea. It was a different climate down there. A different world, for that matter.

A couple of miles farther on the track entered a narrow gully, briars and the previous year's winter-bronzed bracken brushing the sides of the Range Rover as it bounced over the ruts. I involuntarily ducked as the vehicle scraped beneath a small rowan tree. A heron took off from the banks of a little stream that was in full spate and flapped away like an affronted umbrella only to be mobbed by crows. After driving parallel to the stream for a short distance I forded it and the track then climbed steeply, almost like a river bed itself with water flowing into it off the surrounding slopes.

For some distance the track ran alongside a leat, the water as clear as molten glass, long green tresses of waterweed shivering in the current. Then, with a thunderous roar, hail blotted out everything. I slowed the car and pulled up at a point where the track appeared to veer sharply to the left, waiting for it to stop.

It was actually ten days since our weekend in the Bath area and the first opportunity for me to have a day off with a clear conscience. People imagine when you tell them you write that you drift around for most of the time in long flowing gowns thinking Higher Thoughts while sipping from a delicate tall-stemmed wine glass. I thought back over my ten days: I had written not a word. Instead, there had been an every-evening crash course in punctuation for Matthew after an out-of-the-blue discovery that he was struggling with English; Katie was still at home with (another) chest infection, necessitating two trips to the doctor's, and I had spent a lot of time with Justin who is in trouble at school with behavioural problems. In short, he is noisy, stroppy and just like his father at that age. Vicky, bless her sweet little soul, is no problem at all and being with her had been a salve for all the other worries.

Somehow I had found the time to ride George – Patrick had been unable to get home – as although a real gentleman he gets bored and breaks out of the field to jaunt around the district if not regularly exercised. Katie's pony Fudge follows along and the pair snack in any gardens where people have unwisely left the gates open. He had recently inflicted upon himself a nasty cut from the barbed-wire fence. The field is not ours but we had paid to have all the wire replaced with post and rail fencing. George had subsequently put Plan B into operation and started jumping out, again with Fudge rattling along behind.

The children have a nanny, Carrie, and there is other help with housework, but I cannot expect them to cope with the other events that had occurred: blocked drains, a young jackdaw falling down the living-room chimney and then flying about, covering everything in soot before it could be released through a window, all of this culminating the previous day, while I was out shopping, with Justin climbing a tree he had been specifically forbidden to as it overhangs the river. He had fallen some fifteen feet from it to land in a pool, cutting his head on a rock, the intrepid Carrie plunging in to rescue him. There were now three stitches inserted in a large bump on my son's forehead and I had promised him faithfully that his father would have a few thoughts on the matter to share with him. The fact that Justin had been incredibly brave about the stitches and that he had managed, his head pouring blood, to swim to where Carrie could grab him mitigated things a little – here again, surely, was an action replay of his father's boyhood. And no, we were not going to chop down the tree.

The hail petered out to be be replaced by rain and I leaned over to gaze out at the bleak Foxtor Mires that were now

unveiled to the left and below me. This was the 'so horrible
a place' renamed the Great Grimpen Mire in Sir Arthur
Conan Doyle's *The Hound of the Baskervilles*. Deadly
dangerous to the unwary, it all looked pretty innocuous
from up here but the lurid green patches, literally rafts of
mosses floating on deep water above the impermeable
granite beneath, are warning enough to the knowledgeable
walker. There are ways across the mire, used only in the
summer months, but one needs to be in the company of an
experienced guide.

I could see from my vantage point that the track was
flooded for a short distance about a hundred yards from
where I had stopped, water gushing across it and then down
into the valley. The track acquired a lot of black, peaty mud
after this and then forked, the left-hand route sort of slith-
ering down towards the boggy ground and disappearing
from sight around a rocky outcrop. I was not perturbed: I
had an Ordnance Survey map and the farm was marked on
it. I set off again and as soon as I had crossed the flood
my mobile rang. I pulled up.

It was Patrick, asking after Justin and relieved to know
that, although being kept off school for the day, and quiet
– which was different and wonderful – he seemed perfectly
all right.

'Should we stop his pocket money for a month, do you
think?' Patrick suggested.

'No, that would be counter-productive because he's saving
up to buy a book from the school book fair,' I said. 'I think
that as he's had a real fright you just ought to stick to the
talking-to.' We had already discussed the behaviour problem
and were hoping to address it by Patrick taking some leave
and devoting more time to the boy. I thought that in the
long term more would be achieved by sending him to stay
with his grandmother – after all, Elspeth had sorted Patrick
out, hadn't she?

'Thinking of stitches, you remember when James went
off during the match to have his cut attended to and a substitute came on?'

'Of course.'

'The man's been missing from home for a week and his body's been discovered in a wood. He was murdered, shot in the back of the head.'

'That's dreadful!'

'James is upset as he knew him quite well – the guy was a DS working at HQ in Bristol and, obviously, they'd trained for matches together.'

'Is the killing to do with the job, do they think?'

'There's every chance that it could be as he was part of a team tackling some nasty outfits that have moved to the West Country from London. But of course it's early days yet: the body was only found this morning.'

'Did James ring you with the news himself?'

'Yes, he did.'

'That might mean he's hoping SOCA will get involved.'

'That occurred to me too.'

I suddenly recollected that players temporarily brought on to replace injured team-members are referred to as blood substitutes.

Two

I drove on, the going getting rougher and rougher and, not for the first time, wondered how people make a living on these remote Dartmoor farmsteads. The answer, I suppose, is that they do not and that most are now lived in by people who seek wild places and have other means of support or those who are retired and want to keep a few animals as a hobby. But what was a Scot doing in the fastnesses of England when he had the whole of his native land available to him?

I spotted Sheepwash Farm another half-mile farther on, the ancient steading seeming to huddle beneath a promontory that jutted from Fox Tor and looking like a house built just below the prow of a stone ship. The road climbed towards it and then, just past the entrance, appeared to come to an end at a gateway that led to the higher open moorland on the flanks of the hill. I stopped the car and looked at the group of buildings through my binoculars: it seemed to be a ruin. This called for a more direct approach than originally planned and so I drove closer.

The place was indeed mostly in ruins, the walls of the old barn and byres that fronted the central yard crumbling, their roofs open to the sky in places. The house was little better, with slates missing, vegetation growing in what guttering remained and from holes where stones were missing in the chimney stack. The upstairs windows were either shuttered or boarded up on the inside and the curtains were drawn on the ground floor. I drove between the leaning gateposts – there was no gate – into the yard and turned off the engine.

It had stopped raining and a deep and utter silence flowed

in with cold, damp air when I opened the driver's window. Then, in the distance, a lamb bleated. A swallow swooped from one of the byres, skimmed over the roof of the house and went from sight. Nothing else moved; there were no vehicles here unless they were inside the barn and no tracks because the yard was surprisingly clean: it appeared to be deserted.

I got out of the car, the quiet sounds I made a violation of the silence. I did not slam the door, just gently pushed it to before walking slowly towards the house, which was actually no larger than a cottage. The blank windows seemed to stare back at me and for some reason I shivered.

I banged with my knuckles on the front door as there was no knocker or bell. There came no echo from within as there might in a house devoid of furniture, but instead there was a kind of dead resonance. I had a story ready should anyone answer the door – that I was on a hunt for a relative – but nothing moved inside; no one came. I knocked again, louder, with the same result.

Wondering if anyone was outside in a garden at the back I went down the narrow passageway between the house and the barn – the house was joined to an open tractor shed on the other side – but there was nothing that could be described as a garden at the rear, only a tiny paddock overgrown with bracken and rushes. Three large wooden packing cases – empty, I saw when I went closer – were stacked up against the rear wall of the house.

I went back around the front.

'He's deid,' said a man who was standing as though waiting for me to return. He was wearing hiking clothing, the full kit: over-trousers, gaiters, walking boots and a very expensive anorak. The binoculars on a strap around his neck looked top-of-the-range too. He somehow belonged to this place: a chill emanated from him, possibly from the cold blue eyes.

'Deid?' I echoed.

'Aye, deid. Early last winter.'

I decided to take a risk and tell the truth. 'It's Archie Kennedy I'm looking for,' I told him.

'Aye, that's him. Deid.'

'That's a shame. Were you a friend of his?'

'In a manner of speaking.'

I went a little closer to him. 'Do you know if there are any other relatives I can contact?'

'No.'

'Are you living here now?'

'You ask a lot of questions.'

'Sorry, I write books for a living – people and places interest me.'

He did not thaw by one fraction of a degree and said roughly, 'There's nothing here for you or your stories.'

'It has a strange atmosphere,' I replied defensively.

'It has a violent history.'

It was obvious that he was not about to be more forthcoming so I had no choice but to tell him it was lovely to have met him, wish him good day, get into the car and leave.

I rather felt that I had masses of material.

'*Do* you reckon he was living there?' Patrick asked later when I told him of my encounter.

'There are no other houses nearby that could have suggested he was a neighbour,' I replied. 'I actually think it's a strong possibility he not only lives there but is Archie Kennedy himself. He spoke with a strong Scottish accent. To have two Scots living in the same area – the middle of a bunch of bogs six miles from Princetown – is too much of a coincidence.'

'He could have been a regular hill-walker from the village; it's quite large. And if you look at the map you'll see that the road takes a long route following the contours of the land – Princetown is only really a couple of miles away just over the hill to the north.'

'If you survive crossing the various mires and don't fall down the mineshafts,' I said sarcastically.

'Ingrid, I cut my special operations teeth on Dartmoor – they chuck you out there clad in only a thin tracksuit and armed with a bluntish knife, two snares and some fishing line. I know what I'm talking about.'

I love this man of mine to bits but the moor covers 365 square miles, give or take a few, and even he is sometimes prone to trumpet-blowing. Waggling a finger at him, I said, 'And I happen to know that on one of your very first evening sorties the six of you went straight into the Plume of Feathers in Princetown, four formed a barbers' quartet, someone else played the piano and you did impressions. I gather you ate and drank very well on the proceeds and were allowed to sleep in the camping barn that night.'

'Who told you that?'

'Your mother.'

He grimaced. 'I didn't tell her about the aftermath – how we were rounded up, given a thorough dusting and then chucked into Crazywell Pool before being told to stick to the rules for the rest of the exercise.'

'And did you?'

'No, we trotted ourselves dry across to Chagford and repeated the performance there.' Laughing, he added, 'You don't find out until years later that they only pick the real anarchists for Special Ops.'

It was two days after my own sortie on to the moor and late evening. Patrick was home for a short weekend. He had been on another training course, which were for SOCA these days and not so physically demanding, thank everything holy, and had flown to Plymouth from London as there always seem to be engineering works on the railways at weekends.

'I don't really know what to tell James,' I admitted.

'Tell him what you've just told me,' Patrick said after taking a sip from his whisky nightcap.

'But you've just rather rubbished my conclusion.'

'It's up to James what he reads into your findings. From what you've said though, it doesn't appear likely that anyone's living in the farmhouse as it's uninhabitable.'

'It could have been made to look like that. Oh, I forgot to mention the packing cases by the back door.'

'Packing cases?'

'Yes, new-ish wooden ones. The sort of things valuables might have been packed in for shipping.'

'They could have been acquired to be chopped up for kindling.'

'So is someone living in the place, or aren't they?' I retorted, exasperated.

He gave me an unnerving grin. 'There's only one way to find out – conduct a night offensive.'

'That doesn't seem necessary somehow,' I replied after a pause. 'I don't think James expects us to go to those lengths.'

Patrick did not answer, unaccountably going outside into the yard for a few moments. When he came back he said, 'There's a three-quarter moon, not a breath of wind and the weather's settled. Let's go for it – I could do with some fresh air.'

'What, drive out and sneak up on the place *now*? That's daft!'

'I'll go on my own then.'

And he actually poured the rest of his tot back into the bottle.

I was glad when Patrick offered to drive as, from the turn-off in Princetown, this would have to be achieved without lights. Car headlights are visible for miles in wide open spaces, especially ascending hills when they shine up into the sky or illuminate things you don't want them to. The moonlight was quite bright so finding our way was not a problem, the only hazards being rocks sticking out from the sides of the track that were visible in daylight hours but now hidden in deep shadow and likely to inflict real damage on the wheels or suspension if struck at speed.

Everything looks different at night; colour eradicated, shade taking on a solidness that makes a medium-sized boulder look like a car, a leaning tree like a giant bull about to walk into the road. Patrick had ghosted at walking pace over the cattle grid to prevent a giveaway rumble – sound travels for miles on a still night too – and we both ducked this time when the vehicle scraped beneath the rowan tree.

'I forgot to tell you the latest on that cop whose body

was found in woodland near Bristol,' Patrick said. 'He'd been tortured before he was killed.'

'How horrible,' I murmured. 'What was his name?'

'Cliff Morley. Carrick rang me with the news this morning and he'd only just found out himself. It appears that Bristol CID are keeping all this very close to their chests. Strictly speaking it isn't anything to do with him but James is not happy about the reticence at all and is making waves at HQ, his attitude being that police departments, especially those in the same force, shouldn't keep secrets from one another. He also thinks they might have lost the plot with the case as the criminal outfit involved – a fairly new one to the area, which is the number one suspect – is an offshoot from one in London and too big for them to handle. And, understandably, he's wondering what information, if any, his killers managed to extract from poor Morley before they killed him – he can't think there was any other motive for torture.'

'This gang sticks to the usual recipe of drug-trafficking, robberies, organizing prostitution, extortion rackets and so forth, I assume.'

'They appear to have got as far as holding up a building society branch, armed robbery of a jeweller's shop, stolen a few expensive cars and other crimes of which I don't know the details. They've also finished off some of the local opposition, which some cops might think a good thing as it saves them work, but murder's murder, whichever way you look at it.'

Patrick might have become a little distracted here, telling me this, for the vehicle encountered a large boulder while crossing the stream and stalled. Swearing under his breath he restarted it, reversed out again and chose a different route. 'How far now?' he asked.

'About a quarter of a mile along this straight bit above the mires and then steeply downhill to the left for a short way, another straight bit for several hundred yards before a tight turn to the right and then a climb up to the farm.'

A short distance farther on he spotted a recess in the rocky hillside immediately on our right, drove across a

narrow grassy area tufted with rushes and edged the Range
Rover into it, leaving just enough room for us to open the
doors and get out.

There was a breeze up here, blowing towards us as we
faced our destination and bringing with it the wet smell of
peat and bruised greenery. Patrick scented the air like an
animal.

'Something's disturbed the ground,' he whispered. 'But
I can't smell sheep or ponies – not close by anyway.'

'There are people who go hiking on the moor at night,'
I whispered back. 'Properly organized groups, I mean.'

'Umm.'

We set off, walking on the grass at the side of the track
so as to be as quiet as possible. Occasionally Patrick
paused to look and listen, the reason I do not walk closely
behind him. Cattle grazed not too far away, over to the
right and up wind of us on the slopes of the hill – I could
actually hear them tearing at the coarse grass. A fox
yapped.

Patrick immediately crouched down, I followed suit and
we stayed quite still for at least a minute. The breeze rustled
though the grass, water trickled in a tiny rivulet near my
feet, strange ribbon-like clouds sailed past the moon, but
that was all.

'It was probably a real one,' Patrick said under his breath
and carried on walking.

In the moonlight the mire looked unworldly, the vivid
green of the mosses defying the etiolating effect of the
moonlight, appearing a sickly yellow. 'Islands' with stunted
trees growing on them that I had not noticed before stuck
up like the petrified remains of giants that had been trapped
in the bog.

We slithered down the steep section, far muddier than on
the day of my visit as there had been more heavy rain, and
set off on the final straight stretch. We were much closer
to the mire now and there was the unmistakable sound of
frogs croaking. Then, somewhere around to the right, a light
flashed.

Again, Patrick stopped.

'A military exercise on the firing ranges?' I breathed in his ear.

He shook his head and turned to whisper, 'I reckon it was small and close by rather than large and far away. But we mustn't overplay this – there could well be someone living in the house, which might not have any electricity.'

We went on and reached the bend just before the bottom of the final slope. Patrick motioned to me to stay where I was and disappeared into the heavy shadow in the lee of a small rocky hillock that stood alone, almost a miniature tor on the right of the track. He seemed to be gone for rather a long time and then I heard a slight noise and he reappeared from the other side of it, beckoning to me.

We went the way he had returned, following a rough path and then left it to climb a higher grassy knoll, crawling the last part until we lay on our stomachs on the top. Below us and quite close by were the farm buildings. Moonlight only illuminated the byres on the right-hand side of the central yard; the rest was in virtual darkness and no details were visible. There were no lights at the front of the house. Patrick nudged me and we slid backwards and descended again, but in a different place, crossing the track, carrying on in the same direction and then finding ourselves on the banks of a ditch behind one of the outer walls of the barn on the opposite side of the yard. There was a lot of water in the ditch and it smelled terrible, almost certainly raw sewage.

Following the ditch, but in the opposite direction to the main entrance to the yard, we went slowly towards the rear of the house. Leaving the buildings behind us we deliberately stayed behind the cover of the wall of the little paddock and eventually arrived at a gateway. I peeped around a granite gatepost but could see no lights within the house from here either. Patrick signalled to me to stay put again and, cautiously, bending low and not moving in a direct line, he went forward, through a gap in the wall and towards the back door, finally going from my sight into shadow.

Ears tuned to the slightest suspicious sound – this place really gave me the shivers – I waited where I was. After a couple of minutes I saw a light inside the house, a flash as of a torch beam and realized that Patrick was inside. I went across to the open back door.

'The place has been turned over,' Patrick reported, hearing my approach and coming to the doorway. 'Not all that long ago either. Someone was living here all right, and quite comfortably too, despite using oil lamps and candles.'

'We didn't hear or meet any other vehicles,' I said.

'I would guess that whoever it was left at about the time we reached the village. There's a still warm cup of tea on the kitchen table.'

'Were they taken away? Or did they manage to escape? Should we search in case someone's been attacked and hurt somewhere?'

I did not expect Patrick to be able to answer any of these questions and he made no attempt to. We put on crime-scene protective gloves to avoid leaving fingerprints or traces of our DNA and walked through the house towards the front door where Patrick called up the stairs. Silence. He went up them but, oddly, there was a door at the top. It was locked. Leaving that for the moment he came down again, opened the front door, which had not been forced, and we both went out into the yard. The paving by the door had been blown dry by the wind and there were no foot-prints. But there were several some yards away where there was a patch of mud and in it the tracks of what looked like two cars, both sets of tyres different but wide and probably fitted to four-wheel-drive vehicles. Walking to one side of them and well away from any potential evidence we crossed the yard towards the barn, both doors of which were ajar. There was a Land Rover inside, a new-looking Defender TD5.

'Theft of this wasn't the name of the game then,' Patrick muttered. 'They fetch a good price too.' He examined the tyres of the vehicle and securing arrangements on the barn doors, which lay on the ground having been jemmied out of the wood, the padlock still intact. 'This made one set of tracks outside,' he concluded.

We followed the other tyre tracks for a short distance.

They turned left from the yard and went in the direction of the gateway on to the moor. The gate was wide open.

'They came this way too,' Patrick said, crouching down to look at the ground. 'And such is the slope I reckon you could just ghost down here, making hardly any noise at all.'

We went back inside the house. Touching nothing, we searched for anyone who might be in the building but found nothing. There did not seem to be signs of a struggle even though a table had been overturned. Nothing was actually broken and although we made it a priority to look, we could find no bloodstains. Patrick, I knew, was itching to open cupboards and have a really good look around but the whole place was probably a crime scene so he had to contain himself. We were both keen to force the door at the top of the stairs – for all we knew someone might be up there – but had to observe protocol. Finally, after a few fruitless minutes, Patrick called the police. We were asked to wait at the property.

In order to search the house properly we had been forced to light one of the oil lamps. It had still been warm, as had another: further evidence of recent occupancy. They were not modern utilitarian ones but antiques. Other items of furniture suggested that they belonged to a person of taste. The one living room, where the table had been overturned, had an open fireplace but there were only cold ashes in the grate. The other room at the front had been used as a bedroom, blankets and other bedding folded up on a large old sofa covered by a patchwork quilt. A kitchen and storeroom of sorts were at the rear, the latter a muddle of boxes and packing cases, a suitcase dumped down in the doorway where anyone might fall over it.

'You know, I reckon whoever lives here had only just got home,' Patrick said while we waited, eyeing the suitcase.

I went back outside and put my hand on the bonnet of the Land Rover. Like the lamps, it was still warm.

'Whoever lives here must have only just come in and lit the lamps to see what he was doing,' I said, having related this information. 'The ungodly had been waiting for him – I think we must assume it was a him – up on the hill with their engine and lights off and when they saw him arrive, pounced. But did they take him with them? Or did he manage to get away?'

The police arrived very swiftly – there is a prison in the vicinity after all – and, on Patrick's urging and after producing his SOCA warrant card, the door at the top of the stairs was forced. Nothing was up there but buckets standing on heavy-duty plastic sheeting spread over the floor of each room to keep any rain from the leaking roof from penetrating the ceilings downstairs.

'Why put a door there and lock it though?' asked the man in charge, a sergeant from Tavistock.

'The upstairs windows are rotten and by no means burglar-proof so it must have been a security measure,' Patrick told him. 'Do you know who normally lives here?'

The other shook his head. 'No, sir, I don't. And to be honest I'm not sure a crime's been committed even though it's obvious someone left in a hurry. No forced entry's been made – you said yourself that both front and back doors were unlocked. But I will make enquiries as to the identity of the occupant and get back to you. Until that's established . . .' He shook his head sadly.

Patrick looked grim but this was what we had half expected.

'Tell me,' he said, as the police turned to leave. 'Where does that track lead that starts at the gate there?'

'Into a maze of other tracks, I shouldn't wonder, sir,' was the sergeant's reply. 'Some passable by vehicles, most not. If you were lucky you might reach the Two Moors Way and end up near Ivybridge. The Ordnance Survey map will give proper details should you care to refer to it.'

'This place has a bad reputation,' one of his colleagues put in.

'In what way?' I asked, remembering the remark the man I had met had made about the farm having a violent history.

'Apparently some woman servant was raped here by the farmer and threw herself in a cattle trough and drowned.'

'When did that happen?'

'Back in the sixteenth century, I was told.'

And, breathtakingly polite to the last, they left.

'Folk round here certainly have long memories,' Patrick muttered.

Three

For over an hour – until the batteries of both Patrick's little torch and another rechargeable one in the car had run out – we searched the vicinity for anyone who might be hurt or even unconscious and found nothing. I for one was haunted by what James Carrick had told us about the man he was assuming to be his father. Where there are criminal connections no one is safe. Few details of inter-gang warfare and the murders and maimings they generate reach the media. There is little public sympathy for the victims but often they are just that: victims; innocent family and friends of those who have gone decidedly wrong in life.

Was the man to whom I had spoken Archie Kennedy? I know that if the person who had named me as his next of kin had just been released from prison where he had served a sentence for involvement in serious crime – and been associated with heaven alone knows what other un-detected offences if the truth were known – I would be cagey about identifying myself to a complete stranger who might be the tool of someone bent on settling old scores.

With only the moon to light our way now we went back to the farmhouse, closed both outer doors, secured the barn as best we could and started to walk back to the car. Tired and not a little depressed, neither of us spoke until we reached it.

'I suggest we come back when it's light and try to follow the tracks of that vehicle,' Patrick said. 'For all we know they beat him to a pulp, carted him off and threw him out somewhere on the high moor. But there's no justification for calling out the Dartmoor Rescue people.'

I said, 'I think there would have been more evidence of that. Nothing was actually damaged indoors and there were no bloodstains. The way that suitcase was dumped down just off the kitchen suggests whoever arrived without warning burst in the front door while the person who lives there ran out the back.'

'I really hope you're right,' was all Patrick said in reply.

The next day early summer recommenced with a bright sunny morning; small fluffy clouds sailing in a pale blue sky, the sunlight glittering on patches of surface water on the mires transforming the whole area into something that was almost idyllic, even the old farmstead assuming a quaintly fairytale identity below its rocky crag. Swallows swooped in and out of the ruined byres, lambs were playing chasing games over the broken-down walls of the old paddock, a buzzard took off from the top of a wind-blasted goat willow that was somehow still clinging to life and soared up into the blueness with its mewing call.

We had not yet contacted Carrick, feeling it preferable to present him with as complete a picture as possible. Part of our task this morning was to look over the farm in daylight and we were hopeful of finding clues that might tell us what had happened here.

It is illegal for unauthorized vehicles to venture off public roads on to the moor – which is a National Park – so Patrick had obtained permission from the park authorities. The police had already reported a possible disturbance the night before to them so all he had to do was quote the case number and clearance was readily given. We were asked to stay on tracks and it was emphasized that we went entirely at our own risk.

As we approached the house – on foot, having left the car outside the yard – nothing appeared to have changed. But it had, for although both doors of the house were still unlocked the Defender had gone from the barn. Its tyre tracks could be clearly discerned in the mud patch over-laying those made previously.

'Did you get the registration?' I asked Patrick.

'No, I was too busy looking for the owner,' he replied tersely. 'Damn.'

'They must have changed their minds about stealing it.'

'Or whoever lives here came back and used it to get right away. I wonder if they took any possessions.'

I followed Patrick indoors and we both gazed at the suit-case, which was still across the storeroom doorway. It was quite a large one and scruffy, as though it had been battered around for some years on airport luggage reclaim conveyors. I went to pick it up to see how heavy it was but Patrick grabbed my hand.

'What's wrong?'

'Gut feelings. Why do I want someone from the Bomb Squad to give this thing the once-over?'

I took a couple of quick steps away from it. *'Really?'*

'There's no TV here, not even one that runs off batteries. Yet I distinctly remember noticing a remote control in one of the front rooms somewhere.'

'What else uses them other than music players?'

'Entertainment systems generally. I'm not too sure about stand-alone radios.'

We went into the living room and there it was, on the floor by the overturned table. It was exactly what he had said it was, complete with all the usual buttons, not a wire-less mouse from a computer or anything similar. Patrick picked it up, very carefully, looked at it for a few seconds and then replaced it on the floor.

'You think this could be used to detonate something in that suitcase?' I asked. 'But, surely, whoever was doing it would blow themselves up as well!'

'No, it's more likely it's used to render it operable or safe. It might detonate when operable if the case is moved.' He gave me a crazy sort of smile. 'Or is this bloke overdue for his zimmer frame and bus pass? There's only one way to find out.'

For one ghastly moment I thought he meant to pick up

the case himself but he merely took his mobile from his pocket and went outside to use it, the signal indoors being weak. I went with him as I felt the suitcase was sort of staring at me.

Within virtual sight of three army firing ranges, and if you have the right connections – in other words have been a Lieutenant-Colonel in the Devon and Dorset Regiment (now absorbed into the Rifles) – and know the right people, it is child's play to find an explosives expert. This person arrived three-quarters of an hour later, with two colleagues, during which time we closely examined the outbuildings. They yielded nothing of interest except a baby swallow that had fallen out of its nest, which Patrick, using a rickety ladder with some of the rungs missing, put back.

The experts sent us away to a safe distance and there was nothing for it but to sit on a grassy bank in the sun and wait. I do not bite my nails but almost wanted to, expecting the whole place to go to Kingdom Come at any moment.

'They know what they're doing,' Patrick told me, sensing my apprehension.

Finally, while I was thinking morbidly that all three probably had young children, someone came to the farmhouse door and waved. We went back, finding on the kitchen floor a maze of wiring, several small packages of explosives and what looked to my fairly untrained eye like tiny detonators and circuit boards. But I need not have worried; after examining the suitcase and the remote control with their electronic detectors they had taken the batteries out of the latter before touching anything else.

Sophisticated was the verdict, put together by a professional. It contained enough explosive, should it have gone off, to have made a sizable hole in Devon.

Again the police were called, we gave our account of affairs, to an inspector this time, and finally the various vehicles bearing those representing national security and law and order departed, taking with them the evidence.

'I'm really glad we were able to rescue that baby

swallow,' I said as we drove through the open gateway on to the moor.

It was immediately obvious that it would be impossible to follow the tracks of the vehicle in which we were interested as others clearly frequently used the same route. There were tyre tracks of quad bikes, older Land Rovers with smaller, narrower wheels, even mountain bikes. Some were very recent, made that morning as people went out to check their cattle and sheep, and also footprints made by hikers wearing walking boots. After a mile or so of bouncing over the rough track Patrick pulled up and turned off the ignition.

'Sometimes I wish I still smoked small cigars,' he murmured. 'I'd light one now and have a good think.'

'Have a mint instead and think,' I said, offering the packet.

He pulled a face but took one anyway and sucked it gloomily. 'So, what the bloody hell do we have?' he said after a minute or so. 'A house in the middle of nowhere, lived in by a bloke who's supposed to be dead, but isn't? Or is he really dead and the place is inhabited by the bloke you spoke to? Is the bloke you spoke to Archie Kennedy and he's lying about being dead? Someone comes calling with what we assume is malice aforethought and someone else does a runner, leaving behind what can only be described as a large bomb. Later, persons unknown return for a Land Rover. The house is left unlocked, a real booby-trap, the set-up to professional standards. And by that, you must understand my old friend Peter did not mean professional criminal standards but military or mining engineer ones.'

'It's criminal as well since any nosy passer-by could have been killed if they'd gone in.'

'Or anyone looking for Kennedy,' Patrick said. 'You could have been blown up had you gone there this morning instead of a couple of days ago and shifted that case out of your way.' He restarted the car. 'I suppose we ought to carry on and look for bodies in ditches but I don't think we'll find one or any answers up here.'

It took us all day but we covered most of the tracks marked on the map that were passable to vehicles, plus a couple that were distinctly borderline, scanning the moor through binoculars and ending up in Ivybridge having found only three dead – very dead – sheep and a pair of run-over binoculars.

Commander Michael Greenway, Patrick's boss, did not appear to work from an actual base, borrowing an office at various police establishments when he needed to or, like this morning, meeting people in a café or restaurant. He seemed just to need a laptop and mobile phone in order to accomplish everything he wanted to, the former of which he carried in one of those flat as a pancake briefcases that come from Harrods, can accommodate sufficient possessions for a skiing weekend and cost well into three figures. We discovered at a much later date that this method of working not only suited his restless character and low boredom threshold but ensured that the underworld bosses who had put a price on his head were never able to find him.

We had received the phone call the previous evening, Greenway merely saying that there had been a change of plan as far as Patrick's next assignment was concerned – so far, as a 'rookie', he had been given fairly straightforward short-term jobs – and requesting that we meet him in Roberto's, a café near West End Central police station, at nine thirty the following morning. It must be said that Greenway seemed to imagine that Dartmoor lay a half-hour drive down the M6: we had set off from home at just after four. He had finished by saying, apparently as an afterthought, that I might like to accompany Patrick as there was a possibility that the meeting would interest me.

'He's devious,' I commented sourly as we waited for him to arrive. 'Men usually say things like that when they want to pick women's brains.'

Patrick had just organized coffee for us and went away again to add, I shortly discovered, a large Danish pastry to the order, for me, as he had immediately recognized a severe case of going-without-breakfast grumps. I had eaten it and dealt with sticky fingers, thankfully, a matter of moments before Greenway arrived. Everyone shook hands.

'Do you know anyone in Bristol CID?' was Greenway's opening query to Patrick after an exchange of pleasantries.

Patrick shook his head. 'No.'

'Only someone by the name of Reece, Superintendent Paul Reece, has specifically requested SOCA's assistance – *your* assistance – on a case.'

'I don't know him,' Patrick said.

'Could this be anything to do with your friend at Bath, Chief Inspector James Carrick?'

'If it is he hasn't mentioned it to me.'

Greenway sat back in his seat, looking thoughtful. He was a big man, tall and broad without being overweight, fair-haired and with good-natured, if somewhat battered features. Always formally dressed in a suit he looked just like a city banker, possibly a deliberate decision. His hands though were not smooth like those of someone who sat at a desk all day and I had an idea he had a large hairy garden in the countryside somewhere.

'No matter,' he went on. 'And no doubt the mystery will eventually be explained. It was a fairly urgent request and I've a mind to let you get on with it right away as it involves the murder of one of Reece's team, DS Clifford Morley. You might have heard about the finding of his body in woodland near the city.'

'Yes, we did,' Patrick replied. 'Carrick did contact me about that. He and Morley played in the same police rugger team. Ingrid and I were actually at the match where Morley was Carrick's blood substitute. He was quite upset about his murder. I understand he was tortured before being shot.'

'It was very nasty,' Greenway said quietly. 'It included some bastard carving his initials on the poor guy's chest.'

We absorbed this in silence for a few seconds and then Patrick said, 'Readable initials?'

'It looked like RK apparently.'

Neither Patrick nor I made any comment on this revelation, did not even exchange glances.

'Along with quite a few other people Morley was trying to track down one of several gangs that have moved out of London and taken themselves off to the provinces,' Greenway continued. 'Probably because we've made life too hot for them here. All the nice little earners: extortion, drugs trafficking and so forth. As you probably already know they nearly always shift out the local boys, mainly by killing those who don't take the hint and head for the hills. As far as Bristol's concerned it would appear that the hood in charge might be the brother-in-law of a mobster who runs his empire from somewhere in the Walthamsden area of east London. The real worry is that Morley was working undercover. They rumbled him. Reece wants to know how, who they really are and then would like their heads parboiled on a plate. I know that you worked undercover for MI5 and this is not work I'm familiar with. Any theories as to what can go wrong?'

'You get very tired, exhausted actually, and then it's easy to allow your guard to drop,' Patrick said. 'Success depends on what kind of person you are: sometimes you're expected to do things that go against your own moral grain and that can be extremely difficult.'

'Behave really yobbishly, you mean?'

Patrick shook his head. 'We're beyond talking with your mouth full, or even drinking until you pass out or throw up. No, beat people up or help kill them – with a snarl on your face. Was he right inside the gang?'

'You'll need to talk to Reece about that but from what he said probably not,' Greenway answered, but was not to be sidetracked. 'This might be naive of me, but *you've* done that?'

Patrick finished his second cup of coffee. 'I've given downright thugs a going over, and I'm not proud of the fact that, following orders – MI5 orders, I mean – I killed one, but to answer your question properly, no.'

'How, and not give yourself away?'

'I did say one might be *expected* to do things. You can fake a lot of stuff but I never allow the situation to develop where people, those in charge that is, expect me to do anything that I don't want to.'

'That's a huge risk, surely. *How?*'

'I tend to make myself indispensible – and what someone recently described as daunting.'

Greenway was about to say something further but the words froze on his lips as the man to whom he was talking became very daunting indeed. I have never been able to explain it: I am Patrick's wife but when he is like this he is too big, too close and too damned dangerous. I have wondered if hypnotism is involved for when he somehow cranks the intimidation up a notch, which he did now, he trapped Greenway in a stare, his eyes resembling crazed living pebbles, from which the other man was unable to tear away his gaze. You find yourself thinking of animals paralysed with fear in the headlights of the vehicles just about to kill them. Then Patrick chuckled, breaking the spell.

'You insisted on knowing,' he said.

Chin jutting out, Greenway said, 'As I said just now, Reece'll give you all the details. I told him you'd get there around lunchtime.'

It was just after ten thirty now – Greenway had been somewhat late – and Avon and Somerset Police HQ is at Portishead, which is about as far as you can go in that part of the world without ending up in the Bristol Channel. It is a four-hour drive and we had just completed a five-hour one.

'Hinton Littlemoor for dinner tonight then,' Patrick said to me, getting to his feet. 'Fantastic to have met you again, sir,' he said with a winsome smile to Greenway, whereupon everyone shook hands again and we left, the SOCA man looking a trifle bemused.

'Sod that for a game of soldiers,' Patrick muttered when we were outside in the street, reaching for his mobile. He punched buttons. 'James, it's Patrick . . . Yes, I can hear that you're in a debriefing. Just a quickie. I take it Paul

Reece is an oppo of yours? . . . Sort of an oppo. Good. Can I have his number? . . . Yes, we're on the job as of tomorrow morning . . .' He waited. 'Thanks. I'll be in touch soon.'

I had just come to the conclusion that Greenway knew perfectly well how far Lydtor and Portishead are from London.

'So, leaving aside the sadism bit for now, why carve your initials on someone?' Patrick said when we had rearranged our time of arrival to the next day with Superintendent Reece. 'And is it a coincidence or not? Robert Kennedy or someone completely different? Is that why Carrick wants us on the job and has persuaded his sort-of chum in Bristol to pull strings? Is he hoping that we'll be able to handle any involvement of his father in this with more sensitivity that anyone else?'

'No to the last question,' I said. 'He's hoping we'll get the right results.'

'We have some fairly interesting stuff to tell him already.'

I thought that, with bombs involved, this was an understatement.

James Carrick lives quite close to Hinton Littlemoor, where, as previously mentioned, Patrick's father is rector and where we were staying the night, so we arranged to meet him in the Ring o' Bells which fronts on to the green in the village and is, as Patrick once put it, 'only a short staggersworth from the rectory'. Carrick brought his wife Joanna with him.

'I told her everything that's gone on,' he explained. 'I can't be doing with sneaking out to meet people, especially when they're her friends too.'

'Quite right too,' said Joanna, a vivacious red-head, robustly. 'I used to be your sergeant, after all.'

'Any joy at the farm?' Carrick asked us.

I related the full story while Patrick organized their drinks.

'But it's bloody mind-blowing!' James burst out when I

had finished. 'What did this character look like? The one who told you Archie was dead.'

'Around five feet ten and of stocky build,' I told him. 'Thick grey hair that was probably once fair, blue eyes, fresh complexion. He spoke with a Scottish accent.'

'Like mine?'

'Yes, similar.'

'From the description it could be Archie himself,' Carrick muttered. 'But as you said yourself, we won't know until we hear back from the local authorities regarding who pays the council tax. He's a distant cousin of my father's on the Carrick side. I've never met the man but he could well have been on the boat when Robert went overboard.'

Joanna said, 'You could ask Ross, Lord Muirshire.'

'Aye, I will. But don't forget, it happened a hell of a long time ago.'

'But the suitcase, James,' she said. 'What on earth was that for?'

'God knows.'

'Insurance,' Patrick suggested. 'In case "friends" of your father's turned up looking for him.'

'Which rather puts Archie in a different bracket from someone just living quietly in retirement on Dartmoor,' I commented.

There was a reflective pause before Patrick said, 'I gather it was you who put in a word about us with regard to the investigation into Cliff Morley's death.'

'I did, but Paul'd already said he'd like SOCA on the job. I hope you didn't mind.'

'Not at all. It sort of keeps it in the family.'

'I haven't mentioned any possible connection with the initials and anyone in *my* family. Until evidence turns up that makes a connection, that is.'

'No, of course not; it might muddy the waters and waste a lot of time. Tell me, did the records give your father's latest known address?'

'No, it said "of no fixed address". I found that strange.' Carrick then said bitterly, 'But I'm being stupid as that's the norm with most hoodlums; they keep on the move, shacking up with cronies.'

I was sure that, under the table, Joanna took his hand.

To James I said, 'Is there anything at all that you can tell us, on or off the record, that might help track down Cliff Morley's killers? Any remark he made to you in connection with his work?'

'No, I can't think of anything. You're only too glad to forget work and concentrate on your sport.'

'I don't understand how he was working undercover in a mob and yet could play rugby for the police at weekends,' Patrick said. 'Someone could have recognized him.'

'Oh, he'd finished his stint of duty on that case and was due to take long leave and visit his parents in Cumbria. It was his idea to play in the match – a very bad one as it happened.'

'Surely Reece warned him.'

'He did. But Cliff was a stubborn man. He reckoned he lived far enough away from the trouble zone to be safe for a couple more days.'

'In Bath?'

'Yes, up near the university. He had a flat in a big house up there.'

'I take it Reece's team have been over it.'

'No doubt.'

'What were his particular strengths – the characteristics that made him so suitable for undercover work?'

'Well, again, you'll have to ask Paul, but I reckon it was his ability to blend into his background. As you saw yourself, he was a big guy but he had a way of being part of the scenery. Just a bloke reading a paper, someone prodding around under the bonnet of a car.'

'And yet they rumbled him,' Patrick observed.

'Not necessarily,' I said. 'He could have just got up someone's nose.'

'You're forgetting,' he said, 'Morley was tortured.'

'That doesn't definitely mean they suspected him of being a *policeman*.'

'Solving his murder might hang on what he told them, if anything.'

So might the lives of those doing the investigating, I thought.

Four

'He had a way of not arousing the suspicion of the villains among whom he moved,' Superintendent Paul Reece said. 'A man-in-the-street sort of person – or at least Cliff could make himself look ordinary. He had a knack; he was a natural. We're all bloody angry at what happened to him.'

'What went wrong?' Patrick asked quietly.

Reece was of short stature and dark-haired. Despite obviously having been briefed by Carrick he did not seem to know quite what to make of us, this one-time Lieutenant-Colonel and his lady in their dark business suits, and there had been some unfriendly stares from those few members of his team who were on the premises, inhabiting an untidy office that resembled a collection point for a jumble sale. Everyone seemed to be wearing baggy jeans and yesterday's sweatshirt and had not acquainted themselves with soap and razor for a couple of days. There had been no females in sight.

But these were, I mentally told myself sternly in the next breath, amazing and brave people who had to look scruffy because they worked within the criminal underworld and who, for professional pride reasons, resented the arrival of outsiders in the shape of the Serious and Organized Crime Agency.

'We don't know,' Reece said in response to the question. 'The plan to lift him out had been well planned. We knew he would be driving someone else's car in a certain location with the owner as a passenger so we got Traffic to pull the vehicle over on the pretext that it was in an unroadworthy condition. Morley was in on the plan and, as pre-arranged, refused to cooperate with the law, actually putting up a fight. The man he was with did a runner and got away, as it had been decided he should. Morley and the car were then taken into custody and everyone congratulated themselves that the ruse had worked. Morley was de-briefed, went home to Bath, played in a rugger match the next day and was due to drive up to his parent's place in Cumbria the following morning. He did not; he disappeared.'

'What was his brief?' Patrick asked.

'I'll have to fill you in with the background before I do that,' Reece replied. 'Can I get you some coffee first?'

Patrick smiled. 'Did I see a machine in the main office on our way through?'

'Yes, you did.'

'Then allow Ingrid and me to get you some.'

Reece said nothing, but I detected a little surprise.

There were four of them, busily engaged with computers, phones or files, but there was a slight pause in the proceedings when we walked in. One individual with red hair stopped what he was doing altogether, throwing down his pen, and subjected Patrick to an unfriendly stare, as he had at our first appearance.

'Is this a getting-to-know-the-lower-decks exercise then . . . sir?' he asked, pointedly ignoring me.

'No,' Patrick said as we circumnavigated a rucksack and a pile of outdoor clothing on the floor on our way to the coffee machine. 'Right now it's using four hands to fetch three coffees. Would anyone else like some?'

'No thanks,' said the man, answering for all.

'There's no need to call me sir; most SOCA people are given the rank of constable to enable them to arrest people. Patrick will do fine. This is my wife and working colleague, Ingrid. Was Cliff Morley a good chum of yours?'

'He was,' the other man answered stonily. 'A *very* good chum.'

'I shall value anything you might be able to tell me about him and what he was working on.'

'We don't need outside help. We're perfectly capable of finding the bastards ourselves.'

'You might need someone to out-Herod Herod,' was all Patrick said, seemingly absently-mindedly, organizing poly-styrene cups.

'Sergeant Cunningham's taken Morley's death very badly,' Reece said on our return, having seen, but not heard, the exchange through the glass screen between the offices. 'I sincerely hope he wasn't offensive.'

'Not at all,' Patrick replied. 'I could tell he was upset when we first arrived. Is he closely involved on the same case as Morley?'

'No, he's not working on that at all.'

'Nor now, on the investigation into his death?'

'No. I thought it best if he stayed right out of it.'

'I suggest you rope him in in some capacity. Let's get all that grief and burning resentment properly channelled, shall we?' Patrick opened his briefcase. 'Now, please give us as much relevant information as you can.'

He did not think of himself as a mere constable, obviously.

'This appears to be one of those cases where a bunch of urban thickoes with truckloads of form headed by a brainier version jump into a black BMW with tinted glass windows and head for a city in the provinces either because of disagreements or because home is too hot to stay in,' Reece began urbanely. 'These people are unknown to us and although the Met *think* the boss-man could be the brother-in-law of someone calling himself Ernie O'Malley, who runs his dirty little empire from a council flat in Walthamsden when he hasn't given the Met the slip, there's no proof. They seem to keep their heads down and play it respectable when they're not actually breaking the law. I'll be perfectly honest with you and admit that we haven't yet made any progress in establishing who they are. It's almost as though several neighbours from somewhere in the Smoke got bored, decided to rob a building society branch, realized that the life was for them and took it from there. It's that incomprehensible. But they mean business. One of them, or possibly two, carry weapons – knives and handguns – and know how to use them.'

'Are you clear in your mind that these people you speak of were responsible for Morley's death?' Patrick enquired.

'No, but there's a tenuous connection which I'll tell you about in a minute,' Reece replied. 'Its all we have.'

I made notes. My shorthand, a mostly outdated concept these days, is still pretty good and has the advantage of being utterly unreadable to nearly everyone else should someone acquire my notepad or try to read over my shoulder. It also means I can be as rude as I like about those doing the talking and record any suspicions about them.

Reece continued, 'We've actually got recent CCTV footage of a couple of them where you can see their faces. One was a jewellery shop robbery – the proprietor was shot dead – where the scarf that was being used as a mask by one of the gang slipped and you get a good view of the man wearing it. The other was when a Ferrari was stolen at knife-point in a station carpark and whoever was holding the weapon wasn't even trying to hide his face. We've enhanced the pictures and sent them off to the Met and, as they haven't the first idea who they are, I think their theory is wrong. As I said, newcomers. They probably go home afterwards and mow the lawn.'

'Illegal immigrants?' Patrick said.

'They *could* be, but the masked ones making most of the demands don't appear to have foreign accents; more like what's referred to as "estuary English".'

'You reckon it's the same bunch on both those occasions?'

'Yes, because one of the guys involved is extremely tall and bony-looking. He dresses like a scarecrow and wears a balaclava. He doesn't have to carry weapons – his appearance frightens the victims silly. They say he has a strange squeaky voice and moves in an odd way – probably for disguise purposes.'

'He could be the leader,' I commented.

Reece looked at me as if seeing me for the first time, a phenomenon that I have come up against quite a lot since working with Patrick.

'Yes, I think he is,' he acknowledged.

'So these people just come out of nowhere, do a job

and then vanish?' Patrick said. 'What was Morley doing then?'

'Hanging around trying to spot and get an angle on the tall man. This character doesn't appear to go in the kind of pubs that dodgy people use – and we really are talking about a very tall individual; he's at *least* six foot six or seven and bone-thin. Up until a short while ago the snouts we use were as in the dark as we were, or so they said. Then Morley got a lead from one of them about someone who'd moved into a new estate in Bradley Stoke and immediately started upsetting all the neighbours – boorish behaviour, big aggressive guard dogs, the bloke tall and thin and always ready to pick an argument. Morley was given an address of sorts but when he went out there he couldn't find the place. He asked the snout to take him as he didn't want to use his own car for obvious reasons and the guy agreed but said he was banned from driving so Morley would have to. Then *another* snout hinted to someone else on my team that the first snout was involved with the gang and I became worried that Morley was at serious risk. I didn't want him to be seen anywhere near the area. So we lifted him out. During his de-briefing I warned him to keep his head down but he was keen to be available for the rugby match the next day before he headed up north. On reflection I should have made it an order. You know the rest.'

'Both snouts could be dodgy,' I said. 'And in the pay of whoever runs this gang.'

'That too is possible,' Reece said.

'So they both need to be taken apart by persons unknown in order to get at the truth,' Patrick said.

Reece's eyes widened in alarm. 'Do you have that kind of brief?'

Patrick shrugged. 'I could always make a point of asking my boss afterwards.'

'But there can't be seen to be a connection with anything like that and a police department, surely!'

'There won't be. The day I look like anything emanating from a police department when I'm on a job I shall deserve to be chucked out.' He smiled placatingly. 'No, it's fairly simple to give every impression of belonging to an aggrieved local godfather's outfit.'

'All these people could be operating under stolen identities,' Reece went on after a short pause. 'And, picking up the thread of what we were talking about just now, we did subsequently check on the address that Morley had been given. There was no house of that name in the road mentioned.'

'All the more reason to do a little investigating on those snouts,' Patrick said. 'Would you like me to do that first? I mean, you're not going to trust them sufficiently to use either of them again, are you?'

'Do re-phrase that, Patrick,' I urged. 'Or Superintendent Reece will think you're going to make them disappear for good.'

'Unfortunate use of words,' he agreed. 'I should have said "otherwise you're not going to trust them sufficiently to use them again."'

'They would have been brought in for interview already,' Reece told him. 'But the pair of them have gone right off the map. Needless to say, we're looking, but by all means act independently.'

I said, 'One of the worst aspects of this is that Morley was tortured before being killed. I understand that the initials RK were carved on his chest. Have you any idea who that might be, or is it possible that the marks made with a knife only resemble those letters?'

'No, it's fairly clear it's someone signing their handiwork,' Reece answered. He reached for a file on his desk. 'To spare the family we've omitted to mention that he was mutilated as well. There are photographs in there, taken of the body as it was found, if you both care to look at them. But I warn you, they're not pleasant.'

'I'd rather you didn't distress yourself,' Patrick said to me, leaning over to take the file before I could touch it. 'Remember what happened on the arson job.'

There had been no arson job. But as we have our own codes that involve the deliberate telling of lies I went along with this knowing that he would explain his reasons later.

He opened the file and I could tell from his face that the photographs were ghastly – I could see only that they were in colour – and on looking at one of them this ex-soldier of mine got to his feet and walked over to the window to try to prevent us from seeing him retching.

'God,' he whispered. He stared at Reece hard. 'Did he have the kind of information that would be of real use to serious criminals?'

'Well, the names of all his colleagues and those in charge, of course, but that's about it. He certainly wasn't in possession of the kind of stuff that's mostly inside my head. And we're not that high-flown a department, merely CID with a few knobs on.'

'That begs the question of who they might have *thought* he was. Are these people, one wonders, into the kind of activities that would attract the attention of the Anti-Terrorism Branch or those sectors that were merged to create SOCA? Or I suppose it's possible inflicting such torment wasn't in an attempt to learn anything but just to make some sadist feel all nice and warm inside.' These last words had been uttered, as he handed back the folder, in a voice choking with disgust. 'Perhaps you'd be good enough, Superintendent, to let me have a copy of the case notes contained in this. And the pictures of those characters that you sent to the Met.'

'Certainly,' Reece said. 'You can have them right now. Will you visit the scene where Morley's body was found?'

Patrick nodded. 'Yes, probably straight after we leave here. Not that I would presume to discover anything that your people have missed. We find it helps, that's all.'

'There's a map marked with the exact location in the file. I'll get that copied for you as well.'

'You're not very good at hiding your feelings,' Patrick explained when we were on our own. 'That's why I didn't want you to see anything that might possibly be the work of James's father. He'd know, just by looking at you, that you were upset and an abomination had taken place.' He added, 'But I'm glad you didn't see them for your own sake, too. I almost threw up.'

'But you must have seen all kinds of ghastly sights when you were a serving officer,' I said, actually quite shocked at how it had affected him.

'I did, but in time of enemy action your real concerns are tactics, your responsibility for the living, and you learn to concentrate on all that. The worst things were the bomb disposal people who got it wrong when I was in Northern Ireland.'

The media descriptions of the finding of the body in 'woodland near Bristol' appeared to be inaccurate and after wending our way along country lanes we found ourselves bouncing over rough ground and scrubland on the edge of a rubbish tip near Bradley Stoke, the second time the place had featured that morning. Patrick was doing the navigating – we were at the correct grid reference but at the follow-your-nose stage – and we duly topped a slight rise and headed down towards what was indeed a small wood. Incident tape was stretched between some of the trees, creating a restricted area. There was no sign of any police presence now but the ground was churned up from the recent movements of vehicles.

As we went downhill, now on a track of sorts, the ground became wetter. I could see that it was very dark within the wood, water glinting in a couple of places where light penetrated the leaf canopy and, when the engine was turned off, the sound of a trickling stream could be heard. But this was not an attractive place, the air sour with the smell of rotting rubbish on the nearby tip, the thin grass yellow and sickly-looking. The stream, looking more like a polluted run-off, was a strange grey, almost metallic colour and in the small pools that had formed revolved large blobs of revolting yellow scum.

Neither of us spoke as we left the car and walked down to the edge of the trees. Over to our right seagulls circled in the dusty air above the tip and excavators growled somewhere out of sight in the distance. Huge piles of topsoil had been dumped right up to the trees and I could see a day, soon, when this little wood would be buried for ever.

We ducked under the tape and entered, pausing to allow

our eyes to accustom to the gloom. The spot where Morley's body had been found was quickly obvious; the vegetation, such as it was, in a shallow ditch flattened and bruised with a kind of greasy sheen to it, footprints everywhere. I knew that when investigations had ceased all traces of murder would be removed and wondered why no one was here to prevent incursions by the curious or ghoulish. Then I saw that there was indeed a police presence; a patrol car just visible through the trees over to the left. It appeared that we might have arrived by the 'scenic' route. Surely they had heard us.

'Say nowt,' Patrick whispered. 'It would be polite to go over and say hello but . . .' His voice trailed away as he crouched down on the edge of the ditch from which arose the smell of putrefaction.

I felt sick. Looking around, it was obvious that the trees were dying, leaning on one another, the trunks at ground level black and slimy, the bark, in places, falling off. Branches had also fallen and lay, one on another, rotting into the wet ground. The pools of water had an iridescent gleam as though oil lay on the surface. It probably did. Dark, Sherlockian and bog-ridden? I had been very naïve: I now knew what those words really meant.

I turned and went away.

After a few minutes Patrick joined me in the Range Rover.

'You've been crying,' he observed softly.

'This is an evil and disgusting place,' I whispered.

I could not write the book now.

As Bristol CID had undertaken a search of the whole area, even raking through the pools, without finding any clues, there was no point in us lingering. Patrick did have second thoughts about making ourselves known to the crew of the area car and went back to speak to them. It turned out they had been expecting us, having been given our vehicle's registration. Then we left.

'Will you be offended if I ask you to go home for a few days while I endeavour to chase down these missing informers?' Patrick said as we were driving away.

'Because I'm getting all emotional?' I queried, hearing the resentment in my voice.

'No, because I can't see the point in dragging you around neck-end Bristol pubs, which is no doubt where they usually hang out. I was wondering if you'd undertake a little discreet surveillance at Sheepwash Farm – I don't think we're finished with the place yet.'

'I might,' I said grumpily.

'But please don't go inside any of the buildings. Someone might have returned and rigged up another nasty surprise.'

'But surely the local police will have sealed them all off.'

'They may well have done. But don't take any chances.'

I should, after all this time, have got used to Patrick just walking away, taking one of the small bags containing a few necessities that we always keep in the car and going from my sight, either into the countryside, or as now, a busy city centre. I have not: I have a horror that, one day, it will be the last time and I will never see him again. He did not want the car, it was of no use to him, even a hindrance on this kind of job.

My only comfort was that, before he joined the army, Patrick went off by himself and learned all kinds of things; his survival package, he calls it. He has not burdened me with full details – most wives probably would not want to know any more – but it meant that when he started training for Special Services he could show the instructors a thing or two. It is actually a side to him that I prefer not to dwell on too much as I have witnessed what he can do. But it keeps him alive in the most dangerous and nightmarish situations.

I had a nightmare that night; of a tall, shambling scarecrow figure climbing the creepers on the cottage wall outside my bedroom window, all the while making strange hissing sounds. The mouth and eyes were just black holes in a strange sacking mask it was wearing but within, in the malevolent darkness, there seemed to exist a being. When it got into the room and I was trying to fight it off I discovered that although immensely strong it was, after all, just made of straw. Then I woke up, drenched in sweat.

Despite what he had said, I was sure now that Patrick had felt the need to remove me, temporarily, from the forefront of the investigation into the case of the horribly murdered policeman. This occurred to me when I was sitting in the kitchen sipping a mug of tea after my dream. An over-active imagination is the penalty you pay when you write books, I was all too aware, a fact that was not lost on the man in my life either. It was a little before six, the morning already light, the sound of birdsong entering through the window I had just opened.

I heard movement and Matthew, another early bird, came in. He closely resembles his uncle at that age, especially now with this grave expression on his young face.

'Are you all right, Auntie?' he asked, not used to seeing me at this hour. Both he and Katie call me that for their mother is still alive. She is an alcoholic and since illicitly trying to gain possession of valuable jewellery their father left them in his will has no legal access to them.

'I had a bad dream, that's all,' I answered.

Normally, and as previously mentioned, Patrick and I live in the converted barn across the courtyard. My return home had meant that I could give Carrie, the nanny, time off, and she had gone into Plymouth to see friends and spend the night with her mother. I had slept in the spare bed in her room.

'What was it about?' Matthew wanted to know when I had given him some tea.

'A horrible scarecrow.'

He gave me a reassuring smile. 'You were remembering the ones in *Doctor Who*. They were *terrific*! Just men inside though, actors.'

Just a man inside, I pondered. Just a man, acting, a common-or-garden crook.

So he was.

As we had arranged, Patrick kept in touch. We did not speak; he merely rang the landline or my mobile number for the next couple of evenings, allowing it to ring three times and then hanging up. It saved any conversations being

overheard by the wrong people and, with the criminal frater-
nity becoming ever more sophisticated as far as electronic
gadgets are concerned, prevented calls being traced. All I
could gather from this, of course, was that he was still in
one piece and on the job.

I could picture the scene: the scruffy, unshaven individual
leaning on the bar or playing darts with the locals,
succeeding in looking the worse for wear after drinking
hardly anything at all, blending in, keeping his eyes open.
He might decide to start a fight at closing time and even
get himself arrested. There is a side to him that enjoys
making trouble and blacking a few of the eyes of the ungodly
if he thinks he can learn something useful from it. He would
have made a first-class criminal.

I thought the business of my keeping discreet surveillance on Sheepwash Farm rather a ploy on Patrick's part
to make me feel as though I was still being useful. But, as
usual, I did as requested on the third day at home, setting
off mid-morning, the first two being devoted to the children and things like paying bills and organizing the farrier
for George and Fudge.

The weather was absolutely appalling, a real Dartmoor
downpour, so by the time I had fought my way over the
flooded tracks I had reached the mental state of 'bugger
everything', decided to drop the 'discreet' and drove all the
way to the farm. I was damned if I was going to get soaked
to the skin and not for one moment expected anyone to be
around.

But there were plenty of people around; mostly police
by the look of it.

Five

I found somewhere to park on the rough hillside, put boots
on and sploshed my way towards the entrance to the yard,
the steep stony path a fast-flowing stream such was the
force of the rain that somehow turned sharp right and disappeared into the byre when everything indicated that it
should carry on straight though the front door of the house.
I suddenly remembered the name of the senior officer who
had arrived when we had found the booby-trapped suitcase.

'You can't go in there, madam,' said the very wet constable
standing by the gate.

'Serious and Organized Crime Agency,' I snapped, the rain
thundering on the hood of my anorak. 'What's going on?'

He stared at me, I stared back and he then decided to
answer the question. 'Two unidentified males have been
found dead in the house.'

'Who found them?'

'We did. There was a tip-off.'

'Is Inspector Hume here?'

'Yes, he is.'

'My name is Ingrid Langley. Please be so good as to tell
him I'm here.'

He looked dubious but went away, returning quite quickly.

'You were with Lieutenant-Colonel Gillard?'

'That's right.'

'You may go in.'

I threaded my way between the vehicles, endeavouring
not to slip over in the mud that had arrived in the yard.
Lights had been rigged inside what I already knew to be
the house's normally gloomy interior, a generator humming
in the comparative shelter of the open tractor shed. Stepping

over cables, I went indoors. The hallway seemed to be full
of people but the two dead ones lying on the floor in the
cordoned-off front room where figures wearing anti-
contamination suits worked took centre stage.

It was obvious, right from the start – in other words due
to the stench – that they had been there for several days.
One did not have to be very clever, or observant, to see that
they had been subjected to severe torment, exposed areas
of skin bruised, the clothes blood-soaked and not related
to the cause of death, a single shot to the head from behind.

'What brought you here, Miss Langley?' asked the man
standing nearest to me: Hume.

I told him, adding, 'Do you know who they were?'

'No, not yet. There's no identification on them.'

For some reason I found myself stammering. 'Are . . . are
there letters or initials carved on the bodies?'

He gazed at me in surprise. 'We haven't got that far yet.
What makes you think there might be?'

'Patrick's working on the Cliff Morley case and I'm
wondering if they're the two informers he's looking for in
Bristol. There are similarities between the state of these
bodies and Morley's.'

Hume appeared to find this far-fetched but said, 'Well,
we won't be able to tell until the PMs are done – not with
all that bloodstaining. We're still waiting for the pathologist to arrive – I reckon he's got himself well and truly
lost.'

I doubted it was the same two men – I had not seen any
mugshots of the Bristol pair, if indeed they had criminal
records – as it seemed too much of a coincidence. To Hume
I said, 'It might save a lot of work if you sent photos of
these two to the Avon and Somerset force – Superintendent
Paul Reece. He's at HQ in Portishead. Would you do that?'

'You mean it might not be my case at all?' he enquired
after due thought.

I gave him a sweet smile. 'No.'

He did not give me a straight answer and carried on
directing the procedings. I hung around. The pathologist,
from Exeter, eventually turned up, furious because he had

damaged his new car on a stone wall negotiating a tight turn. After an interminable wait while he did what he had to, during which time I went outside for some fresh air and to check on the baby swallows, Hume came out, hurried through the rain into the building where the Land Rover had been housed and called me over.

'I asked Doctor Greene to examine the bodies for any knife marks,' he said. 'It meant swabbing down their torsos but yes, you're right. I'll get those pictures off to Portishead as soon as possible.'

'Could you make out any actual letters?'

'Not really. Not under these somewhat primitive conditions. Possibly BB or RB. As I said, we'll know more at the post-mortems.'

'Could they be RK?'

'It's possible.'

'Has the pathologist any idea if they were killed here, or elsewhere?'

'We haven't discussed that yet but seeing there was very little blood beneath the bodies when they were moved I'd say they were dead, or very nearly so, when they arrived.'

It was important to get hold of Patrick. This I endeavoured to achieve, sitting in the car, by doing what he had done, calling his mobile, only letting it ring four times. I knew he would not return the call immediately, not unless he was right away from his search area, and he did not. But later that afternoon, when I had called the number again and was beginning to worry, the phone rang.

'Me,' he said laconically, sounding very tired.

Cutting the facts right down to the bone I gave him the news.

'I'll get a train. Can you pick me up in Plymouth?'

It was quite late when a dishevelled figure got off the train, tumbled into the car and slept all the way home. I said nothing, just giving a bristly cheek a wifely peck in passing and waited until he had showered, shaved and had a tot of his favourite single malt before attempting to communicate. This first approach, I had discovered years previously, would have to be of a strictly practical nature if there was going to be any discussion on the case that night. I wanted there to be: I am an impatient sort of person.

'Steak and kidney pudding?' I asked.

'Surely you haven't gone to those lengths now,' he said.

'No, I decided some time ago to make individual ones, freeze them and use them for emergencies.'

He allowed himself a few seconds to bathe in the warm glow of anticipation. 'Wonderful. You're a saint.'

When pudding, new potatoes and homegrown broad beans were inside us both – I had decided I needed a good meal too – and I had given him the whole story I said, 'I've a really funny feeling about all these events.'

I got Patrick's full attention: my 'funny feelings' have quite often proved to be useful.

'This business of someone appearing to sign their ghastly handiwork,' I began. 'Is that really what it is or is someone trying to lay blame elsewhere?'

'To blame it on whoever RK is, you mean, whether that happens to be Robert Kennedy, or not?'

'Yes, especially with these bodies dumped in the house belonging to someone who is – or, according to the man I met, *was* – Robert Kennedy's next-of-kin. If even that's true.'

'And bearing in mind that we don't yet know the identities of the two murdered men. It might be that they were other people entirely, victims of a Plymouth drugs war. Or completely innocent of any criminal connections.'

'Having seen them I'd put money on them being what my dad used to refer to as gallows fodder.'

'Did you say anything about Robert Kennedy to Hume?'

'No, but they should be perfectly capable of finding that out for themselves. It's not exactly a secret who was living at the farm.'

Patrick helped himself to more coffee. 'I agree with you up to a point but nevertheless think the time has come for *us* to bring Kennedy's name out into the open. Just because he *might* be Carrick's father – and we don't even know that yet for sure . . .' He broke off and shrugged somewhat angrily. 'I hate working in the dark like this.'

'Please speak to James first,' I requested. 'Even if one ignores the personal side of it, suddenly having a serious criminal for a father isn't going to do his career any good.'

Patrick looked at his watch. 'It's just before eleven. Is that too late to ring?'

'They're not early-to-bed people.'

Carrick had only just got back home after a difficult day and the two men swopped exhaustion details before Patrick got down to business. It was not a protracted call.

'Well, as you probably heard I've made arrangements to meet him tomorrow to talk about this,' Patrick said. 'He's found out more and has asked me to hold my fire until then. That's reasonable.'

'Did you find out anything in Bristol?'

'Not really. By dint of talking to the mostly sloshed I did discover that the local underworld is scared silly of this character who's moved in. They don't know who he is, only that there's family connections, dangerous family connections, with London. The guy's put that about himself apparently, at a guess to aid his crook-cred. One bloke echoed Reece's theory, that he lives and plans his jobs in an unsuspecting and possibly up-market neighbourhood. I did a spot of surveillance on several houses in the area where Morley was given the false address too and didn't spot anyone exceptionally tall or with big guard dogs. I have an idea that if Reece hadn't got him out then there was a nasty end in store for him on that day.'

'Just for asking around?'

'That's right.'

'Reece should have taken a stronger line with Morley and stopped him staying in the area,' I said, unable to stop fretting about what I regarded as a huge lapse on the super-intendent's part.

'Yes, but Bath isn't really *that* close and Reece would have had no idea then that Morley was in such danger.'

'I hope you were careful.'

'I made out I was a Glasweigian crimewriter researching a book but returning home shortly. I became quite proud of the fact that most people couldn't understand a word I said.' He smiled at the memory.

'I'd like to come with you tomorrow.'

'Fine,' Patrick said. He stretched. 'Well then, bed.'

I found myself fixed with an appraising stare, a little smile playing at the corners of his mouth.

'You've only just told James that you were knackered,' I pointed out, knowing precisely what was uppermost in his mind.

'On reflection it was a hasty and exaggerated prognosis,' I was ponderously told in a strong Scottish accent, his eyes nevertheless glinting with mirth and . . . er . . . lust.

He glanced round and clearly thought about sweeping me up in his arms and carrying me upstairs. But the staircase in this little barn conversion is too narrow. Perhaps subconsciously not wishing to be transported as cargo in a fireman's lift I thwarted that by grabbing him for munching kisses and unbuttoned his shirt, aware that once started we would make love right where we were on the living-room carpet.

There and in bed a little later actually.

It was apparent that James Carrick was almost too busy to see us. He arrived, at speed through the door of his office, arms full of papers and a bulging document case.

'We live in a digital age but no police authority it appears can afford to give its personnel lap-tops,' he announced, dropping his armful down with a thump on a comparatively clear corner of his desk. 'But then again, the local villains'd only steal them.' He gave us a fleeting smile. 'Thanks for coming.'

'I'm on my way to see Paul Reece,' Patrick told him. 'As of this morning he's got a couple of corpses to add to his investigation into Morley's death. Or so it *appears*.'

Carrick nodded briskly. 'I know. He rang me at home. They were the two snouts his team use; names of Kyle Jeffers and Madderly Ritter.'

'Which one of them warned someone on Reece's team that Morley might be in danger?' I asked.

'You'll need to get that from Paul.'

Exasperated, I said, 'What I can't understand is how whichever of the two this was knew Morley was a policeman.'

'He might not have done, just mentioned that someone was asking questions, "that bloke over there guv" kind of thing?'

'Well, the tall man probably knows now,' Patrick observed grimly. 'What do you want us to do, James?'

Carrick, who had so far remained standing, sat in the chair behind his desk. 'I really appreciate that you're asking me but it's obvious that a man who might be my father is out of jail and has the initials RK will have to be brought into the equation. I can't be seen to be shielding him in any way and, frankly, I don't think that I want to.'

But he did, he did, I could tell by the tightly controlled emotion.

'Thank you,' Patrick said quietly. 'Have you been able to discover anything further?'

'Nothing concrete. I've been up to my neck here but have been doing a little research at home. As I've already told you my mother and I went to live with an aunt at Crieff after life at her parents' place became untenable. This aunt is now dead but she had a daughter, Louise, who is my cousin, of course. I managed to contact Louise via the internet as she and her husband run an hotel in the same area and we've subsequently spoken over the phone. I gather that my mother and auntie had long conversations about her predicament, some of which Louise was apprised of years later. Louise was staggered to learn that Robert might not have drowned and almost as astonished that he had gone wrong. My mother was very much in love with him, you see, and this must have been conveyed to Auntie along with what a good man he was and all the rest of it. Ross, Lord Muirshire, told me a while back that Robert had said he intended to divorce his wife, who was having affairs, and marry my mother and he too said he was a man of integrity.'

I could see that James was having trouble talking about

this but knew we needed to know the full story if we were to be of any help. 'You never mention your mother, James. Is she still alive?'

'No, she eventually went out to South Africa and married a farmer. She was killed in a car crash ten years ago.' He hesitated and then pulled open a desk drawer to take out a thick white envelope. Within it was a colour photograph which he handed to us to see.

'Such a beautiful woman,' I whispered, gazing at the wedding group of bride, groom and all the guests. 'What was her name?'

'Orla.'

Neither Patrick nor I made further comment: young James had not been present.

'Louise knew all about Archie,' Carrick continued. 'He apparently was a bit of a rogue and drank heavily. She had an idea he'd moved down south, mostly on account of the local laird being after his hide for deer and salmon poaching. He was only a distant cousin of Robert's after all.'

'Yet he was listed as next-of-kin,' I said. 'Is there no other family to contact?'

'None that I, or Ross, know about. I've no doubt one could undertake further research but I simply don't have the time right now. What Louise did have, however, was a photograph. I got it through the post yesterday.'

This time it came out of his wallet and was a small snapshot of friends on a picnic. The girl who must be Orla had moved, her face blurred, but Robert Kennedy stood out a mile, his lookalike right here in the room with us.

'We need to see the mugshot,' Patrick said gently.

Carrick sighed and turned his attention to his computer. After a little all-fingers-and-thumbs difficulty a face came up on the screen. With the prison haircut, the face drawn, thirty-seven years later but looking older than his years, here, surely, was the same man.

'He's been very ill,' I murmured.

'I'm still not too sure it's him,' James said, a catch in his voice.

'It is,' Patrick said. 'Accept it, man.'

'Aye,' Carrick said, and asking us to excuse him, abruptly left the room.

Paul Reece was in the senior officers' canteen and appeared tense and also a little flustered that we had found him snatching a few minutes' break. He organized some coffee and biscuits for us and when we had assured him that we were perfectly happy to exchange news right where we were, reseated himself.

'I fully intend to take a look at this amazing farm on Dartmoor,' he announced, adding, 'Although I'm damned if I know what good my presence there'll do.'

Patrick produced the file we had quickly created before we left Bath's Manvers Street police station. It contained what information there was available on Robert Kennedy, the photograph of him and a background report and the early findings at Sheepwash Farm, in case the Devon and Cornwall Force had not yet forwarded this in an email.

'There's one piece of information that isn't in that,' Patrick told Reece as he handed it over. 'This man could well be James Carrick's father whom he had always thought to be dead.'

Reece stared at him. 'Bloody hell! Do you mind if I look at this now?'

'There's no *real* evidence as far as Kennedy's concerned,' Patrick said when Reece had finished reading. 'Only the connection with the farmhouse and it's strange, to say the least, when crooks start leaving their autograph on their murder victims. One must assume they're either raving lunatics or they badly want someone else to get the blame.'

'Inter-gang warfare then?' Reece mused. 'God, James must be in hell over it.'

'He is. Or rivalry within the same gang?'

'Um. Someone trying to oust the bossman perhaps.'

'They'd have to be RKs too.'

'There's no one known to us around here with those initials.' Reece sighed. 'It's vital we soon get a lead on this tall character.'

'We might have to make things happen.'

Reece leaned back in his chair and subjected Patrick to a steady gaze. 'Like what for instance?'

'You could tell the media that you have in custody a man called Riko Kastovic, an illegal immigrant, for Morley's murder. Or do it with a flourish: all bells and whistles with someone covered with a blanket being taken to a city centre nick.'

'The guilty bastards'll just think we've screwed up and laugh all the way to the pub!' Reece protested.

'Then put it about, via the grapevine, that he's singing his heart out and telling you everything you want to know. *Then* have him busted out of a prison van taking him away on remand by villains unknown. The tall man and his friends will fall over one another to get hold of him, dead worried that somehow he does know a thing or two, and, hopefully, make big mistakes and because you'll have an army of undercover people right on Kastovic's tail you'll be able to grab them.'

Reece frowned. 'They'll know they didn't bust him out of the van.'

'Well, of course. But the villains unknown might just be a rival mob who want to remove the new opposition from their patch for ever and Kastovic knows exactly who they are too.' Here Patrick gave the Superintendent a crazy sort of grin.

After a short pause Reece said, 'This isn't your MI5 days, you know.'

'No, it's my SOCA days and the MI5 experience is why they wanted me,' Patrick retorted.

After a brief silence Reece said, 'I'll think about it.'

'Do you have anything on the two snouts, Jeffers and Ritter?' I asked, feeling the proceedings needed a kick in the pants. 'Has it been confirmed that they weren't murdered at the farm? What about their families, if any? Girlfriends? People they knocked around with?'

The superintendent turned to me with what I felt to be exaggerated patience. 'They were men who drifted around doing odd-jobs, or worked for a short while on building sites as labourers. Ritter had had a job as a warehouseman for a department store in the city, on and off though mostly at Christmas. Jeffers was more of a layabout. It's believed they both came from the north somewhere originally and had known one another for years. You can picture it: drop-outs from school, in trouble with the law from day one. No one seems to know if they had families and they were never seen with regular girlfriends. That's hardly surprising as they probably never had any money.'

Cynical old sod, isn't he? I thought.

'It has been established that they weren't killed in the farmhouse,' Reece continued. 'And there's not sufficient blood at the scene for the knife work to have been inflicted upon them there although how they were transported, dead or practically so, without those handling them and their vehicles getting covered in it is anyone's guess. If they were they didn't try to wash it off in the kitchen sink and apparently there's no bathroom there, just an outside lavatory served by an ancient septic tank that I understand is spilling raw sewage into a nearby ditch. The yard was a sea of mud when the local CID arrived and they satisfied themselves that any tyre tracks had been obliterated by the heavy rain before they drove in. The carpets, such as they were, were taken away by Forensics for examination but as you know every man and his dog had been in the place since the suitcase containing the explosive device was discovered by yourselves. You'll have to give us your fingerprints by the way.'

Patrick shook his head. 'No, we wore gloves – the place was already a potential crime scene when we arrived as the place had been turned over. There was every indication that someone had left in a hurry although they had not gone in the Land Rover we found in a barn. But when we returned the next morning – that's when we investigated the suitcase – the vehicle had gone.'

I said, 'We still don't know if Archie Kennedy's really dead or if he was the man I met.'

'He's not registered as deceased at the Plymouth Registry Office and according to West Devon Borough Council is still the occupier of the farm,' Reece said. 'So if he really is dead it either happened somewhere else or no one's said a word.'

I had visions of a lonely grave somewhere in the rock-strewn, sodden peat wilderness.

Six

'In case you were wondering,' Patrick said to me, 'I have no intention of following up my own suggestion and pretending to be an illegal immigrant by the name of Kastovic.'

I was very glad to hear this, and told him so, adding, 'You're far more use to this case when you're *not* the bait being chased through the sewers of Bristol by armed gangsters.'

We had left Paul Reece to finish his coffee before he was due to attend the post-mortems of the two murder victims – part of the reason, I was sure, for his giving every appearance of being under strain.

'It might be more fruitful to track down Robert Kennedy,' Patrick went on to say in the manner of someone thinking aloud.

'Where would we start?'

'There's only one link that we know of and that's Lord Muirshire.'

'Would an aristocrat remain on friendly terms with a man who had turned to a life of crime?'

'You must know the answer to that question. Yes, a Scot would – they're programmed that way. Loyalty and all that. Quite right too.'

We did not have to go to Scotland to see the Marquess of Muirshire: he came to us, or more accurately, to London.

It was, we discovered, an annual dinner that he always attended, something to do with an Anglo-Scottish tourist association. I also gathered when I spoke over the phone to his estate manager that it was only one of several occasions during the year when the Marquess journeyed south as, to quote, 'his Lordship's not one of those Scots who sits mouldering in his castle brooding over the perceived injuries the English visited upon his ancestors.'

'He would say that,' Lord Muirshire said on a chuckle when I repeated this to him. 'Robin's an Englishman even though he's lived in the Inverness area for most of his life. A real way with words and quite a sense of humour too – although I admit that as far as some of my neighbours are concerned he has a point.' He spoke with hardly a trace of an accent.

I had never met this nobleman before – who had appeared delighted to meet us for coffee at his hotel, the Savoy – but Patrick had. He immediately put us at our ease, insisting we call him Ross. He was a tall, spare but wiry man in his late fifties or early sixties with thinning grey hair and keen blue eyes. Looking at his immaculate suit I wondered if the London trips were also in order that he could visit his tailor.

'I can guess what you want to talk about,' he said, pouring the coffee. 'You're friends of James's and he's been on the phone to me lately asking if I can throw any light on this business of his father. I can only tell you the same: that even after the developments in Devon I'm afraid I cannot.'

'So you were unaware that he was still alive, never mind in prison for serious criminal activities?' Patrick said smoothly.

'That's right. As I believe you already know, I was on the yacht when he went overboard. We searched for him for over an hour but the conditions were terrible with sudden dangerous squalls. If he survived I don't know how and can only think this is a case of mistaken, or stolen, identity.'

'He was neither wearing a safety harness or life jacket? That's staggering, given the weather.'

The Marquess smiled. 'You're forgetting. This was getting on for forty years ago. There wasn't the mania for safety then and Robert, strictly speaking, wasn't part of the crew but a guest. He shouldn't have been where he was on the open deck – in fact had been told to stay out of the way. And I must point out that life jackets were very bulky things in those days and mostly intended for when you had to take to the dingy to abandon ship. Working in them was difficult and people didn't, not on that boat anyway.'

'James appears to have accepted that the man released from prison is his father though. Did he mention to you the photograph his cousin Louise sent to him?'

'Yes, but it's just a snapshot taken at a picnic, isn't it?' Ross replied sadly. 'It doesn't prove anything, other than showing a strong likeness between man and son.'

'The only way to prove anything is to find the man.'

'That might be very difficult.'

'Do you know anything about Archie Kennedy?' I enquired.

'Only that he was a real reprobate and moved south to evade a prosecution on several counts of poaching.' Ross shrugged. 'Whether he really is dead I don't know but I must admit that the man you met at the cottage, Ingrid, is a bit of a mystery. Please, you must understand that with regard to Archie, and Robert for that matter, and my knowing anything about them we're talking about two of a huge family of almost a hundred people who don't even belong to my clan!'

'Are there any other relatives who might know where Robert is?' Patrick asked.

'No, I don't think you'll find there is, at least not in the UK. They're scattered all over the world.'

It was useless to persist with the questioning but on an afterthought I asked, 'Do you know what Robert Kennedy did for a living? I mean, I presume he had a job.'

'His parents were fairly wealthy,' Ross said reflectively. 'A lot of parties, shoots and weekends at friends' estates – young people going madly in all directions really. And obviously, sailing. He went to St Andrews university, I *think*. I know he wanted to come here, to London, but with what career in mind I couldn't tell you.'

And yet there was this photograph of a thuggish-looking

jailbird, I thought. 'Do you know how he met James's mother?'

'Yes, she worked at a village grocer's shop where people used to stop for provisions for sailing trips, picnics and things like that.'

'Something doesn't quite tie up in all this,' I said to Patrick later when we had left the hotel and were walking through fine misty rain along the Victoria Embankment.

'You mean you think Ross knows more then he pretends to?'

'He might well do. But, for goodness sake, the man drips integrity. If he is not telling all it would be for the right reasons.'

'One could understand Robert not wanting to meet James. It would be very difficult for them both.'

'Assuming he's even bothered to find out what his son's doing – one must bear in mind that all he was aware of before he went sailing on that yacht was that Orla was pregnant. For all he knew she could have had an abortion or lost the baby.'

'The only person likely to have been able to tell him about that is Ross. What I find a little odd is that some time ago James told me that Ross had said that he and Robert were really good friends and Robert was a fine man. And yet he seems not to know what he did for a living.'

'I'm beginning to agree with Ross and think it's a case of mistaken, or stolen, identity,' I said. 'What man from that sort of background who had survived drowning at sea would go off without telling anyone?'

Patrick pulled a wry face. 'You've lined me up to say that men are bastards and leave their pregnant girlfriends.'

'I haven't!' I protested.

Stopping in his tracks, he said, 'OK then, oh oracle mine. Fulfil your role as my adviser. Ignore the mistaken identity argument and brainstorm.'

My husband was not altogether joking and probably needed his lunch, I surmised, but also stopped and said, a bombshellish idea having just surfaced, 'You mean if it really is Robert Kennedy and he isn't a sadist and is just out of prison and the man I met is Archie Kennedy pretending to be dead and if I programme in all the other things that happened at the farm and the death of Cliff Morley with the initials RK carved on him and bung in Ross's assertion that Robert was a good sort of bloke in his youth *plus* taking into consideration the good sort of bloke we know James to be?'

'If you like.' There was gentle amusement now.

'Then he either faked his own death or lost his memory after being washed up somewhere and is an undercover policeman, or something along those lines, and someone in the gang he's in, or one in London with a connection, doesn't like him or suspects he's a plant. He could be in great danger.'

Patrick's jaw did not quite drop. '*What?*'

'I'm starving, are you?'

Patrick not recognizing as man-fuel tiny artworks of delicate morsels encased in baskets of plaited lettuce in the centre of a fourteen-inch diameter plate decorated with squiggles of rare balsamic vinegar, we went to a pub where the fare was more robust. I had no health fears on his behalf about this as he is, as a result of sheer hard training, as fit and lean as a racing snake. I noticed, with some amusement of my own, that my statement was actually having the effect of taking his mind off the menu.

'You know what this means, don't you?' he said, laying it aside.

'It's only an alternative theory,' I pointed out.

'It's straight out of one of your books,' he continued, almost resentfully, 'But also has quite a lot going for it. No, it means a change of tactics so we can factor in what you've just said.'

'Can't we find out though? Surely even deeply undercover policeman can be checked up on by colleagues in other branches.'

'No, by no means. It's too dangerous. Just one word to

the wrong person can be the end of someone. I know of a case where even a man's wife thought he'd died – the family only knew him as an out-and-out crook. It went to the extent of having a funeral. He wasn't dead and resurrected himself to shove a whole gang in the slammer for just about ever. It was all set up by the department he was working for.'

'It's hardly a family-friendly way of working.'

'Only a certain kind of person can do it and I understand that it's usually at the end of an operative's career or his stint with that particular branch. They retire, or are transferred and given a new identity thereby disappearing from the dangerous area – together with their nearest and dearest if they're still on speaking terms.'

'Are you having the lamb hotpot?'

'Er . . . yes.'

'I'd like the Greek salad, please.'

'No,' Patrick said all at once, emerging from a deep reverie after we had eaten. 'On second thoughts I don't think we should factor in your theory even though it's growing on me. I remember what it was like when we worked for D12 and someone from another department or the cops crashed into one of my scenarios and ratted everything up. Assuming you've guessed right, or even partly so, I reckon we should allow whoever's running that particular show to get on with it. It's sufficient for the present that we've mentioned his possible involvement in the case to Reece. If Kennedy is in danger – and I also suggest that right now we say nothing of any theories to Carrick – then until anyone asks for assistance we leave well alone. As you say, it's only conjecture and sometimes more damage can be done by the well-intentioned interference of allies than by the enemy.

'Not only that,' he continued. 'Robert Kennedy isn't really part of our brief. If we come across him while locating the tall man who might be the king-pin behind serious crime in the Bristol area and perhaps these killings all well and good. The next question, of course, is how do we find *him*?'

'How did he find Jeffers and Ritter?' I said. 'Or should one say how did they come to know about him? Paul Reece told us that Ritter worked as a warehousemen for a department store in the city, if only sometimes. Which one? There might be a connection there.'

Patrick ordered coffee and then went outside to phone Reece to ask him. (We have a real thing about people who holler down their mobiles in public places for all to hear.) When he returned there was a quizzical expression on his face.

'It was one of the last surviving family-owned large retail businesses in Bristol,' he said. 'A store by the name of Slaterford and Sons and it's been on the same site since the Raj, according to Reece. His great-grandmother used to shop there for flannel to make petticoats in the days when the male assistants wore frock-coats. Somehow, it's survived and although recently taken over is, in his words, still tottering along.'

'Tottering shops are always interesting,' I said. 'Lots of bargains. Shall we go and have a nose around?'

Patrick glanced at his watch. 'You're as bad as Greenway. This is London, the shop's in Bristol several hundred miles away and my expenses don't stretch to choppers. We nose tomorrow.'

The store was situated on a corner in a side street just off the main shopping area, Broadmead. This was not to say that the buildings were inferior, far from it for here was some of the finest and most imposing Victorian architecture of Bristol; the banks, building society and insurance company headquarters, each trying to outdo the other with their titans, chariots and maidens in seemly drapery. It was obvious that the stonework of many of these buildings had been cleaned and netted to keep pigeons away in recent years but this was not the case with Slaterford and Sons, the exterior of which was various shades of sooty-grey, all ledges loaded with bird-droppings. Here, surely, was where the elderly on limited incomes still came to buy the means to keep warm: Chilproof vests, bedsocks, electric fires and small saucepans to heat milk for cocoa. The windows were arranged with a dreary selection of goods; the kind of striped teacloths and towels and candlewick bedcovers that I had not seen since I was a child.

We entered and immediately found ourselves decanted down a few stairs into a bargain basement atmosphere of cut-price silver plate, appalling knick-knacks, 'gifts', tableware, glassware and artificial flowers, all made in the Peoples' Republic of Eyesore.

'Next week's jumble sale fodder,' Patrick said wonderingly, waving around a wafer-thin silver-plated tray.

'Please put it down before it folds in half,' I begged.

We postponed the basement proper – household, lighting, stationery – and wandered up to the first floor to be faced with dowdy dresses, twin sets and other 'fashion' items and then went up again to furniture, bedding, carpets and curtains. People did seem to be buying but none of it, other than what was on the ground floor, appeared to be particularly cheap.

I seated myself on an artificial leather sofa in the almost deserted furniture department. It was in a hideous shade of congealed blood. 'Are you going to make any enquiries about Ritter?' I asked.

Patrick flopped down beside me. 'To learn what, though? The man only worked here on and off – or at least in the warehouse. It might be more profitable to ask a few questions there.'

'This is a weird place.'

He chuckled. 'Like a set for a fifties Elstree comedy. Surely all this stuff has to be bankrupt stock.'

'Do you wish to buy that?' said a woman's voice suddenly and loudly behind us.

Patrick swivelled round to face the speaker. 'No, I think we can face life without it actually.'

'Then get off it. This isn't a rest room.'

I too turned. She was stick-thin, dressed in black, all knees and elbows, and if she had had another six legs would have more closely resembled Shelob, the giant spider in *The Lord of the Rings*.

Not wishing to risk further venom, we got out of range.

I expected Patrick to go back down the stairs but he ascended again towards the restaurant and accounts office.

'Something else to add to one's nightmare library,' I commented when we arrived.

'What is?'

'That woman. I've already had bad dreams about the tall man resembling a scarecrow.'

'That imagination of yours is going to jump up and bite you one day,' he said with a broad grin.

'But at the moment it's earning me quite a lot of money,' I pointed out. 'Tea?'

'My typhoid jabs aren't up to date. Are yours?'

'No, come to think of it, they aren't.'

Even in passing we could see that the restaurant was in fact a drab-looking café with no customers, the dispirited staff standing around like zombies. Travelling purposefully Patrick headed for Accounts, which turned out to be a glass-fronted cubicle, no one on duty within, and then strode down a corridor marked STAFF ONLY. Another corridor joined it at right angles and this had a notice propped up against the wall with the single word PRIVATE untidily hand-printed in marker pen on it. No one was about.

I tried the handle of the door closest to me. It was locked. Running my eye down the corridor all the doors I could see were fastened with padlocks, not just small ones but the kind of thing that would defeat all but the largest bolt-cutters. I silently drew Patrick's attention to this.

Patrick went to explore further but then paused, sniffing the air. He caught my eye and jerked his head back in the direction we had come.

'What is it?' I hissed but he shook his head and did not reply.

Back by the accounts office he stopped to look at a plaque on the wall, the usual legal requirement of company name, head office address and so forth. It looked new and was smaller than its predecessor, an unpainted strip of wall all the way around it. Then, wordlessly, we retraced our footsteps until we were outside in the street.

'The head office was listed at an address in Walthamsden,' I said. 'That's peculiar. Wasn't that where Reece said that London hoodlum who might be a relative of the man running the gang down here was supposed to hang out?'

'And someone was privately smoking cannabis somewhere in their own private Fort Knox,' Patrick said. 'Even more peculiar. Shall we come back and have a proper look round tonight?'

'You no longer have MI5 *carte blanche*,' I reminded him, not for the first time. 'You can't just break into places you think might be iffy.'

This appeared to go in one ear and out of the other. 'There was a security camera right at the end of that corridor but we were probably too far away for our faces to be recognizable,' he said and then turned to me with a gleam in his eye. 'When you think about it the shop might have been acquired as a vehicle for money-laundering. What was behind all those locked doors? Stolen property?'

'And Mr Tall Man was sitting in an office somewhere down that corridor gloating over his loot? I thought I was supposed to be the one with the vivid imagination.'

Patrick merely smiled and, when we were back outside, set off at speed down a narrow lane that separated the shop from the building next door. Grimly, I ran to catch up with him.

There were the usual clutches of fire hydrants, emergency exits, a staff entrance manned by a security man, another wide, dark opening into what I guessed was an underground car park with steel-barred gates across it and, at the far end, a large goods-inwards and outward delivery area fronting partly on to a wider lane that served as access.

Patrick paused, crossed the side road and looked about. 'There's nowhere we could watch the entrances and exits from without creating suspicion. No, damn it, let's leave, I've just spotted more cameras.'

'D'you really think the store might be part of a criminal set-up?'

'You have to ask yourself how such a dreadful establishment survives without some kind of underhand activity taking place. Do they sell stolen goods? The business rates must be sky-high here so if you only tend to sell three cups of tea and a fly-swatter most days . . .' He broke off with a shrug. 'No, perhaps I have caught it from you. If there was anything going on here surely the local CID would have sniffed it out by now.'

We had fruitlessly spent most of the morning at the city centre police station talking to anyone and everyone who might have something interesting to say about the store. We had heard only comments along the lines of 'it was a wonder the place still survived' and how nothing had been done to improve it by the new owners.

I was thinking that the business of not having such a free rein was going to be a real hindrance to this new career when Patrick suddenly removed his leather jacket, thrust it at me and, with a quiet request to stay where I was and keep my eyes open, set off again back in the direction of the main road. Just before he turned the corner there was a transformation into someone else, a stooped, twisted man with downturned head and heavy limp, hands waving around like crabs' claws.

Ye gods, anything could happen now; *anything*.

Approximately twenty seconds later the fire alarm within the store went off; bells and a wailing siren, the latter seemingly emanating from the mouth of the underground area. Then the gates to this began slowly to rumble aside, the small wheels which supported them squealing in the metal groove they were slotted into. No one was in sight so I crossed the road again and went inside, my cats' whiskers yelling at me that this was not a good idea at all.

The concrete surface of what was in effect a curving tunnel sloped quite steeply downwards. I still saw no one, there was no security point here, in fact it was so gloomy that anyone on duty would be hard-pressed to spot an intruder.

There did not seem to be any cameras either and, gazing around looking for the existence of these I noticed that there were light fittings but they were covered in dirt and obviously not functioning. But what about heat sensors? And if there were any would anyone notice another alarm with this racket going on?

To save carrying it I slipped on Patrick's jacket and then, realizing that a large dim space was opening out before me, went quickly over to the right-hand wall where it appeared to come to an end and peered around a huge pillar that marked the corner. The siren wailed on.

The large space thus revealed – as far as this was possible in the lack of light, that is – was indeed a carpark and in the gloom people were moving, running, between the vehicles seemingly to reach their own. I slipped round to the right to conceal myself behind a large people carrier for a few moments, praying that I would not meet the owner head-on coming the other way, and then, bending low, hurried along the row of cars nearest to the wall, came to a corner quite quickly, turned left and, cautiously, headed in the direction of where I guessed the pedestrian entrance into the shop was situated. Some of the cars were in motion now, their headlights on, the already stuffy air thick with exhaust fumes. Luckily, all were facing away from me and over on the far side, near the exit to the lane. Reserved spaces perhaps, for senior staff only.

Caution forced me to pause in the lee of a parked van. Ahead, I could see a dimly lit opening, a doorway through which one or two people were still emerging. Then a small group appeared, four men. One of them was very thin and at least six foot six inches tall. He stared about, examining his surroundings as though sweeping the area for danger. I shrank back behind the van. Here was someone who expected danger. When I dared to look again the four had gone and, heart pounding, I moved on in case they had spotted me and had split up in order to perform a pincer movement. The worst thing was not being able to hear anyone's approach. But no one came and shortly afterwards another set of headlights swung out and away in the direction of the exit.

Rats leaving what they thought to be a sinking ship, or what?

Seven

'Well, I have to say I've never heard of what one must assume to be senior management doing a runner when a fire alarm goes off,' Superintendent Reece said. 'Unless they were rescuing their cars. But their real responsibility lay in first ensuring that the staff and customers were safe, surely.'

'Who all filed out either through the main doors at the front or from the delivery area at the rear,' Patrick reported.

'I understand there was an official complaint to the local nick from the store saying that the alarm had been set off maliciously,' Reece continued. 'The culprit had been clearly identified as a man described as severely physically and mentally handicapped who also assaulted a member of staff. The caller wanted him caught immediately and consigned to a suitable care home – only that wasn't quite how he worded it.'

Patrick laughed. 'I didn't stop at smashing the glass of the first fire alarm I spotted. There was a lumpen security geek just inside the main doors standing by a small desk. Having lured him away from it with a few choice gestures I then heaved him into a display that turned out to be mostly cardboard boxes, had a look at his work station and pressed any number of buttons on a console partly concealed beneath it. Then I made myself scarce. I have to say I didn't expect what Ingrid witnessed.'

'Was the phone call recorded?' I enquired.

'Yes, probably,' Reece said. 'Could you describe this tall man you saw?'

'I only saw him in silhouette against the poor light in a doorway that must have led into the basement of the store,'

I told him. 'Assuming that the men he was with were of average height he must have been at least four inches taller than Patrick, who is six foot two. I would say he was thin, possibly with slightly rounded shoulders and had a small head – although it might have looked like that because his hair was thin or smoothed flat. Despite his long legs he walks with a short stride, which looks a bit odd, jerky. That's all really – I didn't dare look any longer in case they saw me.'

'Gut feelings though?' Patrick prompted. This was for Reece's benefit; he already knew what these were.

'This man is very wary,' I said. 'The men with him were probably his bodyguards and I got the impression they were being careful too – the manner in which the four moved together makes me think that. Their body language towards him was deferential and they all drove off in the same vehicle. He's the boss and there was something about the way he surveyed the car park before he left the comparative safety of where he was standing that spoke of someone ice cold and ruthless.'

Before Reece could comment Patrick said to him, 'Don't discount the last bit – Ingrid might write books but her vibes about situations and the people in them are copper-bottomed.'

Gold-bottomed actually for most of the time, I thought. Sometimes they've saved your life.

The superintendent said, 'The problem is that none of this is evidence – although I have to say the business of all those people bailing out like that was very suspicious. I can't really arrange a close watch on this man on the strength of what you've seen.'

'And for heaven's sake don't!' Patrick implored. 'If he is a hardened criminal with an expert set-up he'll be waiting for other Cliff Morleys to show up. One of those buttons I pressed was probably the early warning system of a police raid – or anything that looked like one. They might be twitchy enough to suspect my little incursion as coming from an undercover department of the law. I suggest you let things settle down for a few days.'

'What about your ruse of us making a phoney arrest?'

'I think that ought to go on hold as well. It's too risky right now – and not necessarily, on reflection, a good idea.'

Not with an outfit that wasn't MI5 anyway.

'Meantime you'll get back to your boss?'

'He'll expect me to tell him what's going on.'

'We can't have too many cooks spoiling the broth, you know.'

'Sometimes you have to let the chefs get on with it,' he was bluntly told. 'By all means investigate Morley's death – that'll be expected of you. Give his colleagues every means and encouragement to catch his killer. You may well find a connection with the man Ingrid saw. But I beg of you to build the bridges properly, by normal methods and by gathering proper evidence, or you'll have more funerals to attend with no results.'

'Do you have the authority to talk to him like that?' I asked Patrick a little later when we were sitting in the car. Just a little worried, that's all.

He shook his head. 'No. He probably called me an arrogant bastard when we'd gone but once in a while your conscience forces you to tell it how it is. He's under no obligation to take a moment's notice of me.'

Patrick then rang Greenway whose orders were immediately forthcoming: go and have a good look round that warehouse – without whoever was running Slaterford and Sons knowing.

By any standards this was not going to be easy. All too aware of his urging Reece to let things quieten down for a short while Patrick had told Greenway he would follow his own advice and endeavour to do the job the following Sunday, in two days' time.

'We don't even know where it is yet,' I remarked.

'We do. While all the fuss with the fire alarm was going on I went round the back and asked a bloke at the goods-inwards door pretending I had a parcel to deliver there. It's down near the old docks.'

'You'll need all your *cordon bleu* skills for this one.'

I found myself on the receiving end of a look that was probably more protracted than was strictly safe as he was driving the car.

'You thought I was being an arrogant bastard too then.'

'You *used* to say things like that.'

'Before we were divorced, you mean? No, I'll re-phrase that: before you chucked me out before we were divorced?'

Wondering if it still really rankled I defused any difficulty with a big smile, a real one as it happened, musing on the sheer impossibility of anything like that happening now. Unless he went off with someone else, of course.

'You're sitting there like the bloody Mona Lisa. Say something, woman.'

'Where are we going?' I obliged, having got him rattled, obviously.

'To Hinton Littlemoor. I thought we'd stay with Mum and Dad until Sunday.'

'Your father will expect you to help at the morning service, or at least to sing in the choir. Then, that evening after dinner, when the routine has always been that you have a chat with him in his study, you're going off to break into a warehouse instead?'

Patrick breathed out hard, or rather, snorted. 'My planets must be all to hell today or something. No, all right, we'll tackle the warehouse on Saturday night and stay over until early Monday morning. Although you don't have to come with me to Bristol if you don't want to.'

'Well, yes I do really as it looks a bit strange if you go out on your own.'

'I wasn't thinking of leaving until getting on for midnight.'

'I'll come. You might need an extra hand to stir the *consommé*.'

'I can see I'll never live that one down.'

We had planned to take Elspeth and John out for a meal but as it happened they had been presented with a large oven-ready duck by a local poultry farmer whose daughter John had joined in Holy Matrimony to a gas meter-reader the previous Saturday. The duck, which had only been in the freezer for half an hour, was duly whipped out and prepared for roasting. I was really happy about this as I did not feel like going out again.

'How's the job?' Elspeth asked her son later when we had gravitated to the kitchen. A slim, still-attractive woman with a keen intelligence, the gaze she fixed him with was as penetrating as his own.

'It pays the bills,' was his surprising reply, and because of who was doing the asking it had to be an honest one.

'You really miss MI5, don't you?'

He just performed a little shrug and smiled at her sadly.

'All the mayhem, explosions, trails of bodies and that kind of thing,' she went on, turning to remove the duck from the oven to check on its progress.

'Let me do that, it's heavy,' Patrick offered.

She passed him the oven gloves. 'We do keep in touch with James Carrick, you know. He and Joanna were over here a couple of evenings ago.'

'And he told you all about the mayhem, explosions, bodies, plagues of frogs and so forth,' Patrick said.

'No, not in so many words. He couldn't know, could he? He just said that he was glad your energies were directed in a less – well – unorthodox direction. I can distinctly remember having armed men in the onion bed here on more than one occasion.'

As it happened James did know quite a lot of what had gone on. But I was not worried about this exchange for Elspeth was merely delighted to see Patrick and often indulged in this heavy teasing. That she was absolutely spot on was another matter.

'You'll be telling me next that it was you, someone who was described as a madman, who set off all the alarms at Slaterfords in Bristol yesterday. It was in the *Bath Chronicle*.'

'Yes, that *was* me,' Patrick dutifully said, bailing some of the fat out of the roasting tin into a small basin.

Elspeth laughed, unsurprisingly not believing him, and then said, 'That reminds me. When Fred Hemmings was here earlier bringing the duck as a thank-you he saw the paper on the table. He asked me if I knew that there's a rumour that someone who's on the management side at the store has bought Hagtop Farm.'

'That's interesting,' Patrick said, his face giving nothing away.

How could anyone forget Hagtop? A huge cattle shed a short distance from the village had been the scene of three stomach-churning murders not all that long ago when Patrick was doing a stint with the local police. He had been peppered with shotgun pellets endeavouring to catch the killer. *I* had found the killer.

'Only this is the farmhouse itself which, as I'm sure you remember, is about a quarter of a mile away from where the bodies were found,' Elspeth was saying. 'Fred said that the house has been practically gutted and old barns and tractor sheds are being converted into extensive living accommodation. He says it must be costing a fortune. Goodness knows where the money's coming from, the shop's dreadful.'

'A truly dire shop,' Patrick agreed.

'Oh, so you do know it then. Apparently it changed hands recently and is worse, if anything. Your father thinks it belongs to the Mafia.'

'Why should he think *that*?'

'Oh, you know John. A bit like you really, thinks it's a government plot when the sun doesn't shine.'

Patrick put the duck back in the oven and left the kitchen. I discovered later that he had run his father to earth in the church where he was polishing the brass. Ladies might wield dusters and vacuum cleaners and do the flowers but John always polishes the brass. I gather that Patrick qualified as a helper to finish the job and the two returned to the rectory quite quickly, possibly on account of the new bottle of single malt Patrick had brought with him now gracing the kitchen dresser.

After dinner Patrick and I went for a walk. I was still unaccountably tired but felt we needed to: it had been a massive main course with all the trimmings – almost like

a Christmas dinner – followed by one of Elspeth's cele-
brated trifles.

'I take it your dad doesn't actually have any evidence to
back up his suspicions about the store,' I said, wishing I
was in bed.

'Not really, but like us, just asking himself how it can
stay afloat in today's cut-throat retail climate. And apparently a local bad boy works there, as a security guard of
all things. He did four years for GBH and being in possession of offensive weapons, a knife and a set of spiked
knuckle-dusters. I wonder if that was the tattooed barrel of
lard I heaved into the pile of boxes. I might need to talk
to James about that.'

'I take it this individual isn't regularly seen in church
weeping tears of remorse.'

'Not a chance.'

I did not have to ask, after following a public footpath
across fields we were striking uphill towards Hagtop Farm.
It was quite late, the evening fine and dry, and, being the
last week of May the sun was only just setting, burning
low and redly through the tree trunks of a copse. A small
flock of wood pigeons rocketed away, disturbed by our
approach.

'Bang,' said Patrick absently.

We dine well at home during the winter months, on game
that he can pot in the garden from an upstairs window of
the barn with an air rifle, other people's pheasants occasionally among the casualties. Once a seriously injured roe
deer – we thought it had been hit by a car – was put out
of its misery with a fine head shot from the Smith and
Wesson that was ostensibly helping to protect the pair of
us from terrorist attack, our names having been on several
such organizations' hit-lists for years. Venison is very good
eating. These days he carries a Glock hand gun, which is a
better weapon whatever the target. I *know* that the
former weapon was handed back to MI5 but had recently
noticed that it, or another one, had miraculously reappeared
in the wall safe.

The murder scene cattle barn came into view over to the

west, roughly halfway up the hill. This, John had told us, had been bought by a local farmer when Hagtop was auctioned off. The rector did not know the name of whoever had bought the house and immediate out-buildings but had promised to try to find out. Patrick had urged caution. His father's response to this, with an ironic grin on his face, had been a robust declaration that it was the incumbent's business to find out who had moved into the district so he could save their souls.

Hagtop farmhouse could be seen on the brow of the hill over to our right and from where we were appeared to be just the same as I remembered it. But as we climbed higher and got closer, crossing a stile into the lane that led to it it was apparent that a lot of work had taken place. As the poultry farmer had said, the house had been almost gutted, the rear part of the roof, the weather side, off with some of the timbers replaced with new wood, all the windows out and the floors between the two storeys just bare joists. The whole place was surrounded with security fencing plastered with KEEP OUT notices and others intimating that it was a hard hat area.

'No one can be living here yet but perhaps we ought to be careful,' Patrick muttered as we set off to walk around the front of the house, skirting the fencing towards the yard, tractor shed and other buildings. He rounded the corner, stopped dead and quickly went into reverse, almost treading on my toes.

'Someone *is* living here. There's a caravan.'

We returned to the farthest extent of the fencing in front of the house and followed it around the other side towards the rear. Here, the builders must have run out of the tall wire mesh panels, a final one lashed roughly to a plum tree that had probably at one time been part of an orchard. Now there was just waist-high grass and weeds between piles of rubble and rotten timbers.

Treading carefully we made our way along the back of the house and over to a stone wall at right angles to it, actually the rear of another building. There was an open doorway in it, a light breeze bringing the unmistakable smell of cooking. Patrick signalled to me to remain where I was and went over to look carefully around the door post. Then he came back to me, shaking his head and we went back the way we had come into the lane.

'Nothing?' I enquired when we were at a safe distance not to be overheard.

'Nothing, just a bloke smoking outside the caravan while his dinner cooked. I'll follow my own advice and leave well alone for now. We could always come back on Monday morning.'

'If you wave your SOCA warrant card at whichever estate agent handled the sale you can find out who this place belongs to now.'

'Good idea. And it was only a rumour. I suggest, just in case, that we go back by another route so we won't be spotted.'

We made our way, bending low and keeping a pile of pallets between us and the house, to a field gate, which was open. We quickly walked downhill in the lee of a thick hedge and after several hundred yards or so – although to me it seemed like miles – picked our way over rough ground, climbed over a stone wall, slid down a steep bank and finished up in a narrow lane. It was now getting dark.

'I wish you'd said it was going to be this sort of walk and I'd have dressed accordingly,' I grumbled, muddy, extravagantly stung by nettles and with my heart for some reason going like a trip-hammer.

'I can hardly be expected to know in advance how things are going to turn out,' Patrick observed.

'You know what?' I shot back at him. 'It would be wonderful if our life together didn't have to feel like constantly being on manoeuvres.'

The man in my life set off up the lane, saying over his shoulder, 'Perhaps you shouldn't have joined.'

Tears sprang to my eyes and then, unbelievably, a huge sob surfaced that I was too late in smothering with a hand. Others followed and I discovered that to stand helplessly in a country lane, unable to stop yourself bawling your eyes

out is a dreadfully humiliating experience. Almost immediately I found myself taken in a hug.

'Ingrid, I'm sorry,' Patrick murmured into my hair. 'I'm
a real bastard. I don't know what made me say that. I didn't
mean it.'

I fought to get myself back under control and then said,
or rather gulped, 'I'm actually feeling pretty exhausted.'

'Home then,' he said decisively

I started to walk up the lane with him but again stopped,
appalled to find how weak and shaky I was and, worse, had
strange ringing noises in my ears. 'I'm really sorry,' I told
him. 'I must have the flu coming on or something. I feel
quite—'

A ghastly stinging sensation hit my nose, throat and lungs
and I coughed. Three worried-looking people stared down
at me.

'Thank the good Lord for that!' Elspeth exclaimed,
screwing the top back on the smelling salts. 'Patrick, that
was far too far to take the girl for a walk when she was
looking so tired.'

'Ingrid didn't say anything about being tired,' said Patrick.

'Men!' snorted his mother. 'I thought she looked fit to
drop.'

Realizing that I was lying on the sofa in the living room
of the rectory I said, 'Where all dilapidated Gillards and
their family and friends are placed to have their wounds
bathed. I'm on hallowed ground.'

Everyone looked worried again.

'Perhaps you ought to call a doctor, my dear,' John said
to his wife.

'No, I'm fine,' I assured them, sitting up. 'Just – tired.'

I discovered later that Patrick had succeeded in catching
me as I fainted but had then been forced to lay me down
in the recovery position in the road in order to call his father
and ask him to pick us up. Really concerned as I was
showing no signs of coming round – I think I was probably merely deeply asleep by this time – he had then carried
me to a road junction to meet John, collecting, I gather,

odd looks from passing motorists. No one had stopped and offered to help.

'Perhaps you ought to go for a check-up,' Patrick said the next morning after I had slept dreamlessly for twelve hours. His gaze became a stare. 'You're not pregnant, are you?'

'I could well be pregnant,' I answered, having done a little mental arithmetic the night before. My internal arrangements have always performed like clockwork: as Patrick himself had once put it, to his chums in the mess of course, 'You could put the moon right by her.'

There was rather a long silence.

Then Patrick said, 'As you know, after I was blown up in the Falklands the medics assured me that I was firing mostly blanks. Then we tried hard for a baby, had Justin, then Victoria by accident and only bothered with birth control when we thought about it. And now . . .'

'I'm getting older,' I reminded him. 'It's quite likely just a false alarm. And don't forget, Vicky was very premature and almost didn't survive so the auspices aren't good.'

Another silence.

'Would you be pleased if I was?' I asked.

Ye gods, a soppy smile infused over his face. 'Of course.'

To be honest I did not know whether I was overcome with joy or not. Possibly . . . not.

'Until we know for sure and to be on the safe side you shouldn't come with me tonight when I have a look at the warehouse.'

'I'm hanged if I'm going to be wrapped in cotton wool!'

'No, I mean it, Ingrid. I'd never forgive myself if anything happened to you – either of you.'

As when husbandly edicts had been previously issued, and aware that once upon a time, a long time ago, I had promised to love, honour and obey, I dissected the wording of this one very carefully. It did, like slightly ambiguous decrees in the past, I decided, actually state an ideal situation. To be on the safe side of course I should not go. But nevertheless I would. This was because Patrick was far more important to me and the four young-sters for whom we were already responsible than a mere question mark.

Eight

There had been no question of my stowing myself away in the Range Rover or anything silly like that, if indeed it was possible. Even stupider would have been to borrow John or Elspeth's car as I could not explain my reasons without causing them worry. So I had done none of these things, merely having gone out into the garden after dinner to make a phone call on my mobile. Then, later, when the rector and his wife had gone to bed, Patrick left, having mentioned to them earlier that he would be going out for a short while. A little later again I had slipped out of the house and walked the short distance up through the village to the junction with the main road.

'You're quite sure he's following orders in taking a look at this place?' James Carrick said, ever cautious as far as Patrick is concerned. He had not said so but I knew was pleased that I had brought him up to date with our hunt for the tall man, although obviously I had not mentioned Robert Kennedy's name.

'Positive,' I told him. 'I was there when he made the call to Greenway.'

We were walking along one of the old cobbled roads in Bristol Docks, the masts and funnels of the restored *S S Great Britain* silhouetted against hazy moonlight in the easterly sky. Most of the warehouses have now been converted into apartments but original corners with what were once old inns remain, some of these now up-market restaurants, where slaves were once brought in on ships and shackled in the cellars before being taken on to work in the tobacco plantations of the southern states of America. I never feel comfortable here.

James was not comfortable either. 'I'm still not too sure why he didn't want you along. Is it trouble he's expecting?'

'I might be, that's all.'

He stopped dead. 'What? You're pregnant?'

'I fainted yesterday and there is a slight chance,' I snapped. 'He always goes off the over-protective deep end.'

'The man'll kill me.'

'I'll tell him the truth – that I didn't let on until we arrived.'

'D'you know where this warehouse is?' he asked after a heavy pause.

'No.'

'Does Patrick?'

'I don't think he knows the exact address – only that it's around here somewhere.'

'I ken the first thing that'll happen is that we'll bump into *him*,' James said unhappily, and as it happened, with uncanny foresight. 'I'd better ask in that pub just up the road there or we'll wander around looking for the place until dawn.'

'Surely it's not still open.'

'According to my colleagues here these places hardly ever close.'

James had been gone for at least a minute before I noticed though the smoky air – someone had lit a fire of waste wood where a building had been demolished – a certain vehicle tucked almost out of sight in an entrance to a defunct yard right next to the pub. I tore after him, mentally running out cannon and manning the starboard braces. We collided in the doorway to the lounge bar.

'Patrick could well be in here,' I told him breathlessly. 'So we might as well make a threesome now.' If I survived the first broadside, that is.

'He can't be. I had to search for the one waitresss who they said might know where the warehouse is – the land-lords are newcomers and most of the staff are Poles. I'd have seen him.'

'You wouldn't,' I replied tersely. 'Wait here.'

'Ingrid, I've been right through the place, the beer garden, bars and all.'

'OK, you go and look in the gents while *I* wait here.'

He returned quickly, shaking his head.

'Wait here,' I said again.

As I suspected, Patrick was in the public bar – a nautical nightmare festooned with anchors, mainbraces, Davey Jones' lockers and stuff like that – playing darts, hair all over his face, shirt hanging out of his jeans, a large smear of what looked like used engine oil together with a superior smirk on his face. Whether this activity had anything to do with undertaking in-depth research for his assignment I was not sure but thought not. Does he miss working undercover for MI5? Oh, brother.

I went over to the bar, walking slowly, wiggling my hips, and made an exaggerated play of undoing the front zip of my top a short way – no, quite a long way – in order to take out the ten pound note I had stuffed inside my bra before I left the rectory. Odd, the feeling that you instantly have every male eye in the room fixed on you. Except one, that is: it was his turn to throw and he had his back to me.

'I'll have a Diet Coke with ice,' I said to the barman quite loudly through a length of fishing net that had snared a catch of plastic crabs.

A dart thunked into the wall a good two inches from the board and it was probably due to the resultant demeanour of the thrower that no one laughed.

'What the hell are *you* doing here?' he roughly demanded, but well in character – that is, rough – I was pleased to note.

'Well, with no real man to keep me company I've come looking for someone,' I drawled in a little-girl voice.

The whole bar went 'OooOOOooo', falsetto.

Patrick handed the rest of his darts to someone, came over and slowly stretched out a hand and undid the zip a little more, a smile twitching his lips. I slapped the hand away whereupon he grabbed me, kissed me – yes, roughly – and bundled me out the door to the cheers and some obscene encouragement from those within.

I miss working undercover for MI5 too.

'Ingrid, what the hell *are* you doing here?' he enquired in his own voice when we were at a safe distance. He noticed Carrick. 'No, James, please don't explain. She bamboozled you into driving her over.'

'I'm glad she did as I do have an interest,' the DCI replied soberly. 'Cliff Morley was a friend of mine.'

'So he was,' Patrick said, a hand momentarily on the other's shoulder.

He told me later that he had seen Carrick in the pub but decided to say nothing, wondering if the DCI was working and might not want to be side-tracked. I reckoned this to be not *quite* the truth: undercover, unrecognized, slumming it, playing darts for money with a pint on the bar – heaven.

Carrick had been told that Slaterford and Sons' warehouse was situated in an area due for redevelopment three streets away from the pub 'towards the water'. Due to the fact that water seemed to be in more than one direction from where we started looking and there was a warren of little roads we did not succeed at the first attempt, ending up in a cul-de-sac. We finally found ourselves, according to a faded sign on a wall, outside the correct building.

'It looks derelict,' Patrick commented. 'They're probably due to get a pile of money for the place to be turned into flats. More money laundering?'

'It reminds me of criminal rat-holes in the East End docks before *they* were smartened up,' Carrick muttered.

I reckoned myself forgiven for my transgression having (a) appealed to Patrick's sense of humour, (b) sidetracked him into thinking about that panacea for a lot of things, sex, and (c) brought along meaningful reinforcements.

'We could be barking up all kinds of wrong trees here,' Patrick said to Carrick. 'Has Ingrid brought you up to date?'

'Aye, and tall men or no, I too think it's most odd that a whole raft of folk should do a runner when a certain alarm goes off in a department store. I wish I knew where they went.'

'We could put bugs under a few of the cars that Ingrid

said were parked near the entrance and then set off the alarm again.'

'True, but they could well smell a rat. And, don't forget, this isn't my case. I don't want to tread on Paul Reece's toes.'

'Perhaps not, but that's not to say I can't consult with you regarding my brief and then stir things up a little. Anyway . . .' Patrick chuckled. 'It looks as though Ingrid already has you on board.'

Which was because Ingrid has a lot more faith in brave Scots on the hoof than anyone thrashing away on a computer mouse at a desk in Portishead.

By the poor illumination provided by two street lights we could see that the building looked like a converted railway engine shed and, like the store, was mostly soot black. The windows of the ground floor had been bricked up, but in recent years as these were much cleaner than the rest of it. There were no visible exterior locks on the large wooden double doors fronting the road. The men gave these the briefest of glances, and, moving as one, set off to explore further.

Patrick suddenly turned to me. 'Promise me that if things get nasty you'll take yourself off.'

'I promise,' I said.

'Oh, for a Challenger tank to drive through the front door,' I heard him say to himself as he and James went on ahead, following the outer wall into the darkness towards the edge of the wharf where I could hear water slapping against the jetty wall. I saw the flash of Patrick's tiny 'burglar's' torch and then they had gone and there was just the smell of the sea and the night.

I went after them, slowly, as Patrick had the only source of light, and finished up by meeting them on their way back. The building was joined to a newer one next door and there was no way around. What had been rear and huge side doors were now, like the windows, bricked up.

'I have a better idea,' I told them.

We went back round to the front.

As is so often the case, within one of the main doors was

a smaller one and, along with the car parked nearby I had noticed a couple of minutes earlier, this smaller door boasted both key holes and a bell push. I shooed Patrick and James out of the immediate vicinity and then jabbed a finger on it, hearing a bell ring quite loudly somewhere within. Then, slow footsteps approached. A myriad bolts and locks were undone and then the door was yanked open.

'Charlie?' said a man's voice.

'No, I've lost my cat.' I snivelled. 'I think she came in here.'

'It can't have done. Shove off, you silly cow!'

The door started to close.

'For God's sake, mister!' I wailed. 'She's all I've got!'

The door opened a little again.

More calmly, I said, 'She hasn't come home and I saw her sitting in the road out here earlier when the doors were open. Please let me come in and call her.'

'It's more than my job's worth.'

'I'll only stand just inside. She'll come if I call her.'

'Lady, the people who own the place'll skin me alive and nail it to this door if I let you in.'

Still unable to see to whom I was talking I sort of melted against the door jamb. 'I know you're a kind man really. *Please.*'

There was quite a long silence punctuated by wheezy male breathing. Then he said, 'OK, but make it damned quick.'

I went into what must be a confined space as it was close and fuggy with the smell of sweat and cigarettes. It was too dark to see much but the night-watchman, whoever he was, was a dark shape shambling ahead of me. We immediately emerged into a larger area, our footsteps echoing.

'Go on, then! Call your bloody cat!' the man growled.

'I can't see where I'm going,' I told him.

'Just call! Or I'll throw you out!'

'Mif . . . fy! Mif . . . fy!' I bawled into a huge gloomy cavern-like space, my voice resonating around the roof. 'Miffy!'

Predictably, nothing moved. Well, perhaps a rat or two did.

'But I can't see if she's here!' I cried, getting upset again. 'She's probably sitting somewhere too scared to come out because you're here.'

'The lights stay off!' Raising his voice then brought on a fit of coughing.

My eyes were getting used to the gloom and I could just make out roof lights high up above me, moonlight penetrating through the dirt of ages and cobwebs.

'Look, there's a consignment due any time now,' the man agonized. 'If the boss finds you here . . .' He broke off, seemingly, it was too horrible to think about.

Only seemingly; in actual fact Patrick had just, gently, fingered his collar.

'What's going on here then?' he said in chummy fashion.

'Who might you be?' the man quavered.

'Someone more difficult than your boss should you not now start talking really helpfully. But since you ask I'm from the Serious and Organized Crime Agency and my friend here is a DCI from Bath.' Turning his prisoner around to face him and shining the light in his face, thus illuminating several days' growth of beard and bloodshot eyes, he then asked the man his name.

'Bill Poundbury.'

'What gives here, then?'

'I – I just look after the place at night, that's all.'

'Why at night?'

'They said because of vandals – they try to get in.'

'They'd have a job to – the place is like a fortress. What's stored here?'

'Stuff – you know, goods for the store.'

'And your boss? Who's he?'

'Why, the man in charge, the warehouse manager.'

'What's his name?'

'I – I don't know.'

'You don't know! Tell the truth!'

'It is the truth. He doesn't like people to know. You don't ask questions. Some of the people the top bods knock around with are really scary.'

'Did you know a man called Ritter? Madderly Ritter?

'No.'

'Think!'

'He – he might have been the bloke I took over from. I don't really know. Someone said whoever that was wasn't very bright and got killed in an accident when he was on holiday down in Devon. Please, guv, I don't know very much because I've only been here a few days.'

'Do you know a man by the name of Kyle Jeffers?'

'No, never heard of him.'

The questioning ended abruptly when Patrick fleetingly gripped the man's neck and then lowered his inert form to the floor.

'Did you *have* to do that?' Carrick protested, whispering for some reason. 'It sounds as though he might be perfectly innocent.'

'Quite,' Patrick said. 'That's why I caught him when something fell on his head.' He flashed the torch around. 'There, that one'll do – that box on the shelf there.' He handed the torch to me and lifted it down. It was far heavier than he expected and he could not control the descent, the unmarked box hitting the ground in a cloud of dust. In the beam from the torch we could see that the cardboard sides had split to reveal plastic-wrapped packets of what looked like plasticene.

'What on earth's that?' Carrick wanted to know.

'Probably explosive,' Patrick replied. 'It looks like Semtex.'

A large vehicle of some kind drew up outside.

'Did you shut the door?' I hissed, wanting to put as much distance between myself and this place as possible for several very pressing reasons.

'No,' James said. 'In case the hinges squeaked.'

There was no time to do anything but conceal ourselves. This proved to be difficult to begin with because of what James would no doubt call the gloaming but when several people had crashed into the warehouse, shouting, and someone switched on all the lights we went to ground much more thoroughly.

In the first few seconds of brightness I had received a

fleeting impression of the warehouse walls lined with metal shelving, the floor untidily stacked with packing crates, boxes and pallets loaded with goods. Then I had burrowed my way beneath a shelf unit and lay, my nose inches from what did indeed look like rat droppings, trying to remember anything I might know about the properties of Semtex but having an idea it needed a detonator. I had no clue as to the whereabouts of the two men. As for my undertaking to Patrick to head for the hills if things got nasty – well, it was a bit late now, wasn't it?

'The watchman's here – been knocked out by a box!' a man shouted. 'But what the hell was he doing with the door open?'

'Probably heard us arriving,' someone else yelled quite close to where I was hiding, making me start.

'He usually waits until he's been given a signal,' said the first man.

'Or, disobeying orders, he'd sneaked outside for a fag and shot back in when he heard us coming,' yet another man said. 'Get any keys or things that could identify him out of his pockets and chuck him in the van. We'll get the truth out of him later. No, before you do that check the whole place for intruders. We don't know how long it's been wide open – someone might have sneaked in.'

A new pair of desert boots squeaked by only a foot or so from where I lay and went off into the distance. It occurred to me that the watchman was probably playing dead as the method of rendering him insensible that Patrick normally utilises only results in unconsciousness for less than a minute and, Carrick really ought to be told, leaves no bruising or other unpleasant after-effects. I was hoping he would make his escape when no one was looking. Otherwise, bless his tarred-up lungs, we would have to prevent what could well be his demise.

Feet paced about, moved things and, judging by the sounds, climbed up the shelving. I guessed that there were three doing the searching, while the boss – was he the tall man we were after? – stood waiting. Two or three minutes went by and then, not very far from where I lay, someone sneezed. Immediately, there were the thumps of approaching running footsteps, I actually felt the vibration through the floor.

'Got you, you bastard!' someone yelled amid scuffling noises.

And, in the next second a hand emerged through small packets of some kind on my left, burrowing, groped, and grabbed me by the material of the sleeve of my jacket. I stayed quite still: it was a hand I recognized.

'Who the hell are you?' shouted the voice I assumed to belong to the boss.

'DCI James Carrick, Bath CID. Release me this instant or you'll find yourselves under arrest.'

The man laughed, aped dutifully by his 'assistants', and then said, 'What are you doing here?'

'You've been under surveillance for some time,' Carrick said.

'You're lying!'

'It's the truth. I was passing and saw the door was open and your man some way along the street, smoking. I thought I'd take a quick look around.'

'You're a damned fool then,' said the other coldly. 'But I'm not risking talking to you here.' There was the sound of another scuffle. Then, 'Get him out of here. Right out. Take him to the usual place, the secure area, and hold him there until I come. We might have to stay there for a while until things quieten down. Meanwhile I'll find out exactly what they know about us before we get rid of him.'

'I'm warning you . . .' Carrick began but was silenced by the sound of a series of blows.

The hand grasping my sleeve released it and disappeared. I took this to mean that war had been declared and there was no need for me to stay where I was a moment longer. Patrick was first on his feet, the Glock drawn.

'Just stay right where you are!' he barked. 'And I kid you not, I used to be in Special Services and a bloodbath of gutter rats is no bother at all.'

I had an idea they would go for the bloodbath option and they did, no doubt of the opinion that they could out-gun their opponent as four against one was good odds. I went rapidly to ground again when the shooting started, bullets ricochetting off just about everything, and, when there was a lull – I was fairly sure that Patrick had not yet fired a shot – he called, 'So how much high explosive is actually stored in this place then?'

Silence.

'It's quite safe as long as you make sure you hit the target,' he went on in his best army instructor's tones and commenced to shoot the lights out, one by one, right above their heads, showering them with hot glass, judging by the language that followed.

'Let's play murder in the dark,' he taunted them from a different position.

I risked peeping around the pile of containers behind which I was hiding and was in time to see one of them for the first time. He was masked, definitely in panic-mode and making a dash for the door. As he ran, jinking, he still wildly waved a gun around and when it was smashed from his grasp he screamed in pure terror and then bent over, hugging the injured digits.

Further lights disappeared in clouds of bits, leaving just two still functioning. Then some packages flew off a shelf near me and they risked firing in that direction, sending me scuttling around the other side of the boxes and then down an 'alley' created by the goods stacked there. I have under-gone training in mock-ups along these lines but then, dammit, I had had a weapon of my own.

Amazingly, I got one, running pell-mell into my husband who thrust the Glock at me with the flying whisper, 'Try not to kill any of them,' and then he had gone, shinning up the side nearest the wall of a piled up row of wooden containers that formed one side of the 'alley'.

With huge caution I headed for where I thought at least two of the remaining three were concealing themselves. Patrick must have thought so too for he began to bob up and bombard them with anything he could lay his hands on, forcing them to keep their heads down. Saucepans whis-tled overhead, a small, and probably iron, casserole landing with a crash on the face of an old-fashioned clock on the wall sending glass and springs yards into the air. The casserole plunged down to dislodge what must have been a badly stacked pile of something which fell over, caused a dominoes effect and the resultant roar as a whole lot more toppled, slithered and plumetted down sounded like a liner hitting a jetty. Clouds of dust swirled up, creating a murky fog effect in the half-light.

Hopefully now the opposition would think the one firing had run out of ammunition.

In the medium distance a figure reversed cautiously into my line of view. You cannot be too ethical in such situations. He still had his back to me when I fired, the shot hitting the floor, as I had intended, and embedding his backside and the calves of his legs with small pieces of concrete. He fell over, howling, howled more when the pain kicked in and was in no position to offer resistance when I ran up to him and booted his dropped weapon out of reach.

I saw a movement out of the corner of my eye, spun round and saw Carrick groggily trying to get to his feet in a small space between boxes nearby. There was no time for sympathy.

'Handcuffs?' I asked urgently and quietly in his ear.

'No,' he muttered.

All I could do then was to grab the gun from the floor and take it back to the DCI who was recovering sufficiently quickly for me not to have to worry about him accidentally shooting himself.

OK, kill another light then, just to keep my hand in and the opposition's nerves on the frizzle.

Someone almost killed me then, a dark shape jumping from behind a large crate, a gun in both hands, aiming. But he did not, disappearing before I could react other than by throwing myself to one side. Moments later the last light exploded in a burst of glass fragments.

'Out!' someone yelled.

I stayed where I was. In the blackness there were scuffling noises followed by a loud thud as though someone had tripped and fallen over. Then, footsteps faded into the distance. They were getting away. I decided at this point that it was a good time to keep my promise and refrain from going after them. The van drove off at speed.

For another jittery few minutes not one of the three of us moved in case it was a ruse. But nothing happened and, finally, I saw the tiny beam of Patrick's torch as he made his way towards me.

'Is James all right?' he enquired.

Before I could say anything I became aware that Carrick was standing at my elbow.

'I whispered to you that I intended being taken!' he shouted.

'You *were* taken,' Patrick replied. 'And they promptly voiced their intentions to take you away and make you talk. They would have tortured and killed you.'

It was obvious the DCI was really angry. 'Before I came out here I contacted Lynn Outhwaite, my sergeant, and told her what was going on. I said that in case suspicions about the store were realized I would carry a homing bug and that if I did not contact her within a certain time she would put agreed procedures into place. We could have grabbed the whole lot inside their little empire if it had not been for your interference!'

There was a short silence before Patrick said, 'My main point in reply is that you could have mentioned that to Ingrid on the way over, or to me when we met up. At no time did you intimate that this was, for you, an official, or semi-official mission. The other thing is that these people are not amateurs and would have searched you before you had been taken very far. Even if they had found something they would have gone on to search you *everywhere*. And when they had finished searching you everywhere you would have been half dead already from serious internal injuries. They mutilated Morley. For God's sake, James, where's your judgement?'

Carrick, still not recovered, blundered off in the direction of the exit.

'It was him,' he said in a choked undertone when we

caught up with him outside. 'Robert Kennedy. My bloody father.'

'But how could you know? They were masked!' Patrick exclaimed.

'It was him!' Carrick insisted.

I will never be able to forget the way he stood there, sobbing on Patrick's shoulder.

Nine

'I didn't shoot out the last light,' I said. 'He did.'

'He being the man who changed his mind about shooting you, you mean?' Patrick queried.

'Yes.'

'Are you still sure he didn't fire at you and miss before aiming for the light?'

'Quite sure.'

'Could it have been the man James thought was his father?'

'Impossible to say in the poor light.'

'If your theory's correct . . .'

'It would tie in neatly. He wouldn't want to kill allies.'

'But what the hell would he have really done with Carrick?'

'In that respect the theory's rubbish,' I said. 'And I'm constantly haunted by the fact that Morley was horribly murdered. How could another policeman have been party to that?'

It was the following morning and we were in the garden of the rectory: that little bit of heaven on earth in Somerset. The house is built of the same yellow limestone as the church and Elspeth has planted her garden accordingly; variegated spindle, which has green and white foliage and vivid orange berries in the autumn, on the walls and roses everywhere, peach, white, yellow and cream. The rectory is surrounded by large lawns upon which children are encouraged to play and which always host the church fête in June.

We had handed over the warehouse investigation to Paul Reece's department, and made short statements. They had not been delighted with us about the shoot-out until Patrick had pointed out that if they searched for the slugs from the gang's weapons they might have a match for those that had killed Morley, Jeffers and Ritter even though, so far, only the one that had killed the latter had been found, bizarrely still inside his head. Then we had come back to Hinton Littlemoor. Carrick, subdued but insisting that he was fit enough to drive himself home, had walked off into the darkness towards his car. Patrick had asked a constable to shadow him in case anyone was still lurking around.

'We have, at least, established a link between Slaterfords and serious crime,' I said.

'Yes, but any lawyer worth his salt would make a good case that the warehouse was being used by crooked staff with criminal contacts to store stolen goods and explosives without the management knowing. We don't know exactly what's there yet, of course – it'll take a while to go through that lot.'

'With a bit of luck they'll be able to track down Bill Poundbury, who wisely had taken himself off.'

'Yes, but I don't think he knows very much. He hadn't been on the job long enough.'

'I've just remembered that Greenway told you to take a look at the warehouse without the management knowing.'

'We couldn't have foreseen that anyone was going to turn up with a truck-load of booty, could we? I'd have given anything to have seen what was inside that van.' Patrick pulled a wry face. 'Yes, thanks for reminding me. I'll phone Greenway now so he hears it from me first.'

'Priorities after the slapped wristie, then?'

'To find the location of the secure place that was mentioned. It could be where the three murder victims died.'

'Somewhere in the head office in Walthamsden perhaps,' I mused. 'Wherever it is that's where they've probably bolted to by now. And, please don't forget, they'll be waiting for somebody to follow them – us.'

'I *was* thinking of casting an eye over the place.'

Although I was beginning to discount my theory it kept coming back to bother me. Had the 'secure place' been mentioned deliberately?

As I had predicted Patrick was press-ganged into the choir for the main morning service. He has a pleasant, if fairly ordinary tenor voice, but is apt to chuck in counter-tenor descants for fun in the last verse, at which, a little embarrassed, he is a natural. Sitting towards the back of the church I could hear the high notes soaring and swooping around the chancel in the final hymn, 'Thine be the Glory'.

Still not too sure about such things I do nevertheless always say a little prayer for his safety.

Later that night Patrick said, 'As you know Dad and I had our chat earlier. He told me that the diocese want to sell the rectory and re-home them in a new bungalow that's part of that development on the old station site. He hasn't broken the news to Mum yet.'

'That's awful,' I gasped.

'Apparently the rectory needs a new roof.'

'But those bungalows are a horrible little enclave.'

'I know. No one wants him to retire even though he's getting on for seventy. But I reckon he will and they'll go and live on Sark as they've always planned to do – not that I'm a hundred per cent sure they can actually afford to build a house on that plot they've bought there. I didn't like to ask.'

Occasionally, there is a strange formality between Patrick and his father, and reticence on the former's part, some-thing I have put down to their strained relationship when Patrick was in his early teens. John, it appeared, had not been prepared for his children behaving like most other adolescents, quaintly supposing that the offspring of those called by God were spared rampaging hormones and explo-sions of bad temper. Once, and I did not imagine this, I had heard Patrick call him 'sir'.

'Everyone loses if your dad gives up,' I said. 'They do, the parishioners do and so do our children. The first phase of that bungalow development is like tiny hutches. *And* that area has always tended to flood. When is he going to tell Elspeth?'

'Tomorrow.'

*   *   *

'This hoodlum with a manor in Walthamsden, Ernie O'Malley, can be described as a career criminal,' Michael Greenway said. Turning to Patrick he added, 'You said over the phone that Superintendent Reece reckons he could be the brother-in-law of this guy who's responsible for serious crimes, and possibly Morley's murder, in the Bristol area.'

'The Met thinks so,' Patrick corrected. 'It's just about Reece's only piece of intelligence. Flimsy though, I agree.'

Greenway stared out of the window, unseeing, for a few moments. 'According to the Criminal Record Office O'Malley doesn't have any sisters, married or otherwise. He did, however, have a wife – they're divorced – and she has a brother by the name of Lance Taylor or Naylor. He goes by both names apparently and has convictions for most things that you can think of.'

'Do we have his description?' I asked. 'Or a photo?'

Greenway switched on his laptop, pushed keys and spun it round on the table to enable us to see the screen. What could be described as a middle-aged, sullen, spotty punk with yellow hair striped faded pink glowered back at us.

'How tall is he?' Patrick said.

Greenway repossessed the laptop and stabbed more buttons. 'Five foot nine.'

'Not our man then. What about O'Malley himself?'

'I've gone into his details in some depth. He's on the run, again, having been busted out of a prison van taking him to court. But it can't be him; he's comparatively short as well.'

'Damn.'

Back in London on a hot, sticky day when the traffic fumes seemed thick enough to cut into slices and parcel off to homesick expats we had met Greenway in the inevitable coffee bar. He had made no comment concerning the '1812 Overture'-style cannon and mortar effects conclusion of the warehouse operation, either now or when Patrick had first told him. But now he said, 'You said Carrick was with you at the warehouse and thought he recognized his old man. I can understand that being pretty bloody for him. Do we go after this guy then, not to prolong Carrick's misery? I mean, he's a good copper and what the hell other leads do we have?'

Patrick looked at me.

'Ah,' Greenway said. 'Undercurrents.'

'Ingrid has a tentative theory,' Patrick said slowly. 'She wonders if he's on our side.'

To Greenway I said, 'Frankly, the theory is not made up of the kind of thinking to which you'd give credence.'

'Nevertheless I would be very interested in what you have to say.'

He heard me out and then slowly shook his head, saying, 'I agree that there are strange aspects to this case and I know it's appalling for Carrick but without real evidence it's fairytale. Believe me, I'd like to go for your theory myself but—'

I interrupted with, 'Is there no way at all of finding out if he is undercover with some unit?'

'In theory yes, but as I'm sure Patrick has told you under-cover bosses *never* tell anyone who their people are or what they're doing. Unless someone's in real danger of losing their life, and even then, rarely.'

Patrick said, 'And, as I've already stressed, by interfering we might put any number of operatives in danger. Whether Kennedy's a cop or not he must be aware that someone's going round carving his initials on people.'

'Have you spoken to Carrick about this supposition of Ingrid's?'

'No, in case it was wrong.'

'That was wise. One wonders, if it's right, whether this man knew he had hold of his own son.'

'It's open to conjecture,' Patrick said. 'For although James closely resembles his father at that age he hadn't even been born when Kennedy was supposed to have gone overboard from the yacht.'

Greenway breathed out hard and remained silent for a few moments. Then he said, 'We mustn't lose sight of what we're supposed to be doing here. We're after the bastard who killed Morley. Let's concentrate on the tall guy and his set-up. Get yourselves into this head office or store, or whatever it is, in Walthamsden. Try not to start a war this time. And stay alive.'

'Short of disguising ourselves as Daleks I don't see how we can just walk into that wretched shop,' I said, on reflection not intending to sound so acidic. 'They know what we look like – or at least the men who arrived at the warehouse do.'

Patrick made no comment, brooding, and might not even have heard me. But a few seconds later he said, 'It's pretty obvious that senior staff at Slaterfords are up to some kind of no good but the only connection with Morley is Madderly Ritter, who sometimes worked there. The fact that they and Kyle Jeffers were murdered by a person, or persons, unknown, who left an autograph on their bodies might have nothing to do with the store at all. Ritter could have done all kinds of *other* things in his spare time, been involved with another gang altogether.'

'So we could be wasting our time in going to Walthamsden, you mean?'

'Yes. And end up by stirring all kinds of filthy ponds without finding anything in the muck that connects with this case.'

'But, as we've said before, there are no other real leads,' I pointed out. 'And, don't forget, Morley was after the tall man and making enquiries about anyone with his description.'

'The tall man you saw might be back in the shop in Bristol calmly getting on with whatever he does. They might have a store policy of senior management bailing out if there's a fire alarm or bomb warning.' Patrick shot to his feet. 'More single malt might cure the mental stalemate. Another glass of wine?'

'Perhaps I'd better just have orange juice.'

We were staying at an hotel for the night. For some reason the place was very quiet and the large lounge in which we were sitting before having dinner was practically empty, seemingly a quarter of an acre of dark blue carpet patterned with gold stars a stage for the usual sofas, tables and chairs and huge plants in Oriental ceramic containers. A dozen or so people were seated, several more standing near Patrick over by the bar and a couple plus one other man, the latter wearing evening dress, walking a few paces behind them, just entering through one of the large arched doorways. I always make a point of noticing my surroundings and what is going on – we both do: in some circumstances such vigilance can save your life.

I did not feel unduly threatened when the man on his own approached even though I immediately recognized him as someone I had met before, at Sheepwash Farm.

'May I join you?' he asked.

'Please do,' I replied.

He seated himself in the chair next to the one Patrick had just vacated.

I said, 'So *are* you Archie Kennedy?'

He shook his head. 'No, I told you the truth. Archie's dead.'

'Deid?'

There was the trace of a smile. 'I use my Scottish accent when it suits me.'

I now knew exactly to whom I was speaking and, suppressing a shiver, said, 'Is the mugshot of you in police records actually a photo of Archie?'

'Oh, aye. He was a real villain but it was lung cancer that got him in the end.'

'There's no record of his death in West Devon.'

'No, he died here, in London.'

'You must be taking huge risks coming here tonight.'

'Needs must. I'm unarmed but I know that husband of yours *is* armed and also a fine shot.'

I postponed thinking about the implications of this remark and said, 'I have an idea it was you who decided not to shoot me the day before yesterday.'

'I didn't fire any shots that night.'

Over his shoulder I could see Patrick coming back. He arrived, placed the drinks on the table and said to this wonderfully presentable, but older, version of James Carrick, 'What can I get you? The Macallan?'

'Thank you.'

There were a thousand things I wanted to say to this man but, for now, merely murmured, 'You must have followed us to know where we were staying.'

'You two are too canny when you travel to make following easy. No, I asked Mike.'

'Mike?'

'Mike Greenway.'

I was sure my hair was standing on end. 'But . . .'

'We carefully share intelligence. But he doesn't know me as Robert Kennedy. You can call me that though, it's sort of my real name.'

I leaned forward and spoke quietly. 'Someone else who knows you as that is carving your initials on people.'

'Yes, that must have been on the orders of one of the men in the little empire I'm working to dismantle. It has outposts in just about every large town in the south and west of the country, starting in Reading.'

'So you're working within one of his gangs.'

'As what he likes to call a sub-contractor. I have a gang, only I prefer to call it a unit, of my own – some with genuine, and some with phoney form. The idea is to put him out of business, starting by recruiting his hoodlums, picking their brains, keeping some on and taking the others out of circulation for a while. They don't know they're helping the law, of course.'

'But he knows your real name.'

'I went to prison for six months not so long ago under that name.'

'But he's really on to you. Two police informers were recently found murdered at Sheepwash Farm. That is your hideaway, isn't it?'

'Yes, it is. But no one is actually on to me in the way you mean. The man in Bristol resents my presence; he seems to think I want to force him out, which I do, but not how he imagines. Somehow they found out about the farm and hoped, as with Morley, to lay the blame for the two murders on me. I shall have to sell the place now – I can't go back there. I shall also have to leave the Bristol area for a while. I don't want more people killed because of my presence there.'

'But Morley didn't tell them about it under duress surely – he can't have known about you.'

'No. I don't know how they found me. It's worrying.'

Patrick returned with the whisky.

'Thank you – your good health,' said Kennedy, raising his glass.

Patrick said, 'I take it the purpose of this visit is to deliver a warning-off.'

'Nothing unfriendly. It's more to clear the air and answer any queries you might have.'

'From what he's told me he has to be working for F9,' I said to Patrick, voicing something I had wondered about for a while. 'David Rolt's unit.'

Kennedy said, 'I've heard you have real brains, Ingrid. Yes, but David retired last year to take over the family stud farm when his brother died suddenly, although what he knows about horses is anyone's guess. I was lucky enough to be promoted to second in command of the department. But I don't want the top job, this is my last – then I'm off too.'

I quickly related to Patrick the rest of what had been said.

'So if you carefully share intelligence with Greenway,' Patrick said to Kennedy, 'why are we getting under one another's feet in warehouses in Bristol? What were you doing delivering stuff to the said warehouse and why the hell is it my brief to find out who mutilated and killed Detective Sergeant Cliff Morley when it appears that you knew all along?'

Not remotely put out, Kennedy ticked off on his fingers, 'First, Mike and I don't share everyday *detailed* information as a matter of routine so that convergence was just an unfortunate coincidence. One of the reasons I'm here tonight is to prevent a repetition of such occurences. Second, we were actually bringing the van with a view to making off with quite a lot of what was stored there, to rattle the enemy as well as to see what stolen goods they had hold of. We'd waylaid the real delivery boys – it was a regular run, same time, same night, every week believe it or not – and they're now helping with enquiries quite a few counties away. The idea was not to meet *anyone* at the warehouse. And third, I don't know the real name of this man, only that he looks like a stork, calls himself Steven Ballinger, and is the so-called managing director of Slaterford and Sons, which as I'm sure you must know by now, is a money-laundering tool. It only changed hands recently and they're hoping to get planning permission very soon to knock it down and build more shop units with luxury flats over.'

'Why not just arrest him?'

'I want real evidence. I want to know where they take people to torture and murder them and who else is involved. I want *all* of them.'

'Isn't the shop in Walthamsden their HQ?' I asked.

'It doesn't exist. Or, at least, it's just an empty room with a name board on the door in an office complex.'

'Well, that's nice to know,' Patrick said crisply. 'Greenway told me to look the place over.'

'Your predictable annoyance is another of the reasons I'm here,' Kennedy said.

Patrick was more than annoyed. 'And what was all that posturing and blazing guns about then? Not to mention beating up DCI Carrick!'

'I could hardly be expected to know who you were, could I? Not until I saw Ingrid and remembered that Mike had told me that you were on the job. And there's always going to be collateral damage, even among the local police as we simply can't tell them what we're doing. I would like to point out that your activities ruined a well-planned operation that Bristol CID are now crawling all over *and* you wounded two of my men.'

'Were they cops?'

There was a pause before Kennedy answered. 'No.'

'Thought not; just co-opted thickoes. What were you going to do with Carrick?'

'Pretend to change my mind and shove him out of the van somewhere fairly close by.'

'You could hardly have taken him along to your own secure place.'

'No, only I and my closest, police, colleagues know where that is.'

'MI5 do too,' Patrick said with a little smile. 'You know who Carrick is, I suppose?'

The other looked blank. 'What d'you mean?'

'You don't know. His mother Orla changed her surname to Carrick for the sake of respectability when she had him – she was unmarried. The father went overboard from a racing yacht off the Scottish coast and until quite recently was presumed dead. You're that man.'

I thought the ensuing silence would never end.

'Why didn't you contact her?' Patrick continued.

When he eventually spoke Kennedy whispered, 'I nearly died. Found myself washed up on an island somewhere in the Sound of Sleat where the only inhabitant was a light-house keeper. He can't have found me for a while as I was stone cold, blue, when he did. But the man saw that I wasn't stiff like a corpse and lugged me back to his cottage where he stripped me off and wrapped me in every blanket, garment and rug that he possessed over every hot water bottle that he could find before phoning the mainland. I'd bashed my head and lost a lot of blood too and when I woke up in Oban Hospital I didn't know who I was. I didn't know who I was for the best part of two years and even then, when I remembered, my old life, as I thought of it, seemed unreal. It belonged to someone else, another man.' His voice dropped until I could hardly hear what he muttered. 'No, I couldn't face digging up that past. Things were still in a kind of mist. There were still big gaps and I didn't know what I would find. Orla . . . do you know . . . is she still alive?'

'No,' I told him. 'She was killed ten years ago in a road accident in South Africa.'

Kennedy sat still, eyes downcast. 'He must hate me.'

Patrick said, 'We can't answer for James. But, no, I don't think he does. Not when you tell him the circumstances.'

'It's in the past. I can't . . . meet him.'

'You must!' Patrick exclaimed. 'He thinks you're a criminal!'

'No.'

'At least allow us to tell him the truth!'

'Will he be able to keep it to himself?' Kennedy said angrily. 'If he's pleased by what he hears will he be able to conceal it or will he go round with a big grin on his face? If people ask will he blurt out why he's happy and send ripples of gossip and rumour right through the Avon and Somerset Force and from there to the outside world? No, it's too risky. He knows I exist. Isn't that enough for him?'

'It isn't,' I said. 'Not judging by how upset he was after you'd driven away the other night. Despite your mask he knew it was you.'

'Then you have your answer. The whole operation would be jeopardized by saying anything at all. When it's over and I'm out of it, then . . . well, everything will be different, won't it? Then I'll . . . I'll think about it.'

He then went on, rather coldly, to inform us that he would immediately contact Michael Greenway, who for professional reasons he would prefer not to know his real name. He would tell him that there was no need for the work to be duplicated and that it was his, F9's, case. He assured us that although it was not of foremost importance his department was as keen as SOCA to find Morley's killer, or killers. Then tossing off the last of his whisky and curtly wishing us goodnight, he left.

'He's just like James, isn't he?' I said in exasperation. 'Exactly the same iron-clad technique.'

'Take us the foxes, the little foxes, that spoil the vines,' Patrick said to himself.

I was puzzled for a moment and then recollected that F9 operatives were referred to as foxes, from their call-sign, Foxtrot 9. 'Where's the quotation from?' I asked.

'The Bible, *Song of Solomon*. With that job he has to be a Super.' Patrick laughed softly. 'I liked the way he finished his drink before he went.'

Definitely not amused, I retorted, 'So where the *hell* does that leave us?'

'It depends on Greenway.'

'I see no reason why a policeman's murder investigation should degenerate into inter-departmental gamesmanship.'

'Nor do I,' Patrick said grimly. 'Thought about like that, it's bloody disgusting.'

Bristol CID on one side, F9 on the other and us in the middle, I mused. The situation could not be allowed to continue and, if it did, I could see Patrick relinquishing the job, even if it meant resigning. I had expected Michael Greenway to blow his top when the latest developments were reported to him but he merely requested that we meet him again and, on second thoughts, said he would come to our hotel as he had a later appointment nearby.

Patrick, who I know had lost sleep over it, came straight to the point. 'I can't work like this,' he said. 'The man we met last night, who would prefer you not to know his real name for professional reasons – his exact choice of words – feels he has sole ownership of this case and when he left us was about to inform you of the fact. I can't be expected to tiptoe between policemen with ego problems.'

Greenway was magnanimous enough not to deem himself included in the criticism and said, 'Yes, he did ring me last night and I have to say I was unaware that he has been using an alias. Are his preferences important to you?'

'Only in the sense that he uses his real name when posing as a criminal so, obviously, his personal safety is highly important,' Patrick answered. 'But from the point of view that you'll be kept in the dark with regard to an important aspect of this case if I don't give you the information and I am, after all, working for you . . .' He paused. 'He's Robert Kennedy.'

Greenway swore vividly and then hurriedly apologized to me, obviously not yet knowing that I was married to an enthusiastic exponent of the art. Then, after a few moments' reflection he said, 'It was your old MI5 boss, Richard Daws, who recommended you for this job, wasn't it?'

'So I believe.'

'You must be aware that he's just about running the agency and has done right from the beginning. But it's still quite early days and everyone's carrying on taking the advice of the experts. Daws likes your methods so let's do it like that, his way.'

'I had *carte blanche* in those days,' Patrick observed.

'Bugger that for a minute. Tell me what you'd have done, faced with a similar situation.'

'It only puts a slightly different complexion on things. First, to recap and clarify matters, SOCA received an urgent official request from the Avon and Somerset Force to help solve a murder case. Unbeknown to anyone F9 has been working for some time on roughly parallel investigations, which actually represent a much bigger picture, hoping to catch criminals who have, according to Kennedy, outposts in every city and large town in the south and west of the country. He spent six months in prison – which I gather is one of F9's specialities – in an effort to find out more from the inside. He didn't tell us much, only that the tall man who would appear to be the managing director of Slaterford and Sons is calling himself Steven Ballinger and is probably the bossman of the criminal empire in that area. Kennedy wants *all* of them, not just him, not just a few. In my view it's impossible to collar the lot but I agree with that sentiment – *and* that it's his case.'

Greenway stared at Patrick, thunderstruck. 'I was expecting you to say that you'd lift Kennedy and put him somewhere safe for a while to let you get on with the job.'

'No,' Patrick said with a smile. 'You've been watching too many James Bond films.'

'So SOCA just walks away?' the other asked incredulously.

'Not at all. As you're no doubt aware, F9 is quite a small covert outfit, no one in uniform. You might not know that it operates out of what looks like a perfectly ordinary house near Woodford Green and on the edge of Epping Forest in Essex. They have to call up practically all they need in the way of everyday police equipment, including official vehicles when they need to use muscle, as they just have a few unmarked cars. They'll have to ask for help eventually, when the time comes to make multiple arrests. You're in contact with Kennedy. I suggest that in the light of a conflict of interests not being in anyone's interest, least of all poor Morley's, we start by offering two liaison officers, with immediate effect, one from Avon and Somerset Police and one from SOCA, Superintendent Paul Reece, and me – plus Ingrid of course.'

'He might refuse – we can't force him to agree.'

'He can't. It's too important. And he won't want to keep tripping over me, will he?'

Ten

This being real life there was no plan to break in to F9's headquarters and appear, all smug smiles, arrayed with the cruet on the table in the canteen where Kennedy had his morning coffee, if indeed he ever did such a thing. Such fantasy should reside only in the overactive imaginations of authors. We were relying on Greenway getting Kennedy to agree to see us for further discussions and Reece being able to obtain clearance from his superiors to work within another department for a period of time that was being described as 'short'. The immediate aftermath of both proposals was an extremely loud silence: Greenway had detected reluctance on Reece's part from a personal point of view and could not get hold of Kennedy.

'We don't want Reece if he's going to be fretting about a work overload back at base,' I said.

'No, you're right,' Patrick replied. 'I don't think I want his sergeant with a large chip on his shoulder instead either.'

My mobile rang and it was Elspeth.

'That was to ask how I am and, in case it's important, to tell us that the rumour was wrong and Hagtop Farm has been bought by an executive of Marks and Spencer, not Slaterford and Sons,' I reported.

'Good luck to them,' Patrick replied. 'Good, that clears that out of the way.'

'And Slaterfords has a closing-down sale, starting today.' Elspeth had not mentioned anything about having to move from the rectory.

'I don't know whether that's good or bad news. Does it mean they're pulling out of that area or merely making it look as though they are? For after all, Kennedy mopped up a few of their boys on the delivery run – that must have shaken someone a bit. They could even be brazenly ignoring little glitches like that and going for the big redevelopment scheme.'

'Now we know that the men who arrived at the warehouse were police, or at least the important ones were, couldn't we risk having another snoop round the store? I mean, the place will probably be mobbed for the sale so we're unlikely to be recognized.'

'I'll grow a quick beard. But it rather depends on what happens today.' Patrick gave me a very straight look. 'Do you know for sure if you're pregnant yet?'

'I haven't had time to go and buy a testing kit,' I answered lamely. In actual fact I was shrinking from knowing the truth: in my heart of hearts I didn't want another baby. So for the present, stupidly perhaps, I wanted the question mark to remain one.

Sometimes he seems to be able to read my thoughts. 'But if you are, you wouldn't . . . I mean, if you really didn't want it would you . . . ?'

'Have an abortion? No, of course not.'

No, that would never be on the agenda. Not ever. Ye gods, we would have to give Carrie a big rise.

Later again, when we had snatched a sandwich for lunch and Patrick had gone off to see if he could get a problem with the car's locking and alarm system fixed my phone rang again.

'I've just had a call from Greenway,' Patrick said. 'He's finally caught up with Kennedy. The signal was appalling and he could hardly hear what the man was saying but managed to gather that he wasn't too happy about the arrangement, which I suppose is to be expected. He asked if he could have a chat with you and me again before he made any decisions. I said I was tied up for a bit – they've got the car plugged into some electronic gear to see what the trouble is but the bloke thinks he can sort it out today – so Greenway suggested you went. Would you do that? You're good at talking people round.'

'Where will I meet him?' I asked.

'He's on his way back from a meeting and plans to walk across Hyde Park for some fresh air as he has a hell of a headache. He said he'd be at Speakers' Corner at around two. There's a café, actually in the park, not far from there. Ring me when you arrive and I'll get there as soon as I can – unless you phone again to tell me the arrangement's off. Sorry, I must go, the mechanic's waving me over. See you later.'

I looked at my watch – it was a quarter to one – and decided I needed some fresh air and exercise as well and would also walk. I grabbed my London AtoZ. Our hotel was in Norfolk Square so it would be fairly straightforward to get to Lancaster Gate via Sussex Gardens and head for the Marble Arch end of the park along The Ring, one of the carriage roads just inside the park boundary.

I was going down in the lift to the ground floor when my cats' whiskers kicked in with a very large warning of stinking fish. So when the lift stopped at the next floor to allow some people to get out I went with them, made my way to the stairs and returned to our room, feeling oddly shaky. Thought about carefully, my reservations were twofold; from what I knew about James I was sure that if he had a headache in the middle of a working day he would either swallow a couple of aspirins, or failing those, ignore it, not waste quite a lot of time by going for a walk. I had an idea his father would do much the same. Another thing that was bothering me was the mental picture of Michael Greenway bawling down the phone to someone whom he could hardly hear. Was mobile phone reception in London really that bad these days? Unless Kennedy had been in the basement of a building, well underground. In that case why not arrange to ring Greenway back when he was outside? For security purposes did these people utilize code words that were changed every day, or very frequently? Had Greenway in fact been talking to Kennedy at all?

I took my mobile from my bag and rang Patrick's number but it was engaged.

I was hanged if I was going to risk serving myself up on a plate, dish of the day, to crooks anonymous.

Time was running out. Five minutes later I had decided to go but quickly disguise myself somehow when my mobile rang again.

'It's me,' Patrick said. 'I've just heard from Reece. They found any amount of stolen property at the warehouse and enough explosives and weapons to give a very strong suspicion that they were all ready to be sold to terrorists. He also said he simply couldn't spare the time to liaise with F9, although he would very much like to be in a position to do so. He actually suggested sending Carrick – as he said himself, to get the whole problem over and done with. Greenway can't have given him the whole story so I didn't either because the least number of people who know the truth right now the better. I told him it wasn't a bad idea so he's going to get hold of James's boss – whoever that is – to try to arrange for him to be ordered to get on a London train as soon as possible and he'll be briefed when he gets here. I take it you're on your way.'

'No,' I said. 'I'm still in the hotel but was just about to set off. I have a bad feeling about this arrangement.'

Our working procedures ensured that he did not waste time arguing with me. 'OK, get a taxi to Starbucks at Marble Arch and I'll leave the car here, do the same and meet you inside. If you see anyone you don't like the look of hanging around head for the nearest big shop, go to the fashion department, pretend to try on clothes in the changing rooms and ring me from there.'

Patrick got to Starbucks before I did as I was held up by a traffic accident in the Bayswater Road, finally paying off the taxi and walking the last hundred yards or so. Slouching in one corner as there were no empty seats he looked more like a workman who was waiting for someone to help him dig a hole in the road. I squeezed past a vastly obese woman who paused in her bid for slow suicide with a cream-loaded beverage to scowl at me and, somehow wedging myself into the same corner, finished off Patrick's orange juice before explaining the reason for my lateness.

'So what d'you reckon then?' he said, scanning the crowded interior carefully.

I had already satisfied myself that no very tall men or anyone particularly suspicious-looking were present. 'I just don't like the business of this garbled phone message.'

'It does happen, Ingrid.'

'Do they use security codes?'

'I can't believe they operate without doing so.'

'You think I'm being silly then.'

'No, you're never silly.' He grinned. 'What did that best-selling book say? Men need praise and women reassurance?'

'OK, you gorgeous, gorgeous man, so what if Kennedy *has* been grabbed by someone and forced to lay a trap for us?'

'I'm sure he hasn't but let's go and see what happens.'

By now it was one-forty. Expecting him to head straight for the park entrance I was surprised when Patrick seized my hand and hurried down the Bayswater Road for a hundred yards or so, turned sharp right and then left and very shortly we were in a narrow mews that had the un-mistakable aroma of horses. It was a riding school and there were dozens of horses; some tacked up ready to ride, some with riders waiting to leave, some in looseboxes trying to bite those outside who got too close, others, not required, dozing. And soon, by dint of Patrick's warrant card, credit card and boundless charm we found ourselves with a heavyweight piebald cob that had hairy hooves the size of buckets and a grey arab that gazed around wildly, whinnying, as though trying to locate the nearest group of pyramids.

It is always much more comfortable to ride in the proper gear but at least we had safety helmets, insisted upon by Patrick as they acted as a disguise. He had also insisted on safety grounds that I ride the cob, possibly a mistake as the arab immediately settled down and the cob proved to be half a ton or so of mostly unstoppable muscle. We tacked ourselves on to the official ride – having made it clear that we were on official business and would not stay with it – until we were inside the park and then the others headed off in the direction of the Serpentine. Despite my best efforts to rein him in the cob and I had worked our way up the crocodile until were almost in front but I managed to persuade him to turn left, towards Speakers' Corner.

It was now five minutes past two. The cob thought we were going to be late as well, performed a massive buck as soon as his hooves touched soft ground and set off along the sand ride at a meaningful gallop. When I had succeeded in getting myself back into the saddle from halfway towards his ears I hauled him back to a canter and finally, the usual crowd of people milling around Speakers' Corner approaching at alarming speed the pair of us performed, foam-flecked, one of those ploughing stops usually seen only in old cowboy films. Quite a few people cheered and whooped, others hurried their families out of the danger zone.

Patrick trotted up on the grey, riding it one-handed on a long rein, the bastard, looking pained.

'Would you like to swap?' he enquired heavily.

'No, I think we've reached an understanding,' I panted.

'I don't. I suggest that while I hack about gently here keeping a look-out for Kennedy, or anyone dodgy, you canter, *canter* – galloping isn't permitted – to the other end of this ride and then come back here. That'll take the steam out of him. Otherwise you're in real danger of having a fall.'

I refrained from retorting that this form of surreptitious undercover surveillance had not been *my* bloody idea, merely turned my mount and set off again. He immediately thought he was going home, of course, and, despite my best efforts, went into overdrive. Blinded by his long mane blowing into my face, the huge hooves flinging sand every-where, I could not hold him. When we reached where we had entered the park he did not dash out into the traffic and kill us both but unexpectedly bore left on to a ride that ran parallel to a narrow road. I had got him back in hand a bit by now and was almost enjoying myself. We crossed the road – it appeared to be barred to ordinary traffic – and I released the brakes, just a little. Off he went again. Another quarter of a mile farther on I sensed that he had taken the edge off his energy and pulled him back to a walk. It was difficult to tell who was sweating the most, me or the horse.

I decided that Patrick was perfectly capable of looking out for Robert Kennedy for a short time – by this time I had almost convinced myself I had worried for nothing – and to deal with any possible trouble should it happen, while I too went for a little hack. For after all, he was armed and unlikely to be in personal danger in such a public place.

Magpie and I (I had just noticed his name in small brass letters on the front of the saddle) breezed along at a fast walk, both of us taking deep breaths and enjoying a sunny afternoon. At last I could gaze about and enjoy my surroundings. People sunbathed, walked dogs, children rode their bikes or kicked footballs. Over the muted roar of traffic I could hear the clippety-clop of a lot of other horses in the distance, probably the Household Cavalry.

This was not the first time it had happened to me; taking to the saddle while on a job *and* being carted off by my mount. Perhaps Patrick had remembered the occasion too: he and another, new, member of D12, Steve, had been watching a suspect while pretending to be fencing contractors and taking, if I remember correctly, almost the whole of one day to get a single post in place. My job had been to ride around the village and keep an eye on the inhabitants of the house, a large country mansion. Warwick, the horse, iron of will and mouth, had followed the usual route of the riding school instead and scorched up a hill, performing an historic emergency stop when he saw the fencing men right on his path. I had landed very safely on Steve who, probably still all colours of the rainbow, had left MI5 shortly afterwards and gone to live with an American divorcée who had four children. It must be said that he did not have a well-developed sense of humour. Patrick and he could never have worked together. On the same assignment Steve had been reprimanded for disobeying orders and had then taken a swing at his boss, whom I knew he found absolutely infuriating, the pair of them then fighting like tom cats in the middle of the village green.

I was jerked out of this pleasant reverie when I became aware of a big, black 4x4 with tinted windows purring along slowly in the same direction as me, keeping level. Somehow, I knew that I was being watched. I didn't like it. Nudging the cob into a trot I rode off in front but the car speeded up and again cruised along just a few yards over to my right. Then, all at once, while it was still moving, three men jumped out and made straight for me. Without really thinking I swung my mount round, cut in behind the vehicle, crossed the road again and, urging him on, tore off down a ride I knew to be Rotten Row.

Another road ran by this as well and all too soon the vehicle was back. It then speeded up, turned hard left, crashed through low railings and stopped twenty yards in front of me, blocking my path. The cob immediately veered left on to the grass, almost unseating me again, and we galloped off through the trees. Above the thunder of hooves I could hear that the car was following me.

I really endeavoured to take charge of this animal now and, lying right on his neck, guided him through a copse, the leaves on the lower branches brushing my back. I was aware of men shouting; a woman screamed. I headed Magpie away from people, across the middle of the park. Trees had been felled in places, the trunks still on the ground and, leaving it too late to ride around one of them, all I could do was cling on tight and pray. Magpie soared over it like a stag, obviously extremely happy as he did the same with an unoccupied seat a few paces farther on.

The car was still following, swerving around the obstacles. In front of me were acres and acres of grass crossed by a few paths with nowhere to hide, Marble Arch toy-sized in the distance. There were too many people to avoid. My heart leapt into my mouth for a moment when I thought a man would try to head off the horse, perhaps thinking I was being bolted with. But after running for a few steps he halted and was left behind.

Magpie was tiring and slowed. I heard the car accelerate and, out of the corner of my eye, saw it begin to draw level. They were going to risk crashing right into the horse, killing it even, to get hold of me. This made me boil with rage and for the first time I really urged him on.

There was a crash as the car hit something and it veered away. Then it came back and was right behind us. Desperately, I reined Magpie hard left and as I did so it felt as though he bucked again followed by a loud clang and the sound of breaking glass. The vehicle drew back.

There were far more people here and, unless I changed course completely, there would be serious injuries as, obviously, those in the car did not care a damn. It was going to have to be, I realized, one of those situations where the pilot steers his doomed plane away from residential areas.

As it was I steered towards a man riding a grey horse who was approaching at the gallop, careful at the last moment as he pulled up and took aim not to ride between him and the car. Too involved with manoeuvring my heavy mount without knocking anyone over, people scattering in all directions, I did not see what happened, only hearing shots and finding out moments later that Patrick had taken out its windscreen and then two of the tyres.

They fled on foot, having shot him off the horse.

At least, first appearances gave every impression of it: Patrick flat on the ground rolling about holding his left shoulder, his teeth bared in a rictus of agony. I dismounted, almost toppled off, my legs like jelly, and only succeeded in staying upright by grabbing a big handful of Magpie's mane and leaning on him for a few moments. Someone had caught the grey and I rudely threw my reins to them to hold as well, vaguely aware of two policeman approaching at a run.

By the time I reached Patrick he was sitting up, still holding his shoulder, swearing. I could not see any blood.

'Are you OK?' he asked tautly.

'Fine,' I said. 'Were you hit?'

'No, bloody well baled out when they took a pot at me . . . my foot stuck in the stirrup iron and . . . the horse caught me with a hoof as it spun round.'

'Is anything broken?'

'God knows.'

Fortunately, an X-ray showed that he was just very badly bruised.

It was discovered when the 4x4 was taken away for examination that it had stolen number plates. Until the investigating officers spoke to me it was assumed that the smashed nearside headlights and dented wing had been due to the vehicle hitting a tree. No, that was Magpie's rear iron-shod hooves, I told them, feeling ridiculously proud of him. He did a lot of film work, I had been informed when we returned the horses; costume dramas and things like that, and loved every minute of it. He hated cars coming too close to him though.

Eleven

F9 was resolutely stonewalling all enquiries and would only confirm that there had been no meeting that Kennedy had attended before telling Greenway that he would walk across the park. This still meant it was likely that Greenway had not been talking to him at all. But whoever he had conversed with knew about Patrick and me and that we were in London. I suddenly realized the scale of the organization we were up against.

'There has to be a mole,' I said later that evening. 'Insider information.'

'Or they got the info from Kennedy himself,' Patrick answered soberly.

It did not bear thinking about.

I had forgotten until a few minutes previously that James Carrick was likely to turn up at any moment but Patrick hadn't and had rung the DCI's mobile number to ask him to meet us at our hotel where we had returned in order to await developments. Whatever happened, Carrick now had to be told the truth. The last thing I was expecting was for him to put a completely new slant on the affair.

'We thought there was going to be a breakthrough and that's why you were asked to be here,' Patrick explained when Carrick had a fortifying single malt in his hand.

'It hasn't happened?' James asked.

'No. Do you want the bad or the good news first?'

'In that order, if you wouldn't mind,' the DCI replied stoically.

'It would appear that your father's been grabbed by serious criminals. He's an undercover cop.'

James smiled gently. 'I know.'

'You know!' Patrick and I exclaimed together.

'There was an email in my inbox at work this morning – in Gaelic so I didn't question the authenticity. He gave hardly any details and said he'd knock my block off if I told anyone. But what's gone wrong?'

Recovering from the surprise, Patrick gave him a résumé of what had happened since.

'And it's gospel that he had attended no meeting?' Carrick asked.

'Gospel. Apparently F9 personnel don't do meetings – not when they're on a case. Which is logical when you think about it.'

'So either he lied or someone else was doing the talking.'

'It has to be borne in mind that he might have been forced to reveal what he knew – he might have mentioned Ingrid and me.'

'For some reason I have a feeling that hasn't happened. Anyway, if it has it would have served no purpose to bring you into it – far easier to have said any names, false names if he was under duress. For after all, the man had as good as told you to away and boil your heads.' The last phrase was pronounced 'awa an' bile ya heids', a sign perhaps that circumstances were making Carrick hark back to his Scottish roots.

'That's true,' Patrick conceded.

'There's no indication that he'd changed his mind.'

'Are you saying that he set us up deliberately?'

'It would certainly have upped his cred with that particular criminal empire.'

It occurred to me that James, predictably on a high, found this all rather amusing.

'He could well have been driving the car,' Carrick added. 'I'm sure he knows you can take care of yourselves. He might have decided to abort whatever they intended to do if he thought you were in real danger.'

'Bloody hell,' Patrick whispered. 'So it *is* his case after all.'

'I think you can rest assured that no names would have been passed on.'

Praying that this optimism was well-founded on all points I said, 'But it would appear that someone, probably the man at the Bristol end, Steven Ballinger, or whatever he calls himself – is trying to remove him from the gang by getting him arrested for three murders.'

'That might be why the undercover cop's moved back to town.'

'He said he probably would. But where does that leave us?' I said. 'Going home?'

'And what does he mean to do now?' James said. 'Organize a big heist and catch them on the job?'

'I don't see how anyone could possibly grab all these villains in one go,' Patrick said. 'Heists apart it's hardly the kind of outfit to have an AGM.'

'You just want to catch the big boys initially,' Carrick said. 'To arrange a job where only the most professional bods are required. The rest are nearly always local suspects who can be mopped up later and only too happy to lay the blame on those with the big plans. That's one way of doing it, anyway.'

'I suppose your email came through official channels?' I said to James, mulling over an idea.

'That's right. It's what one would expect.'

'It wouldn't be wise to try to contact him,' Patrick told me.

'I know that. So as we can't confer how about us being helpful by taking out this Bristol mobster before he does any more damage?'

Both men's eyes glowed for a moment before they came to their responsible policemen senses.

'But we can't just—' Carrick started to say before being interrupted by Patrick.

'It depends what you mean by "take out",' he demurred.

'Prove beyond doubt that the tall man in Slaterfords is the big criminal boss man in that area and do something about him, arrest him, I mean. He must have put a tail on Robert and that was how they found his Dartmoor hide-away. If Robert went back there it might provide the bait to make Ballinger want to take care of him himself. We could be waiting. That's if everyone's guesses are correct.'

'All we need then is to persuade Kennedy to drop what he's doing and play ball,' Patrick said wearily.

I hung on to my patience, just. 'No, all we need is a lookalike and a dark blue Land Rover Defender with the correct registration. We have the lookalike right here so perhaps Greenway could find out the reg?'

Before this suggestion could be discussed it was rendered unnecessary. Paul Reece rang Patrick to tell him that Steven Ballinger had just been picked up for questioning in connection with the finds in the warehouse. Did we wish to be present?

'OK, to hell with F9,' Greenway said when immediately contacted. 'Good idea of Ingrid's: nail Ballinger and see what he has to say. Only the Bristol boys have done it for us. Get there. If he won't play ball we might have to utilize Plan B.'

'What did he mean by that?' I asked Patrick, who had made the call and relayed Greenway's decision.

'I'm sincerely hoping he isn't thinking of asking the one-time MI5 honcho to lay on a little mild torture. My torturing days are definitely over.'

'What about me?' Carrick said.

'Yes, sorry, he said that as you've been released for a short time to represent the Avon and Somerset Force you may as well stick with us. He's still hoping to get your father on board.'

The DCI shook his head ruefully. 'I've been on some bloody strange cases since I came into the orbits of you two. Back to the West Country then – and I'd only just got here.'

Steven Ballinger – who had that morning been working seemingly normally at the store – had refused to answer any questions about the warehouse, other than insisting that it had been sold years previously by the then owners of the store to he knew not who and was no longer anything to do with Slaterfords. This refusal, and it was understandable that Reece's team did not believe his story, led to his being taken to a city centre police station. Suspects were not normally dealt with at HQ in Portishead.

'It wasn't normal circumstances though, was it?' Patrick raged to Paul Reece. 'You had in your hands a man who it is now obvious is the kingpin to most of the serious crime this side of Axminster!'

In short, Ballinger had been busted out.

Late that morning three armed and hooded men, one carrying a sawn-off shotgun, the other two handguns, had smashed a stolen 4x4 through the entrance doors of the building, which was a modern one, into the reception area. They had then fired shots into the ceiling and while one man had held everyone at bay the other two had run into the detention block – they knew the way. There, the duty officer had been clubbed to the floor by a gun butt and his keys taken. Little more than seconds later all four had escaped and witnesses had reported they had got away in a vehicle waiting in a nearby side street. This had later been found abandoned and burned out in a narrow lane off the Bath road.

'Was the custody officer badly injured?' Patrick went on to ask, coming off the boil a little.

'No, thank God,' a predictably very worried Reece replied. 'He was taken to hospital and will be kept in for twenty-four hours for observation, but I gather he is basically all right. By a miracle no members of the public were hurt.'

James Carrick was keeping a tactful distance from where we were standing in the wreckage of the reception area, making himself useful to an investigation team. Scenes of crime personnel were examining the car that had been used as a battering ram, a Toyota, the immediate vicinity around which was taped off.

I said, 'I assume Ballinger wasn't actually under arrest.'

Reece shook his head. 'No. There were no grounds to arrest him. He was very agitated and difficult, refusing to answer questions and that was why he was brought here. If he hadn't insisted on having his solicitor present – on the grounds that he fully intended to sue us for harassment – which took about an hour to organize, he wouldn't have found himself in a cell for a while. We were just about to bring him to an interview room when the mob, obviously his mob, arrived.'

'It was obviously a delaying tactic then,' I said. 'What did his brief have to say about that?'

'Made himself scarce, pronto.'

One could not really blame him.

Reece was then called away, wanted on the phone.

'At least we know where we are with this character now,' Carrick called, coming across.

'I can't get over the man's colossal cool in working at the store as though nothing had happened,' Patrick said. 'Was he calmly assuming that the police would unquestioningly accept his story that the store no longer owned the warehouse? I actually spoke to a man in the delivery area, if you remember, and he told me where it was so it must still be used.'

'Arrogance,' Carrick said succinctly. 'Or stupidity.'

'Sergeant Hall thought he had several screws loose, sir,' said a woman wearing protective clothing who was standing nearby. 'Ballinger's a creepy sort of bloke, according to him – he reckons he's mentally unbalanced.'

'Another reason for his odd behaviour,' Carrick said. 'Thank you.'

We did not see Reece again then, although Carrick did. Reece had been told that orders had come directly from the Chief Constable that the force would no longer be involved in the case as SOCA and a covert unit of the Met, which for some time had been monitoring a gang in London thought to be in close partnership with the West Country organization, would be taking over. All evidence and findings in Bristol would go to them via Detective Chief Inspector James Carrick who would liaise.

'Go to *them*?' Patrick queried. 'Has Greenway got F9 on board?'

'Don't you mean has F9 got SOCA on board?' I said.

The question was answered when we met Michael Greenway in what I would call conventional surroundings, a large top-floor room in a house in south-west London that I was given to understand was SOCA's headquarters. For security reasons it was not advertised as such and could have been any one of numberless elegant Georgian mansions in this particular road that had been converted into offices and flats.

'I've never known a job with more cackle and less action,' Greenway complained, placing the inevitable laptop and his briefcase down on what must have once been a boardroom table and around one end of which we had drawn up our chairs. 'And the mobsters are calling the tune – I don't like that either.' He glanced about. 'Where's Carrick?'

'He's stayed behind to gather all available forensic evidence on the vehicle they used on their ram-raid and also to interview the people who brought Ballinger in. He's coming up to London tomorrow,' Patrick told him, omitting to remind him that the DCI had travelled to London and back once that day already. We of course had breakfasted in the capital, which for me had been tea and toast as I had been feeling slightly unwell, flown the return trip to Bristol and it was now getting on for midnight. Having had a stale sandwich for lunch with plastic-flavoured coffee I found myself looking around the room wondering if there was *anything* within its four walls that was edible.

Greenway cleared his throat and said to Patrick, 'As you obviously know SOCA is a fairly large organization. You must also be aware that along with your presence with a mandate to be an adviser and trouble-shooter other people have been beavering away since we were asked to look into Cliff Morley's murder. I must admit that they haven't come up with a lot although they have managed to recreate Morley's movements just before he played rugby for the Ferrets and just after. He went home to his flat. He could well have been grabbed there if someone was tailing him. The flat has been examined by forensics who treated it as though it had been a crime scene – it probably was – twice, once by Paul Reece's boys and then by us. They removed several items including used crockery and a half-eaten Mars bar. It's too early for definite results yet or matches with anyone on record but we do know some of the samples of DNA detected aren't Morley's.

Who knows? Something that matches that might turn up
in the vehicle.'

'Are F9 saying anything about Kennedy?' Patrick wanted
to know.

'Nothing.'

'What, not even to confirm that he's still in the land of
the living?'

'No.'

'So we still don't know whether you actually spoke to
the man over the phone or not.'

'Life's a bummer, isn't it?' Greenway said wearily. 'But,
on the positive side, when I spoke to David's Rolt's successor
– and I didn't even know if he was aware of our suggestion of cooperation—'

'Was he?' Patrick interrupted.

'Yes.'

'That means you *did* speak to Kennedy on the phone and
he then relayed the offer to his boss.'

'God, yes, you're right. I must be tired. Anyway, he told
me that his lot would get in contact as soon as they needed
assistance. It's not much but all we'll get from them at
present. My next question is to you – do you want to drop
this and work on something else?'

'No, I rather think I owe it to Carrick to persevere.' Patrick
turned to me. 'How about you?'

'Ditto,' I said.

'We can't wait long, for cost reasons if nothing else,'
Greenway went on. 'It might mean that you have to get
stuck into something else and then come back to this when
they shout.'

Patrick said, 'I'd rather get stuck into this in my own
way, if you don't mind.'

'And do what?'

'As I said to someone in Portishead recently, out-Herod
Herod.'

'I don't think I want you treading on F9's toes.'

Patrick's mobile rang and he apologized and answered
it. It was Carrick. Greenway and I watched Patrick's face
as he listened to what he had to say. It became grave but

other than a 'Bloody hell! What, the whole place?' and
'Thank you – see you tomorrow,' he made no responses so
it was impossible to guess what had happened.

'There's a serious fire at Slaterfords,' he reported when
the call ended. 'It started while the shop was still open. The
place was crowded because it was the first day of the
closing-down sale and they think people are still trapped
inside.'

I opened my mouth to say something but Greenway spoke
first. 'Is the fire out now?'

'Not yet, and they're already talking about arson as it's
such a fireball. Several other adjacent properties and some
of the shops down-wind in Broadmead have been evacuated and the surrounding roads sealed off.'

I suddenly remembered that Elspeth had told me a friend
had expressed an interest in going to the sale for a rummage
and had asked if Elspeth wanted to accompany her. Had
she?

Greenway said, 'You somehow know it was arson. To get
rid of any evidence or to make it more likely they – or whatever company they'll set up when they've re-established
themselves somewhere else – get planning permission for
the redevelopment? Murdering bastards.' After a reflective
pause he said, 'Do you think you could infiltrate this outfit?'

'It would have to be done properly,' Patrick said.

'Define "properly".'

'I would have to be able to provide things they really,
really want. On the one hand this might be money, security, weapons, things that could be within the scope of an
international crook who wanted a foot on the ladder of
London's criminal scene or, a more hands-on approach,
expertise as might be provided by an off-the-wall terrorist
type with a massive grudge against law and order.'

'The latter's more your kind of thing, isn't it?'

'Yes, but in order for me to earn the right sort of form
you'd have to let me kill someone important first.'

To Greenway's credit he did not head for the ceiling.
'To be staged in an elaborate but phoney way, you mean.
In other words, whoever it was would not really be hurt.'

'At the very, very worst a few cuts and bruises,' Patrick replied soothingly. Was he aware that any security engendered by his words had been somewhat negated by being uttered through a wolfish smile?

'Who though? Got anyone in mind?'

'You.'

'Me!'

'You're quite perfect,' he was assured.

'I don't think we ought to bring SOCA's name into this.'

'It needen't be. You'd just be described to the media as a top policeman involved with the capital's serious crime.'

Greenway pondered for a few moments and then said, 'I'll have to sleep on that. I suggest we meet here tomorrow morning when Carrick's arrived to allow us to collate everything we've got and then decide what to do next. We might have initial findings from the arson investigators in Bristol by then too.' He collected his possessions and we all moved to leave. 'I tell you what though,' he added as he held the door open for us. 'I'd be willing to incur a few cuts and bruises to bring this bastard to justice.'

Twelve

'I take it you've heard nothing from your father since the one email,' Greenway said to Carrick after the introductions had been made.

'No, sir, nothing.'

'Well, I hope to God the man's all right. What do you have for us?'

'It amounts to a short presentation, I'm afraid, sir.'

'Good, I'm sure we could all do with something like that to get it all straight in our minds. And you needn't bother with so many of the "sirs" – we're all in this together.'

It was obvious when the DCI produced a new file from his document case and what followed that he had worked on it for most of the night.

'It's fairly obvious but we must remind ourselves that this investigation started not with Sergeant Cliff Morley's murder but before that when this off-shoot of a London gang went on a crime spree in Bristol and the surrounding area,' he began. 'There are other off-shoots in various towns and cities in the west of England and Superintendent Reece has a theory that all are masterminded by the head of the London mob and that the comparitively recent Bristol set-up came about as a result of a disagreement within the command structure. He has no real evidence to back this up, only the words of grassers and informers, one of the former, now in prison, being credible. I have to say at this point that it is regrettable that F9 is not in a position to share their intelligence with us.

'Robberies, thefts of top-of-the-range cars, often at knife-point – I'm sure you're familiar with the tally – all commited with an arrogance and callousness that can only be described as breathtaking. We have a description of a very tall man who would appear to be the brains behind all this but has subsequently been discovered to be, ostensibly, the managing director of Slaterford and Sons, calling himself Steven Ballinger. Prior to this discovery Sergeant Morley was making enquiries about this man when he was murdered. I need not dwell on the details of his death. Two other men were then murdered, all had been mutilated and the initials RK carved on their torsos. Robert Kennedy, a senior operative of F9, maintains that this is in an effort to get him blamed for the killings as he has infiltrated the Bristol gang. It would now appear that Kennedy has left the area to try to prevent any more killings but we know nothing of his whereabouts or even his personal safety.

'F9 raided the waterfront warehouse of Slaterfords but because of what I shall describe as a collision of police departments it was the Avon and Somerset Force who subsequently searched the place and found stolen property, weapons and a small amount of explosives. Ballinger was questioned at the store, refused to answer questions and was then taken to a city centre police station. Before he could be interviewed an armed gang broke him out of custody. The Avon and Somerset Force has now been relieved of all duties in this case.'

'But for you,' Patrick said almost inaudibly.

'They weren't removed from the scene because of any perceived lapses,' Greenway added. 'It was just getting a little too crowded. Sorry, James, do go on.'

Carrick smiled his thanks. 'And now of course we have the fire at the store, the investigation into which obviously the local police are involved. I understand the blaze is now out but the building is pretty much gutted, especially at the northern end and until the exterior walls and the remaining part of the roof are deemed not to be in danger of collapse no examination of the interior is being permitted. Due to the nature of the business it is impossible yet to know if anyone was trapped inside but it seems inconceivable to me that bodies won't be found in the rubble. Three were recovered from the entrance area while the blaze was being fought – it would appear that part of the ceiling came down on them as they tried to escape. Two people were killed when they threw themselves from upstairs windows in the staff room area at the rear and several more, staff and customers, were rescued when a turntable ladder arrived. In all, one hundred and seventy-five people escaped comparitively unharmed from the building.'

Without saying anything to Patrick I had rung the rectory at Hinton Littlemoor the previous evening. Thankfully, Elspeth and her friend had decided to give the sale a miss.

Carrick continued, 'Survivors from members of staff have reported that when the fire alarm sounded all senior staff immediately disappeared and they got the impression they left the premises altogether. Questioned further some said they had never seen management taking any kind of leading role during fire practices. The fact that they would appear to have left at an early stage was confirmed early this morning when the underground car park was examined – it virtually escaped damage – and it was obvious that the only significant empty spaces were where you, Ingrid, said the cars drove off from before, the area nearest the exit.'

'I simply can't believe anyone with arson in mind would start a fire when the place was full of people!' Greenway exclaimed. 'If you're going to burn the bloody store down why not do it at night?'

'To make it look as if it wasn't arson?' Patrick suggested.

'If so they must have a very dim view of fire brigade investigators,' Carrick said disgustedly. 'No, I reckon they set fire to it during the day as a two-finger salute to the police.'

We digested this for several seconds in silence and then Carrick said, 'Something useful has emerged from this mess. A woman who suffered minor burns to her hands and face went to the police when she left A and E, said she was Steven Ballinger's PA and that she wanted to make a statement, to talk to someone senior, in fact. She actually seems to have acted as secretary to quite a few senior staff at the store. I understand she's being interviewed again this morning but the gist of what I was told last night is that she'd suspected for a while that something wasn't quite right with the place.'

Patrick butted in with, 'Is she being given police protection?'

'Armed protection,' Carrick answered.

'I would like her to be brought here,' Greenway said.

'I thought you would,' the DCI said. 'I understand that Superintendent Reece will contact you this morning following what she says at the local nick to see if you think it worth bringing her all this way, with regard to her injuries and the fact that Miss—'

'I want her here whatever she says,' was the uncompromising interruption from Greenway. 'So Patrick can get the full story out of her.'

'I'll go and borrow some thumbscrews from the Tower of London now,' Patrick said, half-rising from his seat.

Once you have a certain reputation it seems that you can never lose it.

Greenway waved him down. 'No, no, all right. Sorry. I didn't mean that you'd beat the woman up.'

'And the fact that Miss Dean is well over sixty years of age,' Carrick persevered.

'So we'd better wait and see what Reece says,' Greenway decided. 'Anything else?' he asked Carrick.

'Yes. Just before the case's handover yesterday Reece's team discovered both Madderly Ritter's and Kyle Jeffers' addresses. From a snout they lent on heavily, I understand. I say "addresses" but Ritter had been roughing it in a squat as the girl he had recently moved in with – no, started living off – threw him out. Jeffers had a council flat in the St Pauls area of the city. It appears that a somewhat headstrong sergeant, Cunningham, ignored orders to leave well alone until other people had been consulted – in other words, you sir – and he and a couple of others broke in. The place is like a slaughterhouse – it was where they were tortured and killed. That's the next decision. Do you want them to send in their scenes-of-crime people or use your own?'

Greenway looked at Patrick who wordlessly intimated that it was Greenway's decision to make.

'I can see no reason why they shouldn't investigate this,' the SOCA man said slowly. 'And to put matters straight it wasn't at my behest that Avon and Somerset was removed from the investigation. Morley was their man so let them get on with it. I shall just need the findings, that's all.'

Patrick caught my gaze and smiled. This was noticed by the other two who immediately remembered my presence.

'Any comments, Ingrid?' Greenway enquired.

'Only one,' I said. 'This man will pull another big stunt, commit another crime. He's probably raving mad. So if you're going to send Patrick undercover – F9 or no – then I suggest you do it quickly.'

'We'll see what Miss . . . er . . .' Greenway glanced at his notes. 'Dean, has to say first.'

Miss Phillipa Dean, it transpired, did not want any fuss made of her injuries, which she reckoned to be a minor inconvenience, and as she had a sister in west London would be delighted to talk to SOCA on condition that she was taken to her sister's home afterwards. When told that she would be taken to a safe house with her minder, plus a woman constable, where her sister could, if she wished, join her there was reluctant acquiescence.

By this time all of us were sick to death of sitting in offices, talking, and later that day, when Miss Dean was shown into the room, a different one, where the interview was to take place I knew we were doing our very best not to appear as world-weary as we felt. James Carrick was not present. It had been felt that four of us was at least one too many inquisitors. He was not far away though, liaising by phone with Paul Reece on the latest findings on the fire.

Greenway made the introductions and everyone sat down. The venue that had been selected was an informal one furnished with armchairs, a low table, reproduction paintings of old scenes of the city on the walls and even a small vase of flowers. Miss Dean was asked if she had been given refreshments but this was for politeness' sake as we knew already that she had, during which time we had read her statement. Greenway asked about her burns – a small dressing was affixed to her left cheekbone and there were others on the backs of her hands – and was told they were nothing. Further questioning revealed that she had acquired them in trying to push open a fire door in a smoke-filled corridor while clasping her bag to herself only to find that it was red hot. It seemed a miracle that she was here at all.

There was then a mutual eyeing-up.

I reckoned the lady easily to be in her early seventies, her face quite heavily lined, but it had been decided on my suggestion that nobody would be rude enough to ask how old she was. She had moved a little stiffly on entering the room but that could be more to do with sitting in a car for four hours than infirmity. Her hair, brown but greying, was piled on top of her head in an untidy bun, wisps escaping in what was actually a fashionable and engaging manner. And fashionable and poised she was, dressed in an expensive olive green dress and sleeveless jacket with self-coloured embroidery, a heavy amber necklace around her throat and matching earrings. Her eyes were the same colour as the green of her dress and now regarded us shrewdly and steadily.

Although it had also been decided that Patrick would put most of the questions to her Greenway opened the interview with, 'Thank you for agreeing to come and for making this statement. It is all very businesslike and in it you express your suspicions but we need to flesh it out a little. Please forgive me for asking, but do you still find it necessary to work for financial reasons?'

Miss Dean was not offended. Speaking in her low, soft voice she said, 'Well, I won't pretend the money wasn't useful to me. Adrian, my partner, and I go on holiday to Italy quite a lot. We're into gardens and architecture. He's a retired architect.' She smiled to herself. 'We met at a nudist camp, as a matter of fact.'

'So the salary wasn't the main reason for your going after a job at Slaterford and Sons?' Patrick asked blandly and heroically not smiling at all, no, not one bit.

'It was *that* job I went after,' she corrected. 'My typing was still quite good but Adrian taught me to use a computer.

I've always been good with machines – I used to work at Bletchley Park.'

'What, the code-breaking place?' Greenway exclaimed.

She nodded. 'Yes, for over twenty years. Slaterfords was my last challenge. I told Adrian I didn't want to go completely to pot yet.'

'Challenge?' Patrick echoed.

'Yes, if ever a shop was run by a bunch of crooks it was that one. You only had to look at them, the senior staff, I mean, with their shifty eyes, to know that something was going on.'

'So you took the job with a view to finding out more?' Greenway said.

'Yes, my father was a detective-sergeant with the Met. But he refused to let me join the police. He said it was a most unsuitable job for a woman. Women belonged in the home, according to him. I have to say I hated him rather.' She sat up straight and severely addressing us all, added, 'But this wasn't me trying to do a Miss Marple, you know.'

'No, of *course* not,' Greenway said quickly.

'It sounds as though you were very confident about getting the job,' I said.

'Only insofar as I had an idea that if there was something illegal going on they'd seek either to employ a young dimwit to do their paperwork for them or a much older person they could write off as too ga-ga to understand anything else. I made out I was computer literate for letters and so forth and that was all. They didn't want me to get involved with accounts, someone else did that, but it didn't stop me from having a good nose around the whole IT system. They were so confident in themselves they didn't even use passwords. And, look, I won't pretend that I understand all that is there, far from it, because although there was no real security to the system it would appear that nicknames have been given to people and places so it means nothing to an outsider.'

Patrick said, 'Let me get this straight: you applied for a job at the shop because you thought it dodgy on account of certain shifty-looking individuals. Personally, I think you can go in quite a few organizations and take issue with people's *appearances*. Surely there was more to it than that.'

'Yes, it was Ballinger himself. He killed my neighbour's little dog when I was out for a walk with her, drove right up onto the pavement to get around another vehicle and ran over it. He almost hit the pair of us. Didn't stop, just paused long enough to shout obscenities through an open window at her for being in his way.'

'You recognized him from someone you'd seen in the store?'

'Yes, he was prowling and poking around when I was in there with Adrian one day previous to that when we were looking for curtain material. Such an odd-looking man. I asked an assistant who he was.'

I was still pondering present tenses in her previous response to a question and said, 'You said just now that you don't understand all what is in the database and that it can't mean anything to an outsider. But surely it's lost, everything like that must have gone in the fire.'

'No, it didn't. By that time – and I hadn't been there very long – I was more than suspicious after things I'd overheard in conversations and phone calls. It was why I wanted to see someone senior in the police, before I owned up to saving everything on to CD ROMs.'

I thought for a moment that Greenway would burst into tears with gratitude. He said, 'You wouldn't by any chance have brought them with you?'

Miss Dean opened her voluminous, designer, pricey, handbag. I wasn't at all surprised she'd saved it from the fire.'Yes, indeed, they're here.'

The small paper bag and its contents were passed over and immediately delivered into the hands of a computer expert.

'Tell us about Steven Ballinger,' Patrick requested when Greenway had come back into the room.

I had noticed that even while responding to Greenway's questions Miss Dean's gaze had kept straying to the other man present, with perhaps the smallest hint of apprehension in her expression. He can be intimidating even when not intending to be and I thought it time this was allayed.

'*Please*,' I snapped at him.

He got the message and, although seated, performed a courtly bow, whipping off an imaginary hat. 'Please,' he said with a grin.

Miss Dean smiled back at the pair of us. 'I take it then that Ballinger really is some kind of desperado. I know there was a raid on a Bristol city centre police station and someone was set free. It didn't say on the news who it was and no one would tell me when I made my statement early this morning.'

'It was him,' Patrick confirmed. 'He's wanted to answer questions on various serious crimes in the area. What we really need to know is where he lives.'

'I never knew his address. All his private correspondence was sent to the store. He told me that himself.'

'And you have absolutely no idea where he went when he left work in the evenings?'

'No, none. He never mentioned a family either.'

'Please tell us all you do know about him.'

Miss Dean pondered for a few moments and then said, 'Well, obviously, I was forewarned of the kind of person he could be and have to say I was nervous on the first morning. I was worried that he might recognize me even though he had given no sign that he did at the interview. But nothing untoward happened and I thought to begin with that I might have been mistaken in my identification of him as the man driving the car. He was actually rather disappointing; a very tall, thin man whose voice was squeaky until he shouted. He appeared oddly nervous of things – spiders, for example and if one was in his office I was called in to deal with it.'

'Would you say that in some ways he was an ineffectual sort of person?'

'Yes, that's a good question; he was. I think that with some men who are deficient in some way, they compensate – like those of short stature who wear metal tips on the soles of their shoes and strut around. Who knows what the problem is – unless it's his voice, of course – perhaps he's lacking . . . in hidden areas.' Here she smiled broadly at both men as if to assure them that they could not possibly come under this heading and then said, 'Ballinger compensated for whatever problem he has, consciously or not, by flying into rages. Then the man who had driven on to the pavement and almost knocked down two women emerged.'

'Go on,' Patrick said when she paused.

'To re-cap slightly: nothing that happened initially at Slaterfords excited my suspicions. They were very careful about that. I sent out letters in connection with job applications and things like that, dealt with callers, most of whom were hopeful employees. There were other visitors who were whisked straight past me to see Ballinger. His office was next to mine. Things became interesting when there were arguments and he lost his temper. That is the thing I remember most about him, his dreadful temper. As time went by there always seemed to be rows going on. I could hear them through the wall and out in the main corridor. I came to think that the man was mentally unbalanced as he would fly into a rage over nothing.'

'Were you ever frightened for your own safety?' I enquired.

'Yes, a little. I hate it when people shout. I just kept out of the way or had an early lunch break.'

'What sort of nothings set him off?' Patrick wanted to know.

'I once heard him yelling that no one had told him that it was raining before he went out for something and he'd got wet. All he'd had to do was look out of the window. He seemed to have a lot of disagreements with a man called Bob.'

'Do you know his surname?'

'No, no one used surnames. Which was the first thing I found odd, but then again things are much more informal these days.'

'Did you ever speak to this man yourself?'

'No, he wasn't there very often. Oh yes, once. I wished him good morning.'

'Did he reply?'

'Yes, he did.'

'Would you say he was a Scot?'

'He might have been.'

Patrick said to Greenway, 'Professional curiosity makes me want to ask James to come in for a moment.'

Greenway picked up the phone and a minute or so later the DCI arrived.

'Good afternoon, Miss Dean,' he said.

'Did he speak like that?' Patrick asked her.

'Yes, just like that.' She gave Carrick a scrutinizing stare. 'In fact you look like him, only younger.'

Patrick told her who he was and then said, 'Would you mind if he stays or is that too many of us for you?'

She said that she did not mind at all and James seated himself.

'So what was the general atmosphere like on a day-to-day basis?' Patrick asked. 'How did these people behave towards you?'

'When I first started working there the various men – no other women worked in the admin department except the accounts clerk – spoke to me in a very patronising way, as though talking to a child, possibly on account of my age. One of them was actually a bit sneery and made remarks about geriatrics taking over the planet. I retaliated by correcting all his grammatical errors when he was speaking to me and he soon gave up. They soon realized that I could string a letter together and didn't wreck the office photocopier so attitudes improved and on the surface all was fairly polite and businesslike. I didn't deliberately set out to be myself, or too clever, as I wanted to find out what was going on without creating suspicion.'

'You were Ballinger's PA as well, I understand,' Patrick said. 'What did that entail?'

'I booked air and rail tickets for him, arranged hotel rooms and acted as a go-between for the members of staff at the store and Ballinger. By that I mean those who worked on the retail side. They were very grateful to me for that. Most of them were scared of those in charge.'

I found this revealing with regard to this lady sitting facing us. Either a bunch of crooks minded their Ps and Qs when she was around or she was much braver than we had first assumed.

Patrick said, 'You said in your statement that Ballinger went to London quite a lot and also to Southampton. You also made holiday arrangements for him and his wife, Ella: a fortnight in Turkey. Were you asked to undertake any other duties?'

'She wasn't his wife. And to answer your question, no.'

'Who was she?'

'A rather upmarket Croatian prostitute he was besotted with.'

'Did he ask you to do anything else – different from that everyday kind of job?'

'No.'

'He didn't ask you to deliver parcels or packages to anyone?'

'No, nothing like that.'

'When Ingrid and I had a snoop around the store we noticed that all the doors in one area of the upper floor had padlocks on them. That's pretty unusual.'

'I never saw what was kept in some of the rooms. Ballinger was security mad and has what my father used to call a "garden-shed mentality". A big padlock looks more secure to him than modern electronic or dead locks.'

'Is there anything else that you'd like to add that isn't in your statement?'

'No.' She was looking nervous again.

'Think,' Patrick encouraged softly.

'No,' she said again.

Patrick got up from his seat and went over to the window. 'Miss Dean, there's something worrying you and you're much too nice a person for me to have to get annoyed with you for not telling me what it is.'

I cleared my throat. 'We think Ballinger is a murderer,' I told her. 'One of his victims was a policeman.'

There was a painful silence, during which I tried to catch Patrick's eye and when I succeeded gave him a look that said he was *not* to get annoyed with her.

Not yet.

The silence continued and our witness visibly became more distressed. Then Carrick suddenly said, 'That Scot you met, Bob. You're right, we are similar and that's because he's my father. He's an undercover cop and, right now, I'm not at all sure about his safety. Share your worries with us and it might mean we catch Ballinger all the sooner.'

'Oh dear,' Miss Dean whispered. 'It's not going to make catching him any easier but nevertheless something I wanted to tell you right from the start. It probably means I shall end up in prison. What is it called, "being an accessory"?'

Patrick sat down again. 'How could that be?'

After another long pause she said, 'Ballinger paid for one of our holidays to Italy.'

'That doesn't make you any kind of accessory to crime,' Greenway said.

'He said it was in recognition of the efforts I'd made,' Miss Dean continued as though no one had spoken. 'I had a good idea he was a crook by then and I should have refused. But I didn't. I found myself absolutely delighted with the gift at the time, especially as the air tickets were first class. I've been disgusted with myself ever since.' It all became too much for her and she took a tissue from her bag and sobbed into it quietly.

Patrick does not normally go down on his knees in front of comparative strangers but did so now. 'Thank God you accepted,' he said quietly. 'For we now know that if this man suspects *anyone* around him of working for the law or closing in on him in any way he kills them – in ways that are quite unspeakable.'

It was clear that Miss Dean did not find his close proximity on the floor unnerving, or even unusual, and I began to admire her retired architect. She said, 'But I shall have to stand up in court and admit it, won't I? My conscience will see to that.'

Greenway said, 'There's no earthly reason why what

you've just said should go further than these four walls and I can assure you that we're going to end up with an extremely complicated and protracted court case where a trip to Italy will seem an irrelevance. Ballinger will be too worried about saving his own skin to bring you into it.'

'But the money must have come from *crime*,' she whispered, eyes brimming.

'Look, Miss Dean, PAs always get perks, whatever the company and wherever the money comes from. Quite a few people in this country think all governments are run by crooks but civil servants still sleep soundly in their beds at night.'

Thirteen

I should have known already, of course, but when Patrick told me that under no circumstances would I be able to go undercover with him on this job my disappointment was boundless. There was nothing vague in the instruction, nothing to which I could put my own slant, this was Lieutenant-Colonel Patrick Justin Gillard ordering his working partner to go home and stay there for her own safety. The only concession he would make was that if he needed help of the kind I could provide, he would contact me. If it was at all possible he would contact me anyway. It was all I had. That Greenway was the instigator of the instruction went without saying.

What was worse was that other than saying that they had ditched the idea of Greenway's mock assassination he refused to go into any details about how he intended to undertake the mission. There was a part of me that knew why: on an assignment for D12 when he turned himself into a Hell's Angel he had got himself tattooed and still has the shadowy outlines of those brutal disfigurations on the backs of his hands, more visible in the winter when he is not so tanned. I had wept bitter tears upon seeing them for the first time.

So this then, I reasoned, was bound to be another belt and braces change of appearance. I had to admit it was necessary for there was still the worry that our faces had been visible on video footage of the CCTV cameras at Slaterford and Sons when we had first wandered around the store, and in the side street afterwards before Patrick had gone back and set off all the alarms. Even his removing his jacket and giving it to me prior to re-entering the shop might have been recorded and closely scrutinized.

I went home, taking the car: it was of no use to him. When I arrived I found a huge and gloriously scented tied bouquet waiting for me, amazingly from Michael Greenway. The words on the card were, 'Don't think that he's on his own. The entire system is behind him.'

'No, he is and it isn't,' I said out loud, my eyes misting as I put the flowers on the dresser. 'He's missing a piece of *his* system – me.'

I knew that James Carrick was staying in London for the time being, and was rather hoping that I could count on his sending a few trickles of intelligence in my direction. But over the next few days during which I threw myself into domestic matters, the children, the horses, and a house-to-house charity collection in the village, I heard nothing. Late on the fifth day, a Saturday, I could stand it no longer and rang James's mobile number. All I got was his recorded voice requesting me to leave a message. I did.

Still I heard nothing. I had been at home for almost a week.

My writing had come to a standstill: the idea of producing something dark, Sherlockian and bog-ridden as out of the question now as when I had visited the place where Cliff Morley's body had been dumped. Perhaps I ought to go back to writing romance, I thought dully, and this time not permit the hints of intrigue and lawlessness to permeate and finally take over my novels. Or perhaps go in for humour. For what I needed, surely, was to laugh a bit more.

I cried instead.

On Sunday night I had the nightmare of the scarecrow climbing in through my bedroom window again, so vivid, so *real*, that when I awoke, sweating and shivering, I told myself that I must be sliding into mental or physical illness. Unaccountably, I then fell asleep again to slumber dreamlessly until six thirty and when I woke up this time I knew, going bananas or no, what I was going to do.

Fortunately, this week was half-term. Elspeth had already suggested I might like to take the children to Hinton

Littlemoor but we had put the idea on hold as she had gone down with a bad cold. I knew though that she was disappointed and at just after eight I rang her. Minutes later – she told me was feeling much better – and after telling her the absolute truth that I felt I ought to stay near to home in case Patrick needed my help I had arranged for Carrie and the children to go to Somerset for a few days. Carrie could help with the extra work but would be given plenty of time off, the older children could take sleeping bags to save washing and they would all be right away from Dartmoor and any possible danger.

I hated not being involved with the investigation and for a short while on that Monday morning, when Carrie and the children had left, I contemplated driving out to have a snoop around Sheepwash Farm. Common sense prevailed, mainly because I had no idea what Patrick was planning to do. For all I knew some vastly complicated sting operation had been put into place there and by turning up I would hazard everything.

Common sense held the high ground until the next morning, a bright and sunny one, when, unable to concentrate on writing but loath to completely abandon the basic plot for the book on which I was supposed to be working, I picked up the phone and borrowed a Land Rover.

The Series 3 was old and belonged to a local farmer friend who would lend it to anyone he knew who would top up the petrol tank afterwards, the vehicle, as he put it, always reluctant to pass a filling station without stopping. I had driven it before and although it was noisy and a bumpy ride it stormed up the rutted Dartmoor gradients in jolly and unstoppable fashion that was great fun. More important to me now was that it was a 'normal' kind of vehicle in this landscape and would not attract attention like our somewhat top-of-the-range Lichfield conversion Range Rover.

To the right of the drive to our cottage is a small pasture field with a ridge down the centre that runs roughly parallel to it where there was once an ancient boundary. Glancing over the hedge as I drove up it on the short journey to the farm I noticed, not far from the gate that opened on to the road through the village, a scarecrow that I could not remember seeing before. You don't put scarecrows on grassland unless it has just been reseeded, surely.

Do you?

'It's nothing I've done,' had said the owner of the Land Rover, whose field it was. 'There's a village in Cornwall where I've heard they have scarecrow-making competitions. I expect it's something to do with the school.'

I left the sunshine behind: central Dartmoor wreathed in strange low cloud that enveloped the higher ground and tors like a grey hat, the top of the tall communications mast at Princetown actually sticking out into the sunshine above it. Visibility in the village was not too bad but by the time I was heading for wilder areas it deteriorated until it was down to about thirty yards. I persevered for a little longer and then pulled up in a passing place to mull over the wisdom of continuing. I was just setting off again in order to look for somewhere to turn round, having decided to give up for the day, when my mobile rang.

'It's me,' said Patrick's voice. 'Is everything all right?'

He sounded strained. I told him everything was fine and that the children were at his mother's.

'Where are you?'

Interested in his reaction, I told him, adding, 'Only I'm going home now; it's too foggy to see much.'

'I'm glad you are. Please stay away from that area. Sorry, I really can't talk now. I'll try and get in touch later.'

I stared at the phone when he had rung off. Had he rung just to check on my whereabouts?

Whether the mist really did thin a bit then – that's what I told myself anyway – or it was just my own bloody-mindedness I nevertheless started off again and continued along the track. I knew it quite well now but the mist concealed all landmarks, both large and small. I almost hit a bullock that I had assumed was a rock on the verge until it heaved itself to its feet and walked into the road at the last moment. At least I could console myself with the thought that I could not get lost because there were no turnings that I could inadvertently stray off on to.

A little later I realized I knew exactly where I was: on the straight stretch above the mire. I decided that I would drive right by the entrance to Sheepwash Farm, as any farmer going about his or her business might, and make for the gate that led on to the open moor. There I would pause for a few minutes before turning round and heading back. That was if there was nothing interesting to see.

The ground rose and there, ahead on the left, loomed the gateway into the yard. I slowed and glanced over. No vehicles were in sight, the outline of the house only just visible. All looked empty and deserted but I had learned that appearances here could be deceptive. I drove on until I reached the gate a short distance away and saw that there was room to turn without going through it. For a heart-stopping few seconds I got stuck in a boggy bit, engaged four-wheel drive and the vehicle hauled itself out, shedding dollops of thick black mud.

Again I paused as I went past the farm. This time the house was slightly less obscured and I saw that smoke was coming from one of the chimneys. At this point I decided to do as Patrick had requested, that there was someone in residence could be reported when we next spoke. He was hardly likely to divorce me over it.

When I got home the scarecrow was farther away from the gate, closer to the cottage.

It not being anywhere near April Fools' Day or Hallowe'en I donned wellies, walked up the drive, into the field and approached the object in question. I had not imagined it; the scarecrow was now a good fifteen yards from where I had first seen it earlier.

And here it was, constructed around a stake, the no doubt pointed end of which was firmly rammed into the ground. The body was made of a plastic fertilizer bag stuffed with straw – there were bits poking out of holes in it – tied in the middle with string. A straw-stuffed pair of trousers were fixed to this, no boots or shoes, and the jacket it wore, buttoned up, had merely been draped over the top, the sleeves inserted inside a wooden cross-member. The head had been made out of one leg of a pair of tights stuffed with screwed-up fabric of some kind, topped with what looked like a hank of false hair, a party wig perhaps, and an old cap.

I noticed these details afterwards, when I had recovered from the shock. What I saw first was the face, a laminated life-sized photograph of a man who must surely be Steven Ballinger. He smirked at me, the defiant and superior smile of a gangland thug, a murderer, who knew where I lived.

I have an idea I stood staring at this thing for a full two minutes, numb with shock.

Did I leave it here or not? Did I inform the police? Did I mount a watch on it, staying up all night if necessary in order to see who was moving it? I found I was shivering, not able to make any decisions. I could not remember telling anyone about my nightmare other than Matthew. Yes, and Patrick. But where had I mentioned it to him? I remembered; it was in Slaterfords, when we had gone up to the top floor. The whole area must have been bristling with snooping devices.

This female is not the kind to lock herself in a house and allow herself to go down with a monumental attack of the heebie-jeebies. I forced myself to be practical and examined the ground. On the top of the ridge here it was quite firm, certainly not sufficiently soft to show any footprints, mine included. I went back to the gate where it was slightly muddy but could see only the imprints of my own boots. There were no tyre tracks on the grass verge by the road either so whoever had brought it had been very careful not to leave any traces of their presence.

But had they? For what I now had, of course, was this man's photograph, if indeed it was him and any number of fingerprints and traces of DNA on the scarecrow itself. Perhaps it was not a picture of Ballinger. I went back and gazed at him trying to remember the figure I had seen in the underground car park at the store. Surely the head had been smaller than this, narrower, thus ensuring that the eyes would be closer together.

I returned to the cottage – I had decided to stay in the main house as the locks on the doors are stronger than on the barn conversion across the courtyard – for a pair of anti-contamination gloves that I knew were in Patrick's briefcase. Then I went back and carefully detached the plastic-covered print from the head of the figure: it had been clumsily stapled on and I was able to remove these with the pointed blade of a kitchen knife. Back indoors I scanned it into the computer and sent it off with an email to Michael Greenway. Fifteen minutes later he rang my mobile number.

'Are you armed, Ingrid?' was his opening question.

'I'm not supposed to be,' I replied carefully.

'I know, but *are* you?'

'A Smith and Wesson that I know was handed back to MI5 has turned up again in the wall safe,' I told him. 'Or another one has.'

'Get it out and load it.'

'It is already. Is the picture of Ballinger then?'

'We still don't know what that bastard really looks like. No, it's Cliff Morley.'

My skin crawled.

They still seemed to be one step ahead of us and someone was watching the house, or at least the drive where it emerged on to the road. There were not many vantage points from where this could be secretly achieved: the cottage was in a dip and there are other houses on the road, one close to the top of the drive itself. Unfortunately, a high hedge screens it from the field so no one would have witnessed what was going on.

I had left the scarecrow where it was, on Greenway's instructions as by moving it I might destroy evidence.

'I must satisfy myself that your car, and landline, haven't been bugged,' Greenway had gone on to say. 'I'll phone you back as soon as I've arranged someone to do it.'

But as soon as he had rung off the phone on the dresser rang. It was Elspeth, with the news that the children were well and happy and wondering how I was. I told her everything was fine with me as well but I was stuck on the writing. Still she said nothing about plans to sell the rectory.

'There's something for one of your stories going on in the village right now. Someone's playing a practical joke with a scarecrow. It started off on the far side of the village green to the rectory and has gradually been moved – at night, no one's seen anyone with it – and now it's just inside the lychgate in the churchyard. People are muttering about black magic, you know what they're like round here, and John gave a couple of them a talking to. The children are all agog that it's going to end up in the garden and I have to say it's making me feel a bit creepy.'

'Have you taken a close look at it?' I asked, trying to keep my voice normal.

'No, but John has. He said its face is a photograph of someone. He doesn't know who. I said he ought to remove it now it's on consecrated ground but he didn't want to be thought a spoilsport.'

'Elspeth, I have to make another call right now. Please stay right by the phone and I'll get back to you,' I said. 'No, on second thoughts, will you switch on your mobile?'

'Yes, of course. The reception's terrible so I'll have to go upstairs into our bedroom and open the window.'

Did I wait for Greenway to ring me back or get in touch with him about the latest development? I agonized for a couple of minutes and then my mobile rang.

'Someone's on their way,' he said. 'The password's one that you already know.'

Baffled by this because I could not remember having been been given any SOCA passwords I nevertheless told him what was happening at Hinton Littlemoor.

'Don't worry,' he responded. 'I'll get an armed protection team there right away and arrange to have the object in question removed for forensic examination. It might be a coincidence and someone playing silly buggers but I'm not taking any chances.'

'Carrie must have been followed. How else would they know where Patrick's parents live?'

'It looks like it. But hold fast, girl. I'm probably going

to end up in prison for killing this bastard with my bare hands.'

I rang Elspeth. As she had said, the reception was terrible but I got her to understand that the police would collect the scarecrow and she wasn't to be surprised if she found armed men in the onion bed.

'Again?' was her reaction to this.

'Please don't worry.'

Was I worried? Yes, I was. Very.

One small reason for this was that my mind was a complete blank on the subject of passwords.

It was now almost four in the afternoon and I had not had any lunch, not that I was hungry. I was shocked when I looked out of the window to see that the mist I had encountered earlier had rolled down from the high tors and the cottage was enveloped in drizzly greyness. I had to go out and check on the horses, in a field about half a mile away, before it got dark. But I could not, I reasoned; someone was coming to check on the phone and car. In the end I rang a horsey friend and asked her to do it: she never minds as she lives very close by and looks after them for us when we're on holiday.

'Are you all right, Ingrid?' she asked. 'You sound a bit stressed.'

'Just tired,' I told her. 'I have to wait in as a man's coming round to look at the car.'

'Patrick's not there then?'

'No, he's working.'

The female who was not the sort to get the heebie-jeebies then put the phone down and had another little weep instead. Why did I keep thinking that the scarecrow did in fact move of its own volition and even now, in the fog, was coming closer?

'Because of that bloody stupid nightmare,' I told myself out loud, going upstairs to check that all the windows were closed, and locked. I had already locked the outside doors. I came down again and put the kettle on the hot end of the Aga in order to make myself some tea. It is an indication of the state of my nerves that when Pirate, our cat, jumped up on the kitchen window ledge and mewed to come in I almost dropped the teapot.

Later again I made a sandwich and ate it, still not hungry but aware that I was not helping myself by starving and furious with my own reaction to what had happened. This was what they wanted; that I would stay indoors, frightened. I thought of going to see my sister but reasoned that if the car had been secretly fitted with a bugging device then by turning up on her doorstep I was risking putting her and her family in danger too. And, abandoning that idea, what then after some engineer or other had removed any unwanted hardware in both vehicle and phone? What should I do?

Realizing that I was fretfully pacing around the house I went into the living room and switched on the television. No, that was no good either; I wanted to know whenever whoever it was arrived so I could take a good look at them before I opened the door. I also wanted to be able to hear any other visitors walking around the outside of the cottage, the reason the place is surrounded by gravel paths.

But the scarecrow had had no feet, boots or shoes.

'Oh, shut up, you stupid cow!' I cried out loud and closed the living-room curtains to block out the swirling mist and gathering gloom. It would get dark early tonight. Then I thrust them aside again, so I could see out, see who was coming.

Why couldn't idiotic men realize that I was much safer when I was actually with Patrick, not stuck on a moor a couple of hundred miles away?

I decided that, in the morning, whatever Michael Greenway said, I would go to Hinton Littlemoor, where admittedly there was possible trouble already but at least something was being done about it. Now though, I fetched a blanket from upstairs, wrapped it around myself and, in the darkening room, curled up on the sofa, the Smith and Wesson cold and heavy company.

I must have slept, waking suddenly, a noise of some kind

half heard, half a memory. It was night, the lighter long rectangle of the window the only detail visible until my eyes accustomed to the darkness. Groping for the gun and struggling out of the blanket I went over to the window. Nothing. Putting on lights as I went I walked through into the dining room – the cottage is an old longhouse so everything downstairs connects in a straight line – and for a moment could see nothing unusual. Then my eye was drawn to the window.

The scarecrow was looking in at me. With a new face, only this time a dead one, Cliff Morley's horribly grimacing murdered one, blood trickling from one corner of his mouth.

I have a vague memory of screaming and then the next thing I was aware of was standing in our bedroom leaning on a wall in the darkness, shaking, crying, my legs giving way so that I was slowly sliding down to the floor. I put the gun down on a chest of drawers, even in this state aware that I might accidentally fire it, even shoot myself.

Lights.

Car headlights coming down the drive.

Shocked at how weak I was I somehow made it over to the window and looked out. The security lights in the courtyard came on as a battered van swung round the corner into it and braked to a standstill. I staggered back to fetch the gun, opened the window and waited. As I watched, an Asian man with a shaven head and wearing overalls got out, went round to the back of the van, opened the rear doors and took out a large toolbox. Then, whistling, he came in the direction of the front door.

'That's far enough!' I called, holding the Smith and Wesson two-handed, just the way I had been taught.

He looked up, did a positive shimmy of terror and dropped the toolbox with a crash.

'Oh, lady, and it is only me coming to look at your car,' he said shrilly, doing a fair imitation of Peter Sellers doing a fair imitation of a gentleman from India.

'You passed it in the drive,' I told him.

'And here you are making a good man look like a real

cuckoo,' he wailed, the single gold earring glinting as it caught the light.

I had already lowered the gun, nay, almost dropped it.

Ye gods.

I went down, opened the door and let him in.

Fourteen

'Does that dye wash off easily?' I demanded to know first and foremost.

'No, it's permanent. Otherwise I wouldn't be able to shower.'

'*Permanent!*' I shrieked.

'Insofar as it doesn't wash off but fades over time,' Patrick said.

'But your hair,' I moaned. His lovely black – although now sprinkled with grey – wavy hair was gone.

'It'll soon grow again.'

'You look like a pirate,' I wailed. Then I really did cry, despising myself, hugging my brown, bald man tightly.

'You're definitely pregnant,' he observed lightly when the worst was over. 'You freaked out like this in Canada when Justin was on the way.'

I led him into the dining room and gestured wordlessly in the direction of the window.

'Delete that last remark,' Patrick said softly and, drawing his own gun, cautiously went outside. The thing disappeared; he locked it in the barn. When he returned he said, 'God, these people are bloody sick. We'll take it back to London for tests. The one from Hinton Littlemoor's on its way there too. Everyone's all right by the way and they're well-protected.'

'I hate the thought that they know where we live.'

'It's not the first time hoodlums have tracked us down. I'm beginning to think we ought to move – this place is too far from anywhere.'

'Someone can't be too far away now,' I fretted, nerves still jangling. 'Whoever moved the scarecrow. Won't they wonder why a man who looks like a mechanic is staying the night here?'

'Only if they have night-vision glasses or watch the place all night. Which, somehow, I doubt.'

'Anguished lady householder begs hunky car fixer to chase off yobbo indulging in anti-social behaviour?' I suggested.

'As usual, you're a genius,' he said and went out, taking a flash lamp from the toolbox, telling me to lock and bolt the door. When he returned he would use a series of knocks, one of our codes.

Half an hour, then three-quarters, went by. I had busied myself laying and putting a match to the living-room fire – a basket of logs is always kept by the hearth – even though it was ten-thirty and supposed to be summer, and then sat watching it for a while. I needed the warmth and homeliness. It occurred to me that we would both need something to eat so I prepared the ingredients for cheese omelettes and located oven chips in the freezer.

After an hour and ten minutes had elapsed there came the agreed set of knocks on the door.

'Good idea that,' said Patrick, slightly muddy but triumphant. 'He was perched in a tree at the top of the field with a pair of ordinary binoculars. Not very far up it though, a really useless city yobbo with real city lip. He came down faster than he wanted to when I chucked a lump of wood at him and was then delighted to show me the way to his van where there were two more scarecrows. The faces on those were of the two men whose bodies were left at Sheepwash Farm. It was then just a matter of calling the local police, showing my ID and arranging for the whole shooting match to be taken to London, the scarecrows to the address where SOCA has all its forensics done.'

'He might not have been on his own.'

'I would be surprised if he was. I think we ought to be prepared to repel boarders. Unless they really were only trying to frighten you silly.'

'Someone's living at Sheepwash Farm,' I told him, suddenly remembering.

'I hope no one saw you,' was the sober response.

'No, I was in Andrew's old Land Rover and it was a real pea-souper.'

Patrick can't have been too annoyed with me over this as he gave me a glass of wine, pregnant or no, fixed himself a whisky and said, 'Both Greenway and I realized that it makes no sense; you down here on your own and me and all the back-up bloody miles away. I'll take a look at the car in the morning and we can use the mobile I've got with me – it's hack-proof. Then we must leave – I can't spare any more time here. Do you have a bag packed?'

'I always do.'

In truth I could hardly take my eyes off him – the man was practically unrecognizable – the business of scarecrows a mere bagatelle right now. 'Where did you have to go to get dyed?' I asked.

'To the make-up department of a film studio.' He gave me a careful look. 'It's all over. You can't risk leaving bits.'

'Bits?' I enquired.

Helping me to serve out our supper he snitched a chip and said, 'Bits,' with difficulty through the too-hot mouthful.

I thought it best not to enquire further on that subject and we carried our plates through to the living room to eat by the warmth of the fire. Patrick was alert and wary, listening for any sound outside, and I wondered if we should have left straight away without pausing for refreshment. I dismissed the idea: when your blood sugar is low you make mistakes.

'There's a possible witness to the murders of Jeffers and Ritter,' Patrick said when he had taken the edge off his appetite, speaking quietly. 'Or, at least, to the arrival of several men, four he thought, at the flat in St Paul's – which is on the first floor of a terraced house – where the killings took place. The witness, a retired man living across the street, then looked from his window again when he heard people leaving. The house has a bad reputation, by the way, and local residents have already complained to the police after drink and drugs problems there. Anyway, he saw the same number of blokes get into a van but they were carrying what appeared to be two rolls of carpet, heavy rolls of carpet. One of the men was very tall and thin and the witness got quite a good look at his face and thought he would recognize him again.'

'Were any carpets missing from the flat, do you know?'

'I haven't had time to ask Paul Reece for the latest info.'

Patrick then put his plate on a side table and switched off a lamp that was on it – the only source of light in the room – leaving just the redness of the glowing embers of the fire. I kept quiet; he had heard something outside. We sat in absolute silence.

'Hey, you in there, darkie!' a man's voice suddenly shouted from somewhere out the front. 'We just want the woman. Shove her out of the front door and you'll be perfectly safe. You've got two minutes and then we're coming in.'

'They can't get in,' Patrick whispered.

'Unless they drive a car through this big window,' I breathed.

'Yes, there's a risk they'll hot-wire the van – there's no room for any other vehicles to manoeuvre.'

'If you retaliate you'll blow your cover – they'll know you're not just a mechanic. They might suspect something already now their partner-in-crime's disappeared.'

'There's no connection with *me* though – unless they were watching.' Patrick swore under his breath. Then he said, 'I really do need to take a look at the Range Rover in daylight before we go anywhere.'

'I did check all the likely places yesterday and found nothing.'

'They knew where to come to though, didn't they?' Patrick bolted the last couple of chips and stood up. 'No, it'll have to be emergency measures. I can't risk you falling into their hands. Fetch your bag. After I've gone outside and created a diversion, climb out of the kitchen window and then over the fence into the field where we put in that new section of post and rail and then follow the hedge up to the top. Go through the gate and then back down the drive to where you left the car. Get the hell out of here.'

'But what about you?'

'I'll hope to make it to the other end of the village across the field that runs behind the houses. Wait in the pub car park five minutes *only* for me, no longer, and don't even stop there if anyone suspicious-looking is hanging around. Take my gun. If anyone tries to stop you, use it.'

'Keep the Glock – I have the Smith and Wesson.' I did not argue about anything else. The bag, actually a small rucksack, was upstairs. As I ran to fetch it someone started to pound on the front door.

'All right, all right!' I heard Patrick shout in his Indian voice. 'I am having to persuade this lady to leave. She does not want to and I cannot say I blame her!'

He waved his arms conductor-style and, taking the cue, I shrieked, 'No, please! Please don't make me go out there!'

A shot was fired and there was the distinct thump of a bullet hitting the door.

'I come out now with her!' Patrick yelled, panic-stricken-falsettto, rattling bolts.

I scooped up the rucksack and, downstairs, also Pirate from beneath the chair under which she had just gone to ground and tossed both, in that order with care but no cere-mony, through the kitchen window. I was not worried about the cat, she goes to a neighbour when we're not at home, but could not leave her indoors where she might go very hungry. Moments later I was outside.

Out the front, Patrick, having opened the front door, was having a pretend argument with someone still inside, suppos-edly me. I could hear his entreaties to me to co-operate as I clambered over the fence – thankfully there was hazy moonlight now so I was not blundering blindly around in the mist and darkness – and then, in the lee of the hedge, I headed uphill as fast as seemed sensible.

There was still a lot of shouting going on – I also distinctly heard the front door slam – and then, heart-stoppingly, the sound of another shot. I hurried on, tripped over a protruding stone, fell flat, picked myself up and went on more slowly. Behind me the gun fired again. Another thirty yards or so farther on I could see the gate

outlined against the distant and therefore faint illumination of one of Lydtor's only two street lights. No one
seemed to be lurking there.

Having got over the gate, clumsy with nerves, I turned
left. The top of the drive was a mere five yards away but
I did not rush blindly, forcing myself to stop to watch and
listen for a few moments. I could hear nothing for the
pounding of my own heart so had to inch forward slowly
until I could peer around the corner. In the distance were
the lights of the cottage glimpsed around the bonnet of the
Range Rover parked at an angle in a wider part of the drive.
Cautiously, I walked towards it.

The drive is an ancient Saxon lane, the hedge at this point
high and unclipped thus forming a tunnel making it very
dark. I could see nothing but the lights ahead of me and
there was now an ominous silence. These men must have
arrived in a vehicle of some kind. Where was it?

'Going somewhere?' said a voice from the shadows as I
was approaching the vehicle.

'I'm collecting for the church roof,' I squeaked, backing
away.

'Bit late at night for that, ain't it?'

He moved towards me so I could see him in silhouette
– beer belly, bad breath, BO and all – lining himself up
neatly for a sideways swipe with the barrel of the Smith
and Wesson. Aided by a hefty shove he went down like an
overturned roadroller into the nettles growing in the hedge
bottom whereupon I abandoned caution and tore towards
the car.

Praying that Patrick would be waiting for me in the car
park – the distance across the field is a lot shorter than by
road – I started the vehicle, stalling it in my haste by trying
to drive away with next to no revs. With visions of hoodlums pelting along in my wake I roared up the drive, turned
left at the top and made for the pub. It occurred to me that
I must call the police: the house was unsecured.

With a pang I realized that my home was no longer the
peaceful refuge that it used to be. I did not really want to
live there anymore.

There was no sign of Patrick, no one was about, the only other vehicle a large red saloon that I had an idea belonged to the publican. Keeping a close watch on my surroundings – I had parked right in the centre of the small car park, facing the entrance – I duly glanced at my watch and then found my phone and dialled 999 to report what had happened. I was given to understand that other residents of the village had reported hearing shots. I had to explain that I would not be able to stay until the police arrived and was not prepared to say where I was going. This was in case anyone was monitoring my calls: I had not actually clapped eyes on the mobile phone Patrick had mentioned, never mind made a note of the number to enable me to ring it. Where the hell *was* I going?

Four minutes went by and still dead silence hung over the village. Then the quiet was broken by a car going by without stopping. A dog barked a few times. In the distance, probably somewhere out on the moor, a cow bellowed.

No one came.

I waited for seven minutes and then, utterly wretched, turned the key in the ignition and drove away.

There was only one person on the entire planet whom I could ask to look over a vehicle for tagging devices, who was suitably equipped and reliable, that is. The phone rang for quite a time without any interruptions from answering machines, which was what I was expecting, and then a recorded message did cut in. I said nothing, just pressed 4. There was another wait, a silence inhabited by occasional electonic clicks and mutterings.

'Meadows,' said a voice I had not heard for a while.

'Ingrid,' I said tersely. 'I have a cuckoo clock that's suspect.'

'Where are you?'

'Not far from Exeter. I daren't go where I want to until it's checked over.'

'Are you in danger?'

'I could be.'

'Is the governor not in circulation?'

'No.'

'I take it you're heading roughly east.'

'Yes.'

'I'll meet you at Claridges.'

'Claridges' was the code name for a truly dreadful pub on the outskirts of Shaftesbury that had been used as a drop-off point and meeting place in our D12 days. Terry Meadows had been Patrick's assistant, in the days before Steve's arrival, who had finally left MI5, married our then nanny, Dawn, set himself up in business as a security adviser and was living somewhere in Wiltshire. Last I'd heard he was doing very well for himself.

Expecting to see in my mirror at any moment a following vehicle, or vehicles obviously tailing me, I drove very fast, stopping only for petrol. It was well past midnight when I arrived and of course it was long after closing time so the pub's car park was shut off with large gates. I drove right by and stopped in a lay-by a short distance away.

I suddenly felt very tired, exhausted if I was honest. There was a car already in the lay-by and I had the hand gun securely in my grasp but out of sight when the driver's door opened and a man got out. He came over and I opened my window.

'This is a bloody strange time of day to have trouble with cuckoo clocks,' said Terry cheerfully.

I got out, stiff, not a little scratched by brambles that I had not noticed at the time and gave him a hug. 'I'm so very, very glad to see you,' I said.

He seemed surprised by the warmth of my greeting even though, a long time ago, we had fancied one another slightly, more than slightly on my part. But no, we had not gone to bed together and I now thought of him, although he was younger than me, as a big brother.

'And a few tears,' he observed, giving me his handkerchief, not for the first time. 'You sit in the back of the car while I fetch the gizmo.'

When Patrick looks for unwanted electronics he has to undertake screwdriver and spanner wrangling, having gone on a course to learn how to access and put back together again vital parts of our vehicle. The piece of equipment that Terry brought was a laptop computer in a small carrying case that he merely plugged into the Range Rover's own electronic diagnostic system. He soon found what he was looking for.

'Patrick had trouble with the locking system in London,' I told him, having got out of the car to hold the torch for him. 'He had to take it to a main dealer.'

'Well, that was probably when this little job was fitted,' Terry told me, waving it under my nose, having briefly dismantled the front passenger-side doorlock to find it. 'If Patrick wants to stay ahead of the game he'll have to get SOCA to buy him one of these detectors.'

I rather thought that SOCA would decline.

'I've deactivated the bug. Do you want to take it to show somebody?'

'Are you sure there isn't the smallest sign of life in there somewhere?' I enquired, looking at the tiny device dubiously.

He trod on it with a hefty boot and then gave me the flattened remains. 'Quite sure. So where *is* Patrick?'

'I don't know whether he's dead or alive,' I whispered, and then briefly told him the story.

When I had fallen silent, he asked, 'Ingrid, is this new career of Patrick's really worth it?'

'No, I'm beginning to think it isn't.'

'Where are you going now?'

'I'm not too sure. I can go to Hinton Littlemoor because there are members of an armed-response unit there. But I shall have to report to Greenway tomorrow. I'm very angry with him. This wouldn't have happened if he hadn't ordered Patrick to send me home.'

'Look, it's already after midnight. You can't knock up the rector and his wife now. You ought to come home with me.'

'It's all right, I have a key.'

'Dawn would love to see you – she's expecting our second,' he said proudly.

I kissed his cheek. 'Then I won't disturb her – she needs her sleep.'

I thanked him again, got back in the car and drove away.

I did not drive far, forced to stop to think over what I could only describe as the outrageousness of the situation. Terry's question still rang in my ears. No, it simply was not worth it. All we had done was to hold innumerable briefings with Michael Greenway and achieved absolutely nothing. These criminals had run rings around us and still appeared to be in a dominant position. While they had apparently been forced to abandon the Bristol area, temporarily or not, leaving more evidence behind than they might have wished, we were still no nearer to finding out who these people were.

And here I was, running back to tell teacher again.

No.

I did not go to Hinton Littlemoor, spending what was left of the night at an hotel in Shaftesbury. I hated having to stop but I was beginning to feel dizzy from lack of sleep and hunger. In the morning, and after a large breakfast, I headed back to Devon. To hell with scarecrows; dead or alive, I was going to find Patrick.

I rang Greenway near Okehampton, in the mood now to tell him go to hell as well, but desperate to know if he knew where Patrick was. He did not and, predictably, refused to say much over an ordinary line, even a mobile one, in the circumstances, and told me he would ring me back shortly. I waited.

'There's no one been seen with gunshot wounds at any of the A and E departments of hospitals in the Plymouth and Tavistock areas and a search of the area around your home by local police found nothing suspicious,' he duly reported.

'That means he's either dead in a ditch somewhere or this bunch of murderers has got hold of him,' I retorted. 'Because he would have contacted me by now if he was living rough in the countryside or hitching a lift somewhere.

I mean, I take it you've told him to disappear from your own radars now he's using a disguise.'

'Yes, I have. Unless it's an emergency.'

'By wrecking our working partnership you've compromised the work on the case,' I furiously told him. 'You might even have been responsible for Patrick's death.'

'Ingrid —'

I cut him off.

For the sole reason of looking for evidence – and what would the police have discovered by way of clues in pitch darkness? – I went home. I had seriously thought of asking James Carrick to come with me but that would have meant more delay until he arrived and remove a really useful person from the investigation.

With all due caution, the Smith and Wesson handy, I drove slowly down the drive in bright late-morning sunshine. I was banking on this being the last thing they – Ballinger, whoever – would expect me to do but there was still a chance that someone had been left on watch. No strange vehicles were in sight, nor had been parked in the village street, no oddly waving or weighted branches in nearby trees. No scarecrows. No van, which was interesting.

I turned and parked the vehicle so that it was positioned for a quick getaway and then, the full commando training kicking in, shot into the garden behind the barn, weapon two-handed at the ready. No one. Back in the courtyard the front door of the barn showed no sign of forced entry. Neither did the main house. I rang both doorbells, wary of possible booby traps should I just unlock the doors and breeze straight in. No one came. No blood stains.

Leaving the courtyard by the narrow pathway that runs around the other side of the barn I examined the ground-floor windows. Still no evidence of forced entry. I repeated this at the house with the same result. Then, standing in the small back garden of the cottage I searched the ground for anything that might tell me what had happened. If Patrick had got away and taken the route he had planned to it would have meant climbing over the low wall that separated the garden from the field and then heading west at the top of the long and quite steep slope that runs down to Lydford Gorge at the bottom. Examining every inch of the way I clambered over the wall, carefully surveying my surroundings before moving off. I then walked along what was, in effect, a meandering sheep path towards where I knew a stile gave access into a lane between houses that eventually led into the cark park where he had said he would meet me.

There was absolutely nothing to see. I deviated from the path a few times to look under hedges and in a large hole in the ground where an ages-old rabbit warren had collapsed under the weight of a tractor the previous year, my heart in my mouth with the thought that I would find a body at any moment.

Nothing.

I reached the stile and saw that it had been repaired recently with a new top bar and steps. The job was badly done, the wood left rough with quite large splinters sticking out. On one of these was caught a tuft of wool. Not that from a sheep but dark blue in colour, from someone's sweater. I knew that Patrick had such a sweater because I had bought it for him but he had not been wearing it beneath the overalls. I forced myself to dismiss the cosy thought that he had somehow had time to change and then come looking for me. This was, after all, a sort of a right of way for those who lived on this side of the village: the wool could have come from any one of a number of people's garments.

Mounting the stile I walked up the lane, emerging half a minute later in the car park. The mobile library van was parked in it, the usual group of village ladies chatting at the bottom of the steps. One waved, the others gave me sideways looks. Of course, the police had been at the cottage the previous night. People had heard shots and here was the mad author who must have criminal connections in order to give authenticity to her stories.

I suddenly felt very bored with the lot of them and, worse,

had learned nothing by coming back. Once more I got into the Range Rover and left. This time it seemed that I was leaving my life behind. I could never remember feeling more miserable.

Fifteen

Miss Philippa Dean was being watched over in a one-time police section house a stone's throw from Olympia. Her sister was staying with her for a few days but was out when I called, having taken a bus into the West End to do some shopping. Miss Dean seemed pleased to see me.

'I'll be in the next room,' said the woman police constable on duty.

'You don't have to go,' I told her. 'This isn't a private matter.'

But she went, saying she would make tea in a short while.

'Is that young woman armed?' asked Miss Dean wonderingly.

'No, but there's someone who is in the front room,' I answered. *And someone who is right here*, I did not add.

I had had no choice but to ask Greenway if he would arrange the meeting, aware that the man did not actually know what to do with me. He could hardly order me home again and was probably praying, after what I had said to him, that Patrick would turn up and we would then work together. It did not need me to tell him that this situation was highly unsatisfactory to all concerned.

I had gone on to ask him about the CD ROMs that Miss Dean had brought to London with her and he had only said that he did not want to go into details over the phone.

I said, 'I just have a couple of questions and won't keep you long. I was wondering if there was *anything* you can remember about Steven Ballinger that will help me to find him.'

She seated herself in one of the dreadful green armchairs

in the rather dreadful room and thought about it. 'No, I'm sorry, I don't think there is,' she said after a few moments.

'The store's head office was listed in Walthamsden but apparently that's all it is, an empty office. Do you know why that was?'

'No. The address was on the notice board, wasn't it? I'm afraid that not knowing much about retail business I never gave it a thought. I heard Walthamsden Cinema talked about though.'

'Cinema?' I echoed.

'Oh, it's not one of those modern multi-screen places. This is a little old cinema in a back street somewhere that's art-deco and Grade 2 listed that Ballinger's been trying to buy. Needless to say he wants to knock it down and build flats on the site. No, that's wrong: he's hoping to redevelop the entire area.' She finished by adding disparagingly, 'They've probably burned it to the ground as well by now.'

'Do you know any more details?'

'Well, I have no idea where it is, other than it's in a rundown area that's due for improvement. There's a Save Walthamsden Picture House Society been formed to fight the proposal. Ballinger cursed them daily.'

'Was the name Ernie O'Malley ever mentioned?'

'I don't *think* so.'

'He's supposed to be Ballinger's brother-in-law.'

Miss Dean smiled. 'They were all brothers-in-law.'

'How do you mean?'

'It was the only time I ever saw anyone there laugh. It seemed to be an in-joke. I assumed it meant they were crooks-in-law, or lawless brothers – a bit like the Mafia.'

I thanked her, telling her that it was useful.

'And your working partner?' she enquired. 'Or shouldn't I ask?'

'He's my husband actually.'

'I thought you had a long-standing relationship by the way you communicated.'

'I don't know where he is right now,' I admitted.

She gazed at me sympathetically. 'You must be worried.'

'I am.'

'He doesn't look the kind of man to get too unstuck. Who is the person he loves most in the world, other than you?'

'His mother.'

'Ask her. She might know.'

Why hadn't I thought of it before?

'Please be careful, my dear. These people are monsters.'

Still fearful of eavesdroppers, even on mobiles, and not in possession of one with more firewalls than Nero's Rome, I determined not to ask Elspeth outright if she had heard from Patrick. It soon became apparent though, after she had assured me that the children were well and happy, that she was choosing her words very carefully.

'Any – er – other family news?' I stammered.

'No, not really. It's not family but you might like to know that the Fieldings have a new baby boy. And Donna Warrington's engaged to that boy who fell in the river last year and almost drowned.'

I hadn't the first clue who these people were. Then it occurred to me that they might not even exist and there were other forces at work here.

'Oh! And we have a new gardener. He's just arrived,' she went on as though being prompted. 'He's really good at his job. I didn't know people from Delhi liked gardening, did you?'

'No,' I gasped.

'Would you like to speak to him? I've asked him in for a cup of tea.' She actually giggled. 'Indian, of course.'

Ye gods.

Before I had had time to think, let alone reply, a quiet sing-song voice said, 'Hello, Mrs Gillard. Would you be having a nice day?'

'Yes, thank you,' I managed to say. 'Are you staying with the rector long or would you like to come and work for me?'

'I am very pleased to stay here until the usual gardener comes back from his broken leg. Then I shall be free.'

My heart sank. 'How long will that be?'

'Tomorrow.'

'But you just said he'd broken his leg!'

'Not broken at all badly. No, not badly at all. Just a very small tinge broken.'

I bit my lip hard to stop myself exploding with laughter.

'You know where I live,' I said.

'Yes, the big house with the trees. Goodbye, Mrs Gillard.'

'Goodbye until tomorrow,' I whispered.

The 'big house with the trees' like 'Claridges' was a code name and more correctly the Elms Hotel just off Piccadilly. It had been one of our occasional haunts when we worked for D12 and I personally had not stayed there for years. Tending to be the kind of place frequented, and often lived in, by ladies who looked like Barbara Cartland it was, for the purpose of keeping our heads down, perfect.

By a complete coincidence Patrick and I arrived in the foyer together. He was, I noted, as brown as ever and must have had his head freshly shaved because it possessed the polish of a freshly harvested conker.

'Sorry about the complete balls-up,' he said in my ear as we were checking in.

'I waited for longer than you said,' I whispered back.

'I know, I saw what must have been your tail lights disappearing down the road.'

I turned to him in real anguish. 'Why didn't you ring me?'

'That's why I'm apologizing. I'd left the phone indoors and didn't have a key on me. By the time I'd returned home and remembered where a spare was hidden then checked that the mobsters really had gone it was too late to call you back. I'd just left, in the van, when I saw half the Devon and Cornwall Force arriving. But I didn't go back, which saved a lot of awkward questions.'

'I bawled out Greenway,' I said.

'Good. I hope you didn't bring the car.'

'Yes, I did. Terry removed the bug.'

'I can't understand how these people were so close to us that they knew I'd left it at that garage in London.'

I did not want to think about it and to lighten things I said, 'What on earth did the children make of you?'

'Vicky was a bit worried but the others thought it was great fun. Justin wants the ear-ring afterwards.'

'And your parents?'

'Dad saw me first as I was hanging around outside the rectory waiting for someone to turn up – you have our key – and asked me if I was an illegal immigrant. Several had been recently found hidden in a lorry in Bath. Needless to say, he's now annoyed with me for making him look foolish.'

John has always become annoyed with his son rather readily. 'And your mother?' I went on to ask.

'Took one look at me and asked where the fancy-dress party was. Apparently my eyes are the wrong colour and Indian men don't usually have ear-rings so I took it out.'

He had written, in a flowing hand, something mostly illegible in the hotel register: I was sharing a room with His Eminence Squiggle Dash Three Loops.

'It would appear that the CD ROMs hold details of just about all that goes on in this particular branch of the criminal outfit west of London, but not in the city itself,' Patrick said later when we were sitting in an almost deserted lounge, the decor as faded as most of the clientèle, for what was ostensibly a briefing. 'Not that it's easy to work out exactly what's happening because code names have been used for people and places. In its present state the info's not a lot of use to *us*. I reckon we ought to get Miss Dean on to it seeing she used to work at Bletchley Park.'

'I went to see her,' I told him. 'The only interesting thing I found out is that she heard Walthamsden mentioned in connection with an old cinema there that Ballinger and Co want to knock down. Oh, and all the men jokingly referred to one another as brothers-in-law so that might explain that anomaly.'

'That's interesting too as it suggests that whoever gave the Met the information had some connection with the gang.'

'Are F9 saying anything about Robert Kennedy yet?'

Patrick shook his head. 'No, still no comment.'

'That means he is missing. Unless he's at Sheepwash.'

'No, I was told that a couple of cops are at Sheepwash – to await any visitors.'

'James is still going thorough hell then.'

Patrick, who seemed subdued, did not give any indication that he had heard the remark. 'You know, that's not a bad idea – to get Miss Dean to have a look at the info. The computer bods have done all they can and even printed it all out.'

'And then?' I asked. 'Has anything really been achieved this past week and a bit?'

There was a little silence before Patrick said, 'No, only me being turned into a rather poor copy of an Asian.' He gave me a look that I remembered for a long time afterwards. 'I missed you, your ideas, your flair.' He paused. 'Another thing is that I don't think this SOCA venture of mine is going at all well. The very reason I left MI5 – threats to the family, the need for police protection at Hinton Littlemoor – is happening all over again. It can't be allowed to go on.'

'You'd die of boredom if you had a desk job.'

'I might have to adapt to a quieter occupation, for the sake of everyone. Just be an ordinary copper.'

'You do seem to have fielded some exceptionally poisonous criminals in the cases you've tackled over the years. Probably because you've been given the difficult jobs due to your reputation for success.'

Although nothing had been said I knew that this was the last night we would stay at an hotel before we headed for Ernie O'Malley country in Walthamsden to try to find our quarry. I had an idea that Patrick did not really know what to do with me either and was not expecting for a moment that I would be asked to adopt a brown skin and a sari.

'I just want to chuck it all in,' Patrick suddenly said in a whisper. 'Now.'

Shocked, I decided to say nothing right then.

'We have a little boy who is now behaving badly and turning into a bully at school,' he continued. 'A little boy who needs his dad to be around more often to occupy his mind with worthwhile things and take a strong line when he gets stroppy. Matthew and Katie's real dad is dead and the one they've got now keeps going off and having adventures so he doesn't get bored working at a desk all day. Worst of all, Vicky cried when she saw this scary stranger and called for Grandma.' Patrick turned to face me and I was appalled to see that he too was crying. 'Ingrid, I feel a complete *shit*.'

'Abandon the case,' I said decisively. 'Resign from SOCA. Move from Devon to be nearer your parents. Be a family man again.'

Nothing was said for a while, Patrick sobbing silently and privately and, sitting side by side on a large sofa, I put an arm around him. This day had had to come, when other responsibilities demanded priority.

'There's James,' he said in a choked voice at last. 'I promised him I'd do everything in my power to find his father.'

'Then we abandon everything else on the case and do just that. But do tell Greenway.'

He gazed at me, tears on his eyelashes. 'You're being very businesslike about this.'

'I'm doing my oracle thing, aren't I?' I said, my own eyes misting with tears. I blinked them away.

'And as my wife?'

'I hate wives who employ emotional blackmail to make their husbands change their jobs.'

'But what do you *think*?'

'This is about *you*,' I told him. 'About the rest of *your* life. About not regretting certain actions. About not being bitter. It's very difficult for me to be so pragmatic but wives and children are the ones who suffer in the long run when men are bitter and keep wishing for the good old days.'

'So if I decide just to look for Robert Kennedy, hoping the poor devil isn't already dead, where do we start?'

'By talking to a man by the name of Sydney Hellier, who is the founder of the Save Walthamsden Picture House Society.'

*   *   *

As I had discovered, the society had a website and it was from this that I had gleaned the information. Imagining that I would be left keeping the powder dry while Patrick plunged alone into the criminal underworld I had already sent Mr Hellier an email asking if we might meet and have a chat about the cinema. In order to allay any suspicions that I was some kind of time-wasting nutter I had mentioned that I was an author. There was a reply when we returned to our hotel room.

'He's free tomorrow morning and suggests ten thirty,' I called around the bathroom door, Patrick having a shower. 'We need to have a look at this place, don't we?'

'Yes, not that I'm expecting for one moment to find Kennedy. But while we're there I suppose it's worth mentioning Ballinger's name.'

I replied to the email in the affirmative. Patrick's initial reaction to my proposal had been lukewarm and if it had not been for his promise to Carrick would have probably been quite happy in his present mood to have collected the children and Carrie and gone home. Although I had come to the conclusion that what had happened was inevitable I had never seen him so negative before. Was I right to encourage him to carry on?

Yes to that question: James was a friend of ours.

'I get a real shock every time I catch a glimpse of myself in a mirror,' Patrick muttered when he came back into the room, scowling at himself in the one over the dressing table.

'How long will it take to fade?' I enquired.

'God knows.'

'I quite fancy you that colour.'

'I thought we were going down to have something to eat.'

'I didn't *necessarily* mean right now, right this very minute.'

He came over, sat on the bed and proceeded to kiss me silly.

'Yes, OK,' I murmured when he had undone my bathrobe, hands wandering everywhere.

'Right now after all, then?'

Fingers caressed between my thighs.

'*Now*,' I told him.

Now it was, that glorious strength. My own desire for him apart, I wanted to give him something to be happy about.

'They've knocked the old place around already,' Sydney Hellier reported glumly. 'And a few really nice pieces have been ripped out and sold, some of the light fittings, decorated glass panelling, stuff like that. All quite illegal, you know, because it's listed. They're hoping that when the planning people take a look at it they'll say it isn't worth saving. Are you hoping to write a book about the place?'

Hellier lived in a modest semi-detached house that was creaking under the weight of heavy dark furniture that was anything but art-deco. He was younger than I had imagined; probably in his mid-forties and of a type that could be uncharitably labled as 'geekish'. I had turned down the offer of coffee purely on the grounds that everything around me was remarkably grubby and a quick glimpse into the kitchen on our way to a rear living room had suggested the source of the house's sour smell.

'No,' I said, in answer to the question. 'I have to confess that although I'm delighted to add my name to your list of people who want the place saved my main interest is in those who are bent on destroying it.'

My escort had remained on watch outside in the car, hired, the Range Rover having been deemed too distinctive in what was, courtesy of Ernie O'Malley and Co, a sensitive district as far as police departments, covert and otherwise, were concerned.

'They could well be a bunch of crooks,' I added.

'And you're doing research on them, like.'

'That's right. Has anyone connected to a prospective buyer been to see you about it?'

'Oh, the blokes who want to knock it down and build flats – posh flats mind, not for folk round here – have been round. I told them it wasn't my decision but the planning department's. They couldn't understand why folk want to keep the place.'

Regrettably, I was finding myself fascinated by his loose and yellowing dentures. 'Did they threaten you at all?'

'No, but they looked like typical dodgy development bods; shifty. I was glad when they went.'

'Were any names mentioned?'

'Not that I can remember. It took me back a bit, seeing four of them standing on the doorstep.'

'Who owns the place?'

'The local authority. It was left in someone's will to the borough to be used as some kind of community hall or theatre. It needs money spending on it, mind. We're trying to get lottery funding. But it'll be demolished, all right. So-called progress always wins.'

'I'm particularly interested in a man who's calling himself Steven Ballinger.'

'Calling himself? It's not his real name?'

'Probably not.'

'Never heard of him. What does he look like?'

'He's distinctive; very tall, thin, probably has a small head and speaks with a high-pitched voice. Has anyone like that been to see you?'

'Er . . . no.'

'Are you sure?'

'Yes, of course.'

He was lying.

'Mr Hellier, the man who fits that description is exceedingly dangerous. If he has been to see you there might be a risk to your own safety.' I gave him a hard stare.

'Well . . . er . . . that does sound a bit like one of our founder members, Lazlo Ivers. He's a keyholder too.'

'A keyholder?'

'To the cinema.' Hellier uttered a nervous false laugh. 'Not my place.'

'Well, it couldn't possibly be him, could it?' I chortled, heart thumping. 'Would I be able to have a look at it? I mean, if I'm going to sign your petition it would be nice to know what I'm supporting.'

'Yes, I allowed time this morning as a matter of fact.'

'Is it all right if my colleague comes too? He's thinking of making a donation actually.'

'No bother.'

The old picture house was a short drive away. I had already indicated to Patrick that I had learned something important by giving him a nudge. I then introduced him as 'my friend Rahjeed', the first thing that came into my head and for all I knew a brand of Indian drain cleaner. Rahjeed decided to go in for an English public school accent. This was not the time for quirkiness.

Walthamsden is a pleasant enough area, but this particular street looked ripe for demolition, most buildings boarded up, the few that were inhabited sorry spectacles of peeling paint, disintegrating stucco and slipping roof slates. Every entrance to the houses presented an obstacle course of litter and overflowing refuse bins. We parked the car on a vacant plot of land – vacant but for fly-tipped rubbish – and got out into a warm breeze redolent of traffic fumes and tom cats, causing my well-bred companion to wrinkle his nose in disgust.

'There's European Union money ear-marked for the whole area,' Sydney Hellier, who had noticed, told him eagerly. 'It's going to be turned into an Italian-style piazza, no traffic and with lots of little eateries. We want the cinema to be an art gallery-cum-theatre for local talent and events.'

'It'll cost millions,' Patrick told him dismissively. 'Where's the rest of the money coming from?'

'Grants, the heritage people. This place is rich in heritage. For example, that house over there was lived in by a man who invented the idea of flea circuses.'

'God,' Patrick said under his breath.

Hellier briskly rummaged in his pocket for keys. We were, I saw with surprise, standing right outside the cimema, the front of which was almost completely obscured by bill boards covered in posters. It was impossible to tell what the building really looked like, seemingly squashed between those on either side, and I could not see any access into it at all. But there was, Hellier leading the way to one end and unlocking a padlock on a gate in a section of security fencing.

We traipsed through the gate and on up what must have been the original steps into the building. Even these were falling to pieces – we were warned to look where we were going – and were scattered with broken tiles that had fallen from the facade. They had been rather beautiful tiles by the look of them.

The main doors had been fitted with more padlocks and these took a while to undo as they were rusting. I gazed about, seeing the glass cases that had once housed the posters announcing forthcoming attractions, and an advert for Lyon's ice cream almost faded out of existence.

'My dad used to talk about going to the Saturday morning pictures,' I said to myself. 'Cartoons and *Flash Gordon's Trip to Mars.*'

'My father played polo on Saturdays,' said Patrick loftily, well in character. 'He had his own team.'

I tried to imagine John on a polo pony and failed.

Then the doors were open and we went into the foyer. It reeked of damp. As Hellier had said, the interior had been knocked about – vandalized was a better description of what had happened. Even in the gloom it was fairly easy to see where decorative features had been ripped out because of the bare patches, holes even, in the mouldy plaster of the walls.

'There's no lights, the power's off,' Hellier told us. 'But there's a torch kept in a cupboard here if you want to go and have a punt round while I check all the outer doors are properly secured.'

'Fine,' I said.

Hellier went into what had been the ticket office. 'Funny,' he mutttered, moments later. 'It's gone.'

'I have a flash lamp in the car,' said Patrick. 'I'll get it.'

Both men disappeared and I walked slowly towards one of the doors that led into the stalls, opened them and stared into the dark void beyond. *Lazlo Ivers*, said a voice inside my head. Lazlo Ivers. A good name for a scarecrow. We would have to be very careful or Sydney Hellier was a dead man. How would we get an address from him without arousing suspicion? We might even have to reveal our true identities and take him into protective custody.

'The ghosts of film stars past,' said Patrick very quietly behind me, jerking me from my thoughts.

'Lazlo Ivers,' I said under my breath. 'A very tall man with a small head and a squeaky voice who belongs to the preservation group.'

'I shall heap you with gold and elephants if it is him,' said the sahib. We went in and he switched on the torch, which was a large one, illuminating a crumbling, cobwebby cave-like auditorium.

'What did Greenway say when you said we were going to concentrate on finding Kennedy?'

'I didn't tell him.'

'Oh?'

'I just said we might have a lead on Ballinger and were coming here. It's the truth.'

'Yes, of course it is,' I responded, deciding to defer further discussion.

The stage was still there, as were most of the seats in the auditorium, but there was no sign of any cinema screen. Beneath our feet as we walked down the slight slope the remains of the mouldering red carpet sent up clouds of dust that set us sneezing. The torch beam picked out the remnants of gold paint on what had been gold and green wall decorations but here also there were bare patches where tiles and mouldings had been knocked off, anything broken left where it had fallen.

'The whole place has been gutted,' Patrick said. 'Everything of the smallest possible value taken away.'

'It's probably all sitting in the nearest reclamation yard,' I said.

We mounted the wooden steps at one side of the stage – there was even a tiny orchestra pit – and ventured on to the worn boards. They creaked alarmingly. Patrick flashed the lamp into the wings and more empty spaces strung with ropes and wires yawned before us. Facing the auditorium he then shone it towards the back, revealing a balcony of circle seats and above them, the small windows through which films had been projected.

'This is where people in horror films split up and the heroine gets troughed by the resident nasty,' Patrick said, wandering off to the far side of the stage.

'Thanks, and I'm staying right with you,' I told him, catching up.

The place, although very small by modern standards, was bigger than it looked from the outside. Corridors and narrow stone staircases, going both up and down, led off the bare area concealed by a tattered drop curtain towards the rear of the stage. Before its days as a cinema this building must have been a theatre.

'Music Hall,' I said. 'You can almost hear "Knees Up Mother Brown".'

Patrick said, 'I still can't help but feel a modern building wouldn't be more suitable as a community centre.'

'I'm inclined to agree with you.'

We headed down the nearest corridor, wider than the others with several rooms off, and almost immediately found ourselves at what must have been the stage door. Retracing our footsteps we looked into all the rooms, dressing rooms of old probably: they contained nothing but broken chairs and rubbish.

Going back to the stage area we climbed one of the sets of stairs, too narrow to walk two-abreast, and came to a high metal gantry, some of the pulleys and ropes used for moving scenery still in place. Even the metal handrail felt damp and there were black patches of mould on practically everything. Not so much music hall perhaps as *Phantom of the Opera*. Going down again, and discounting the stairs on the other side that obviously ascended to the far end of the same gantry, we picked our way carefully over assorted small pieces of rubble scattered over more steps down into some kind of basement.

'Yes, of course, where the trap door in the stage would have been accessed from,' Patrick commented, his voice sounding oddly dead and muffled. He shone the torch around and the reason for this became evident.

The room, only about sixteen feet square, was practically filled with boxes. He took hold of one of them and was surprised to find it empty. We examined more: they were all empty. There were newspapers in piles too and on the floor near my feet I found three new boxes of firelighters.

'Miss Dean was right,' I said, holding one up for Patrick to see. 'It's a recipe for an inferno.'

Sixteen

'Are they really that stupid they think fire brigade arson investigators wouldn't be able to discover what had caused the fire?' Patrick said wonderingly. 'This is probably how they started the one in Bristol.' He ploughed off through the boxes, tossing them this way and that, stooped to grab something and came back with a plastic container that proved to be full of petrol.

Nothing else was said as we again returned to the stage, hurried down a corridor behind one side of the auditorium, pushed through a door and found ourselves back in the foyer. There was no sign of Sydney Hellier, and, I at least feeling relieved that he was not kicking his heels waiting for us, we went up one of the carpeted staircases that led to the circle. There was nothing to see up here but the stairs carried on up and shortly we emerged on to a landing with two doors off, both shut, dim daylight coming through a small, filthy window in the sloping ceiling.

'Be careful,' I whispered, my cats' whiskers giving me hell.

Patrick drew his gun. 'Too right. Finding that lot changes everything.' He turned the handle on the door nearest to him slowly and then kicked it so that it flew back and hit the wall. A few seconds elapsed during which we remained motionless and then Patrick flashed the torch within. It was a large cupboard lined with shelves that were bare but for a few round cans of the kind that contain film and yet more rubbish; old papers mostly.

The other door had to be to the projection box. It was locked.

'I'll go and find Syd,' said Patrick. He gave the door a

glance. 'Thinking about it, I can't see that anyone dodgy would lock themselves in and risk being cornered.'

'We *have* just decided they're stupid,' I quibbled.

'Smith, Wesson and you should be able to handle it,' he said, and went back down the stairs.

Thinking how strange it is that men are wildly over-protective one minute and abandon you to the wolves the next, I took the gun from my bag and stared at the door, daring it to do anything. There was no sound from within, not the slightest whisper of movement. No sound came from down the stairs either, my writer's imagination kicking in with a description of it; a sullen, clammy silence.

Five minutes went by.

Why the hell *did* anyone want to save this place?

Perhaps they, or rather he – Hellier – didn't.

I was trying to analyse what had caused this odd thought when, deep in the building, a door slammed. This was followed half a minute or so later by the sound of hurrying footsteps and Patrick came into view.

'Plan B,' he announced slightly breathlessly, coming into sight on the stairs. 'I can't find Syd because he's done a runner and appears to have locked us in. He made his getaway though the stage door and got to it just before I did. And I have to tell you that there's a strong smell of petrol with a hint of smoke.' He did not wait for any reaction on my part but, having arrived, aimed two shots at the locked door – the sounds booming down the stairs and echoing below – and when the lock was shattered, barged straight in.

For some reason my heart leaped into my mouth when we encountered two ancient projectors that had been removed from their floor fixings and were standing like dead aliens just inside the door. Patrick shut it behind us and rammed one of them against it.

'We'll be trapped!' I protested.

He merely gave me a big smile on the way by.

Yes, light, I thought, fighting down panic, there was a window in here.

Somewhere below us there was a huge roaring sound and

I actually felt the floor beneath my feet quiver. I tried to shut my mind to it and followed Patrick into what looked as though it had been an office. He wrenched open all the cupboards, some quite large, but other than an avalanche of yet more old papers and film magazines they were empty.

'Oh, dial 999, would you?' he requested calmly, opening and looking out of a large window. 'And, Ingrid?'

'Yes?' I stuttered.

'Cinemas and theatres always have fire escapes.'

With a sense of complete unreality I called the fire brigade.

The projection box itself was actually quite large and it occurred to me that it might have been built on to the back of the roof of the theatre afterwards. There were two other doors on the far side of the room, both also proving to be locked.

'Stand clear,' Patrick said and again, shot off the locks on the one nearest to us.

As though the sound had triggered something there was a huge bang beneath us. The floor jumped and I staggered and must have hit my head on the wall because the next thing I remember was Patrick bending over me, urgently calling my name.

'Thank God for that,' he said when he saw that my eyes were open. 'You've been out cold for a couple of minutes. Get up! They must have planted explosives.'

He was still having trouble with the door but finally barged it open.

It was pitch dark inside and stank like a lavatory. It *was* a lavatory, complete with a basin and a small cupboard on one wall together with a window that had been boarded up. Slumped on the floor, his head under the back of the toilet bowl, was a man. Patrick gave me the torch and hauled him out by his feet. It was Robert Kennedy, unconscious and barely recognizible, filthy, blood dried on his face and with several days' growth of beard.

'He's still alive,' Patrick said urgently, fingers on one limp wrist. 'And the water's turned off,' he went on, wringing the tops of the taps to no avail with the other hand. 'Which means the poor devil's dying of thirst. Add an ambulance to the 999 list, would you? Meanwhile, let's see where the other door goes.'

The staircases would act like chimneys, I knew, and as soon as we opened any windows or door to the outside would suck the flames and smoke up to where we were. I could already smell and see black smoke billowing past the one window of the main room.

The second door yielded, opening into empty space but for a small balcony with railings around it. Patrick was correct in that there was a fire escape but it consisted merely of iron rungs set directly into the wall, going down to quite a large flat roof seemingly a hundred feet below. He lay on his stomach and, leaning down, pulled on the top few to test them.

'It's not too good,' he said soberly. 'The cement's cracking and they're loose. You'll need to go down as fast as you can.'

'But you must save Robert first!' I exclaimed, deciding it was my damned writer's imagination again and the floor beneath my feet wasn't really getting warm.

'No, you first. You're lighter and stand more chance of not pulling the rungs from the wall.' Going back and struggling in the confined space he got Kennedy in a fireman's lift. 'Go on, go!' he yelled at me. 'This place will—'

Directly below us there was another explosion. After a vague period of time had elapsed I discovered that I was lying in a corner, it was very hot and there was smoke emanating from a large hole in the floor that, dizzily and stupidly, I told myself had not been there just now. As I watched, one of the projectors toppled and disappeared into it. I could not see Patrick.

'Are you still there?' he suddenly shouted as though not for the first time from somewhere in the smoke before succumbing to a bout of coughing.

'Yes!' I called, my voice sounding strange.

'Then go!' he yelled hoarsely.

Acrid fumes now tearing at my throat and wondering if I had been knocked out again I crawled to where most of the smoke was exiting, a lighter rectangle in the dimness, for some reason first remembering to ram the gun back in my bag and looping the strap of it around my neck. I could still hear Patrick coughing. Then I was outside, my hands on the cold metal of the grating floor of the fire escape balcony. It was fresher here and I paused before realizing that I was holding everything up by staying where I was.

Could I hear sirens or was it my bloody imagination again?

Although not particularly afraid of heights I was determined not to look down. Standing and holding on to the railings at the top I felt for and found the first rung with my right foot. Testing my weight on it I gingerly lowered myself and found another. It all held and I wasn't even thinking what I would do if anything gave way. Everything would have been much easier if the world wasn't going round and round and if I didn't feel so nauseous.

A huge gust of scorching air then belched through the open doorway to hit my face and I ducked down. My head was now on a level with the grating floor and again I paused, trying to probe the murk for a sign of Patrick. I could see nothing.

Numbly, I went down, feeling the rungs literally moving under my weight. One slowly bent a short way but stayed in the wall. Then, when I had hardly touched it, the next tore right out and I heard it land on the roof below with a thud. My foot groped lower for another one while the cement around the fixings of the one I was gripping in my right hand slowly crumbled before my eyes.

I was going far too slowly. Looking up I could see that I had only descended by about fifteen feet. I risked a look down: it seemed I was almost at the top of a cliff face. Quicker it had to be. The realization that Patrick would wait until I was nearly at the bottom before coming down with his burden then hit me. Otherwise if he fell he would take me out too and the three of us would probably die.

I hurried, treating the rungs as gently as possible and using them for as short a duration as I could. Another three either sank under my weight or broke away from the wall altogether but I was getting into a rhythm, making sure I was holding on with both hands to different ones before I reached down with a foot for the next. Another quick glance below gave me a shock; I was almost there, the height had been an illusion. The sound of sirens had not been illusory though; they were approaching fast.

From within the building there was a thundering crash as of floors and ceilings collapsing and, as I looked up, flames burst out up above the roof. I could not see if Patrick was on his way down or not because of the smoke wreathing around. Then two of the rungs I was on fell out and I nearly went with them. Another twisted as I grabbed it in a panic but I hung on, somehow resisting the urge to drop the last bit and risk broken ankles.

Then my foot touched firm ground and I sank down, muscles like jelly. Crawling again after two failed efforts to stand – uppermost in my mind was the thought that I had to attract someone's attention – I headed for the edge of the flat roof and, still on all fours, looked over. Predictably, I was only one or two storeys up now – it was impossible to tell exactly how high from here – but the street below appeared to be a cul-de-sac and no one was in sight. When I looked round I saw that there was a small square hut sort of structure on the end of the roof nearest the cinema. It had a door in it.

I went back to the bottom of the fire escape and used to it to pull myself to my feet, dully wondering why I was having such trouble with balance. Concentrating hard I made my way over to the little building, realizing belatedly that it existed to provide access to the roof from within. I tried the handle. Yet another locked door in a world of dead-ends.

I was trying not to think of the chances of Patrick succeeding in carrying down what was probably a twelve-stone man without the pair falling. He has never really recovered full bodily strength since being thrashed with studded belts by a gang of bikers when he was working undercover some years ago. He has no sensation in his right

foot, for however clever prosthetic limbs are there is still
no feeling. Peering upwards into the smoke I tried to see
if there was any movement. Should I shout? No, that would
not achieve anything. I felt ashamed when my sense of self-
preservation caused me to move away from the bottom of
the fire escape in case they fell on me.

Now, surely, the fire would be spreading to the building
next door, which I guessed was an old warehouse.
Unsteadily, I went back to the edge of the roof. Access here
only appeared to be provided by the one no-through-road,
actually a lane, but as I was walking around the perimeter
looking for a way down I saw a group of people emerge
from a Portakabin on a bare patch of land nearby and quickly
begin to walk away. They were obviously being evacuated
from the area.

Langleys can really shout if they have to and this one
did.

They all looked up and someone, a man, waved and ran
off. I saw a girl reach in her bag for her mobile. I supposed
I could have done that too but had assumed that the road
below would be filled with emergency vehicles by now.
There was then a gust of wind bringing with it a huge billow
of smoke, obliterating the view below. I turned and saw
that there was a huge cloud of it belching out of the rear
of the cinema, probably through the top doorway. Within
it was the redness of flames.

Somewhere in the murk there were two heavy and sepa-
rate thumps. Once again crawling because of the fear that
I would lose my way in the swirling smoke, the roof now
warm beneath my hands, I went towards where I had heard
the sounds. It was farther than I had thought and it was
only when I almost went over the edge of the roof that I
realized I had lost my sense of direction in the smoke. The
blustery wind cleared it away for a few seconds and suddenly
I could see where I was.

Patrick and Kennedy were lying on the roof at the bottom
of the fire escape, some ten yards from me, not moving.
The smoke closed in again but I had got my bearings now
and found them quickly. Kennedy appeared to be the same,

deeply unconscious. I could not rouse Patrick, and could not find a pulse, so all I could do for the moment was kneel by him, murmuring his name in his ear, rubbing his face. To no avail. The smoke was horribly thick now, setting me coughing again.

I stood up, knowing that I ought to get them both as far away from this area of the roof as possible. Starting with Patrick I got him under the armpits and began to drag him backwards. I could only manage a few feet at a time before stopping for a rest: he was a dead weight. I counted as I went, hoping to judge it correctly so that I did not walk myself right over the edge. I had paused for my third rest, coughing fit to turn my lungs inside out, when I heard crashes and bangs coming from roughly in the same direction as where Robert Kennedy still lay. I left Patrick and went back slowly, bent double so that I could see the floor in front of me, expecting to find that that part of the roof had fallen in, taking him with it.

I could find neither holes nor Kennedy.

I suppose I was mentally confused, still stunned from twice hitting my head when the explosions had occurred, retching for breath, and when I saw a weird figure emerge through the smoke and come straight at me, masked, the eyes just holes in the head, I shrieked. No, I scolded myself, it was not the 'alien' projector that had fallen though the floor restored back to life and coming to get me, merely a fireman wearing breathing apparatus. I never knew exactly how he, they, found the two men, because right then I collapsed.

I was definitely in the mood to shoot off more locks and dealt with the ones on Sydney Hellier's front door with relish. It was broad daylight and I did not care. People saw me; I did not care. I did not care if the entire Metropolitan Police descended on my neck, the prospect of prison positively cheering if it meant I could wring Hellier's scraggy neck. All I wanted to do right then was nail this little shit who had lit a large fire under us and tried to kill my husband. I did not know yet whether he had been successful or not.

Ambulances had taken both him and Kennedy away and after giving me oxygen the paramedics had wanted me to go to hospital for a check-up but I had refused. I had pressing business.

The door hammered back into the wall in a most delightful Patrick-style fashion as I detonated in. I raged through all the downstairs rooms without locating him and then tackled the stairs at a run. Front bedroom, bathroom, back bedroom, box room. The last was where I found him; in a small space almost filled with junk, crouching like a cornered rat, grey with fear.

I yanked him out by his shirt collar, one-handed, amazed at my own strength, and slammed him into a wall on the landing. And again. He uttered a high-pitched shriek and his dentures fell out. I put the gun in my pocket to have both hands free to resoundingly box his ears.

'You rang him, didn't you?' I yelled. 'Lazlo Ivers. The preservation society's all a front, isn't it? You rang and told him people were sniffing around the cinema and he ordered you to start the fire. Answer me!'

He gobbled at me wordlessly.

I rammed the gun into his ribs. 'Tell me the truth or I'll blow your guts out through the back of your spine!'

He carried on opening and shutting his toothless mouth like a half dead fish, all the while puffing bad breath in my face.

God alone knows what prevented me from pulling the trigger.

'Are you up there, Ingrid?' called a familiar voice.

I got a firm hold on the knot on Hellier's stained tie and dragged him to the top of the stairs, banging his head on the wall when he started making choking noises. I was in time to see James Carrick shove a couple of people out of the front door while shouting, 'Police! Sod off!'

He came on up the stairs, gazing at me soberly. 'Do we want him alive?' he asked, even more soberly.

Right then the irony was lost on me. 'I would like you to arrest this man,' I said, trying to stop my voice from quavering. 'For attempted murder, I *think*.' I let go of Hellier and he went down in an untidy heap and stayed there. I stopped myself from kicking him, just.

'Let's hope and pray it's attempted murder,' James said.

'Have you heard anything?' I whispered.

He shook his head. 'No, not yet. Greenway sent me because he was worried you'd come to harm. The man's obviously clueless.' He surveyed me wonderingly. 'Ingrid, *mo ghaoil,* have you looked at yourself in a mirror lately?'

Well, of course I bloody well hadn't.

'Get this dreadful woman away from me and I'll tell you everything you want to know,' Hellier glugged from the floor.

I bent down to be on his level. 'Just confirm that it was Lazlo Ivers who told you to set the place alight.'

'Yes, it was.'

I handed him back his teeth.

The worst thing was not being able to remember how Patrick had looked. Had his clothes been alight? Did he look as though he had been burned? I could remember nothing, not even the clothes he had been wearing. How far had he and Kennedy fallen? Had he, in fact, actually started down the fire escape with the unconscious man before the flames belched out of the door?

James Carrick had called Greenway before handing over Sydney Hellier to the crew of an area car with instructions to take him to Walthamsden Police Station and there await orders. He had then escorted me, nay virtually frog-marched me, to his car and taken me back to the hotel where I had been staying. There, I was firmly delivered to my room and he too came in and shut the door.

'I must find out how he is,' I insisted. 'How they both are,' I corrected.

'I'll do that. Meanwhile, you go and scrub the soot and stuff off yourself and we'll get some food and a hot drink inside you.'

'I don't want anything to eat,' I snapped. I could still taste smoke.

'Fine, but you can't go wandering around looking like

that or someone's going to suggest I take you to the nearest mental hospital.'

The man had a point, I had to concede when I saw my reflection in the en-suite mirror. Privacy brought tears and it was a real covered-in-dust, sooty mess who, sobbing, stared disbelievingly at herself. The only thing that was the right colour was my hair: black. Well, I supposed my eyes were still green but they were surrounded by red instead of white.

He's dead, the inner voice insisted. *You're a widow. Get used to the idea, you silly cow.*

But what had he once joked in similar circumstances?

'I never have a pulse on Wednesdays.'

It was Wednesday.

It was a measure of my tattered and exhausted condition when I happily said, 'That's all right then,' stripped off my filthy clothes and got into the shower. I ended up by having two, such was the dire state of affairs, and when I returned to the room, wrapped only in towels – what the hell, Carrick was a married man, wasn't he? – there was a tray waiting for me loaded with things like a mug of hot chocolate, buttered crumpets and fruit cake. All of which, smoke-flavoured mouth or no, I fell upon, needless to say.

'You're just like Patrick,' James said, from a chair over by the window. 'In the event of trauma, feed.'

'Did you ring?' I asked, cradling the hot chocolate in both hands and, despite the showers, shivering.

'Yes, but there's total chaos at that particular A and E department. They know both of them are in casualty, are being attended to and neither has died. But there's been a major traffic accident on the motorway and people are being ferried in like there's a war on so some of those have to be given priority. And Greenway rang me. He's going to carry on with your project of taking Hellier to bits later. You can be present if you want to, but you'll have to promise me that you'll' – surprisingly, a big smile lit up his face – 'be good.'

I promised.

*   *   *

Greenway gazed at me severely. 'I'm sure you should be in hospital being treated for smoke inhalation,' he said.

'I'm quite all right, thank you,' I told him. I had an idea my lungs were still a bit kippered and had a tendency to cough but did not want to join a queue of seriously injured people who needed help far more than I did, then wait hours only to be told to go home and rest. Carrick had not really wanted to bring me back to SOCA HQ with him but other than by chaining me to the bed there was not a lot he could have done to prevent me tagging along. I was ignoring my sore head.

'I did as Patrick suggested and asked Miss Dean to have a proper look at what's on the discs. She's here now as a matter of fact – it's got her out of the safe house for a while. I'm not too sure if she'll achieve anything though.' The SOCA man shuffled papers around on his desk. 'I've decided to question Hellier personally. I take it you'd like to be present?'

'Yes, please. I can stand in for Patrick.'

'Do we know any more about how badly he's hurt?'

'No.'

More shuffling. 'I have to ask you this, Ingrid. Last time I spoke to him I distinctly got the impression he wasn't happy.'

I felt I owed it to everyone to tell the truth. 'No, he's not. He was of a mind to tell you he didn't want to go on with SOCA any more but would honour his promise to James Carrick to do everything he could to find his father. It was my idea to investigate the old cinema – Miss Dean had said Ballinger had discussed it in her hearing.'

'I see. Is this mind-set of Patrick's due to private reasons?'

'Yes, but not secret ones. He feels it's about time he gave more time to his family. Today has demonstrated how four children are at serious risk of losing their father.'

'And mother,' he added.

'Justin is being a bit of a problem; he needs his dad around a lot more.'

'Thank you for telling me,' Greenway said, and rose from

his seat. 'I've had Hellier brought here too.' He gave me my second bright smile of the day. 'It's great when you get to be commander – you don't necessarily have to slog through traffic jams to God-awful nicks in the course of a day's work.'

Seventeen

Having got the formalities out of the way Greenway opened the questioning roughly with, 'So who is this Lazlo Ivers?'

Sydney Hellier's gaze darted from one to another of us. 'I said I'd only talk if she wasn't around,' he said.

'Is that right?' Greenway said with a nasty grin. 'Well, if you don't start spilling the beans right now I reckon I might just leave you alone with her.'

Ye gods, what had Carrick told him?

It was quite late in the afternoon and we were in a room in a secure – very secure – area in the basement.

'He's just a member of the preservation society,' Hellier muttered.

'Don't give me that load of old baloney,' Greenway said. 'You admitted in DCI Carrick's hearing that he told you to set the place alight. It was all ready to go up with incendaries stacked beneath the stage.'

Hellier gave me another wary look. 'He was just a member *to start with*,' he amended. 'Then all these heavies turned up with him at one of the meetings and he sort of took over.'

'But you must have still kept an eye on the place. Didn't you question all this wildly inflammable stuff being stored there?'

'Yes, I . . . I did. He just told me to shut up and mind my own business.'

'How long had it all been there?'

'A few weeks.'

'These people are the ones who want to knock the place down,' Greenway informed him heavily.

'Well, I wasn't to know that, was I?'

'But did your tiny mind work it out eventually?'

Hellier nodded miserably. 'One of the stupid ones opened his mouth one day when I was there. Ivers threatened me not to tell anyone.'

'That whole area's due for redevelopment and it was highly likely that a building in such poor condition would have been demolished anyway. Why did they have to go to such lengths to take over some piddling preservation society instead of just biding their time?'

Hellier shrugged.

Greenway thumped the table. 'There's something you're not telling me. These people are big-time crooks.'

'They wanted to stifle resistance to a redevelopment scheme. I think they've bought up most of the area,' said Hellier.

'And they stifled your resistance with threats?'

'That's right.'

'No money was involved? They didn't grease your grubby little mitts with silver?'

'No. And I want you to know that nothing they've done is anything to do with me.'

'No, you just tried to burn three people to death.'

'Two!' the man shot back with.

'You admit it then?'

'He made me do it,' the other responded dully. 'As soon as I said I'd mentioned his name to people who wanted to have a look round he went half off his head and said he'd kill me personally.'

'But you must have phoned him or he wouldn't have known.'

'I just thought I ought to get an OK from him. He'd always said he wanted to know if anyone was taking an interest in the place.'

'What's his number?'

'I – I can't remember. No, honest,' he shrilled when he perceived that Greenway was coming to the boil. 'I mean, you put them in the phone's memory, don't you? You can't possibly remember them all.'

'We'll find it in your mobile then.'

'No, I . . . er . . . dropped and accidentally trod on it before you lot arrived. It's bust.'

In the exasperation-loaded silence that followed this statement I caught Greenway's eye and he nodded.

'You knew nothing about the policeman trapped in a room off the projection box?' I asked Hellier.

'No!'

'You've just told us that all the boxes and papers had been there for a few weeks. Did you put it all there yourself?'

There was a silence and then Hellier said, 'Yes. He said he'd set some of his boys on me if I didn't.'

'How long did it take you?'

'I did it over three or four days. I pinched most of the stuff from the recycling dump.'

'So how come some of the newspapers were only a couple of days old?'

'Oh, I tossed in a few more yesterday.'

'You're lying. That's when there was a big panic to get it all ready for burning – when the policeman was brought from wherever he was being held with a view to finishing him off without anyone knowing.'

'No!'

There was a knock on the door.

'Come!' Greenway bellowed.

'Miss Dean would like to speak to you, sir,' said a woman I knew to be his assistant.

'I'm rather tied up here,' he countered.

'She says it's important.'

Greenway stopped the tape, jerked his head in my direction and we left the room. When he had organized someone to watch over the suspect we took the lift to the second floor.

'I'm sorry if I've dragged you away from something important,' Miss Dean began. 'But I think you ought to know that I've had some success with this. Once I had realized that some, if not most, of the code names for people are places and vice versa I made headway. It's an almost childishly simple code. The old cinema is Garbo after the actress. It would appear that they bought a lot of other property surrounding it two years ago when prices in the whole area were at rock bottom. I think we're talking about money-laundering on a large scale. Plymouth is referred to as Drake, Portsmouth as Nelson and Swindon as Bombs – so someone must have studied History and English literature at school,' she ended by commenting crisply.

'So what's Bristol?' Greenway wanted to know, his mind obviously on Slaterford and Sons.

'Duke, I think.'

'Duke?'

'Wasn't Sid James the Duke of Bristol in one of the Carry On films?'

'You're a genius,' Greenway said admiringly.

Miss Dean beamed at him. 'Putting the names of real people to those of places is much more difficult, of course – and some eastern European-sounding ones could be either – but I'm working on it. What I really wanted to tell you was that I went on the local authority website here and there's a report that the old cinema has, in the last couple of days, been awarded money from the Lottery Heritage Fund for its restoration, together with the whole road as most of the properties are Grade Two listed. Everything would be compulsorily purchased.' She removed her half-moon glasses and said sadly, 'It's come too late for the old picture house.'

'They knew,' Greenway said succinctly.

'And because of the award a planning application by a development company has been turned down. I accessed the local paper's website and understand the plans were very unpopular with just about everyone in Walthamsden because it would have meant a lot of high-rise flats and a casino. That would be Ballinger all right.'

'Was the application for lottery funding anything to do with a preservation society?' I enquired.

'I don't remember seeing anything like that mentioned.'

'Did the name Lazlo Ivers appear anywhere?'

'I don't think so. If you like I can double-check.'

'Please do,' Greenway said earnestly. 'I'll look in again later but you mustn't feel obliged to work late.'

We were halfway out of the door when she called, 'Oh! How do you spell that name?'

I told her how I thought it might be spelt.

'Slizaverlo!' she exclaimed, pointing to the computer screen. 'If ever there was a place name on no known map it's that one. It's an anagram,' she explained, seeing our baffled expressions.

'I'm seriously thinking of taking that brainy lady on as a part-time consultant,' Greenway said as we were returning to the basement. 'Do you think Hellier's lying or just stupid?'

'Both,' I replied.

'So do I.'

'Right!' Greenway exclaimed, flinging open the door of the interview room and making Hellier jump out of his skin. 'I want to know Iver chummy's address and how much he was paying you to be his dogsbody.'

'I've never known where he lives,' Hellier stated emphatically. 'He isn't the kind of man you ask anything of a personal nature.'

'And the rest? Your cut for stifling resistance to his presence among the other members of the preservation society, lighting fires for him, that kind of thing?'

'Nothing! I didn't get paid nothing!'

Greenway ignored the contradiction. 'It seems that you're easily intimidated. I think that when most people, even frightened ones, were asked to commit murder they'd run to the police, but you obviously didn't. Why?'

'You don't know him,' was all Hellier said.

'But we're getting a pretty good idea,' Greenway went on silkily. 'I actually think you're now part of his whole set-up and were bought, lock, stock and conscience by him right from the moment he decided to snuff out all local objection to what he wanted to do. You have a website that anyone can access. He might have thought the organization was much larger and had more influence than it has. Well, sunshine, it was all in vain. Not only has the whole area been granted a ton of money to be fully restored but you're in the frame for murder.'

I shot a panic-fuelled look in Greenway's direction, wondering if he knew something that I did not, but he glanced at me and winked.

'He said he'd kill me if I didn't do as he said!' Hellier shouted. 'I knew he must be a crook and would never take his money.'

'I only need to take a look at your bank account.'

'Carry on, I've nothing to hide.'

Greenway took a deep breath and I sensed that we would get no further with our suspect at this stage.

There was another knock on the door.

'What?' Greenway yelled.

His assistant's head came around the door. 'Inspector Rahjeed craves admittance, sir. Sorry, his words.'

'Send him in,' said Greenway. Then, *'Who?'*

Inspector Rahjeed came in.

'They said you were dead,' Hellier said disgustedly. 'Or is that the other one?' he scoffed.

Patrick drew up a chair and sat down. Even with the brown skin dye he looked wan and had limped a little as he crossed the room. When he spoke it was in his normal voice.

'I don't have to remind you that I'm the person who saw you when you'd just lit a match and made sure a box containing petrol-soaked newspapers had ignited before you bolted, locking the stage door virtually in my face. I saw you in the light coming in from outside and I shall get enormous pleasure in testifying against you in a court of law. Right now you're the only one in the frame for this crime so it's in your own interest to tell us everything you know about Lazlo Ivers.'

Stone cold. He had not so much as looked in my direction. I did not need to be told that if ever there was a moment not to show emotion it was this. I bit back the tears of sheer relief and concentrated on the thought that after a lightening visit to our hotel to shower and change he must have witnessed at least the second part of the interview courtesy of mikes and the one-way glass partition situated behind where Greenway and I were sitting.

'So it's three of you now, is it?' Hellier shouted. 'Three against one. This is when you start putting the boot in, eh?'

'He's right,' Greenway said. 'And it's against regulations. I shall go and get myself a cup of tea.' And with another wink in my direction, he left the room.

Our suspect did not appear to be relishing the result of his protest.

Patrick gave him a jolly smile. 'I don't need boots,' he said. 'The question we really need answering is why you lit that match just because Ivers told you to.'

'I've already explained why. He was spitting mad with me for mentioning his name and said he'd kill me if I didn't do as he said.'

'You only had to go to the police. You would have been given protection.'

'His sort find you wherever you are. You can't hide for the rest of your life.'

'Explain to us why you didn't go to the police when you first realized the preservation group had been taken over by a bunch of crooks.'

'For the same reason.'

'You're still lying. You're actually in the pay of this man.'

'Go to hell!'

'When a Detective Chief Inspector from Avon and Somerset Police arrested you at your house he had in his pocket a search warrant that he genuinely forgot to mention to you. I've just had a call from him and it appears that a team working with him from the local nick have discovered five thousand pounds hidden under the floorboards in your bedroom. I'd like you to explain that.'

'Perhaps I don't trust banks,' Hellier said after nervously licking his lips.

'You'll have to do better than that.'

'Ivers asked me to look after it for him.'

Patrick turned to me with a sigh. 'He'll get life for this.'

I nodded. 'And get mashed by Ivers anyway when they're banged up together after we've caught up with him and his hoodlums shortly.'

'You're right,' Patrick agreed musingly. 'I hadn't thought of that.'

'Eh!' Hellier exclaimed. 'They don't do that! Do they? Put you in the same prison? They can't!'

'It's your decision,' Patrick said with an off-hand shrug.

In the long silence that followed I was expecting at any second that he would turn up the pressure, switch to that inexplicable mode, stare at the other man and exude that *threat*. But he did not, half turning his back to Hellier and saying to me,'Fancy a drink later?'

'I'd like that,' I said.

'And then a meal perhaps?' with a winning, come-hither smile.

'That too,' I agreed.

He just carried on sitting there, blatantly flirting with me without saying a word. This was not all acting; the smile said it all. *Thank God you're all right and I love you to bits*.

'What about me?' Hellier said in a small voice.

'Oh!' Patrick said, giving every impression of having been so involved with lustful thoughts that he had forgotten all about the job in hand. 'Well, you could turn Queen's Evidence, co-operate and then be put somewhere nice and safe from Ivers and soon, no doubt, be tucking into a hot meal. As I said just now, it's entirely up to you. The evidence against you is overwhelming.'

'OK,' Hellier said after another long pause. 'But send in that other bloke. I don't trust you not to turn nasty.'

'Before I go I want that mobile phone number. And don't tell me you can't remember it. It must be engraved on what's left of your soul.' He pushed a note pad and pen across the table.

Hellier wrote and shoved it back.

'Is that correct?' Patrick asked. 'Because if it isn't I shall be right back.'

'That's the number,' the other muttered.

'I shall also return if you refuse to tell my colleagues all you know,' Patrick said grimly. 'And next time I shall stay until we've wrung you dry of every last bit of information. Is that understood?'

'We can't have fallen very far,' Patrick said to me outside the interview room after we had sneaked a kiss and a quick cuddle, after which I had given him the important details of what Miss Dean had found out. 'All the rungs my weight was on gave way at once and that was it. I must have hit my head on the ground and knocked myself right out. They wanted to keep me in for observation and all that rhubarb but were quite glad when I opted to go as soon as I felt able to.' He added, echoing Carrick's remark, 'The place was like a battlefield.'

'What about Kennedy?'

'He's definitely being kept in. They were sending him down to X-ray as I left because he was in a lot of pain, probably from broken ribs. He had at least recovered consciousness after being given fluids. A couple of blokes in shades, at a guess from F9, were trying to get to speak to him but the medics were having none of it and sent them packing.'

'Did you manage to speak to him?'

'Not really; his mouth was too dry for him to say anything and he didn't really know what was going on. I just shook his hand as I left and told him I'd check up on him later.'

'Did he know you though?'

'No, hardly surprising in the circumstances and the way I look now.'

'You still smell of smoke.'

'So do you – but I still fancy you enough to take you out for a drink sometime.'

'But I'd only just handed over to you. What the hell did you do to him?' Greenway said when we had relayed the news.

'Nothing,' Patrick answered. 'He's been a loner all his life and sometimes the feeling of isolation is unbearable.'

The SOCA man shook his head, not understanding.

'What d'you want me to do about the mobile number he gave me?'

'What do *you* want to do with it?'

'Phone, pretend I'm Hellier and ask for the wages owing to me for burning down the cinema. He'll suggest a meeting place and be all ready to gun down his now useless henchman. Ivers can't know that Hellier's been arrested unless he's got someone permanently watching his house, which seems highly unlikely. We grab the bastard plus whatever mobsters turn up with him.'

'There's an awful lot of conjecture in there,' Greenway pointed out. 'First, I think I'd prefer to try to find an account address for the number. *And*, don't forget, all Ivers has to do is send someone round to Hellier's place to put a bullet in him now only to find that the house is crawling with cops.'

'He could well do that. But he'd wait until dark. You could make sure all searches have been completed by then and everything was looking normal.'

Eyeing him dubiously Greenway said, 'You're sure you can fool him into thinking you're Hellier?'

Patrick took his mobile from his pocket and waggled it, one eyebrow raised questioningly.

'OK then, phone.'

This he did, first going into a corner of Greenway's office and facing into the right angle of walls in order to muffle his voice. I walked over very quietly behind him to listen in.

'It's Syd,' said Patrick, loosely pinching his nostrils in order to mimic Hellier's flat, somewhat adenoidal tones. 'The whole place went up a treat, them with it. They're raking over what's left looking for bodies now. When do I get paid?'

I could hear the high-pitched, hissy sort of voice on the other end of the line but not what was said.

'Sometime next week's not good enough,' Patrick said. 'I've put myself right on the line for you and you owe me.'

More hissing.

'I *need* the money. I can go to the cops, you know.'

'Do as you're bloody-well told, you little disease!' came over loud and clear.

'I'll be at home tonight, waiting. If you don't come up with the goods I'm off round to the nick first thing in the morning. It was all for nothing anyway – I've just found out you've lost your bid to make a mint of money in the area as it's just been granted funding to be restored.' Blustering and slurring his voice as though he had been drinking Patrick finished by saying, 'So that's what you are, a real loser.'

'You ought to be on the stage,' Greenway commented wryly. 'I just hope it wasn't too over the top.'

Patrick sat down rather suddenly. 'Any chance of some tea and a sticky bun?'

When I had despatched Patrick to SOCA's somewhat upmarket canteen I discovered that Miss Dean had come to the conclusion that most of the information on the CDs involved business ventures – as she had already said, probably legitimate ones to soak up gains from drug-dealing, in other words, money-laundering – records of trading with other criminal outfits and a register of monies received, or not, from small businesses like restaurants, a protection racket. They were all neatly listed under various headings, the place names she had also told us about. There was a lot of it.

'I can come back tomorrow if you like,' she said to Greenway as she was leaving to be taken to the safe house. 'There's still quite a bit to do on the names of people side of things, but now I know that most are anagrams I should be able to sort it all out for you. Unless it's another anagram there might be a woman involved, Lil's Here or Lil Here features in what one must assume is recent information.'

Greenway told her that he would be most grateful if she carried on.

'It has to be S. Hellier,' I said when the door had closed behind her.

Rubbing his hands gleefully Greenway said, 'That's him as good as in the slammer then.'

'So what's the plan for tonight?' I asked briskly.

'The plan is, Ingrid, that you'll be somewhere else,' he replied, and, excusing himself by saying that he had to conduct a briefing, left me.

'I expect he thinks you've done enough for one day,' Patrick said, infuriatingly, when I had run him to ground together with what remained of his sausages, bacon, eggs, baked beans, tomato and fried bread. Oh, and black pudding.

'Look, I'm not going back to the hotel to chew my fingernails to the bone while you're setting yourself up as bait!'

'I agree that after all your efforts it's frustrating for you not to be in at what will hopefully be Ivers' arrest,' he said peaceably. 'But do you really want to hide in a cupboard all night in Hellier's place? You said yourself that it's a fleapit. And it's not as though I'll be unprotected – undercover cops'll be everywhere. Why don't you go and see if you can talk to Robert Kennedy? If he's fit to receive visitors he'll be more likely to give you info that we can use and you can ring Greenway, not me, with anything immediately relevant.'

'He's not going to talk to me with his F9 cronies hanging around.'

'He might. It's his last case, remember.'

'I take it he's been given police protection.'

'Of course, there's an armed guard.'

Greenway was right, of course: after a big dose of smoke I had done more than enough for one day and my stamina did not seem to be as good as it once was. You are getting older, I told myself, if not old, and took a taxi back to the hotel where I intended to put my feet up for half an hour before going to see Kennedy. I had fleetingly seen Greenway again before leaving the building and he had called to me not to worry as Patrick would be only one of several experienced, and armed, personnel who would be waiting for Ivers and any henchmen with whom he might turn up.

I had a snack in the little bistro just off the hotel reception area and then went up to our room where I slept like something dead for four and a quarter hours.

Eighteen

Waking with a jerk I saw that it was now eight forty-five. I tumbled off the bed and went into the bathroom where I splashed cold water over my face, cursing my carelessness in not phoning reception and asking to be called. For, surely, it was now far too late to expect a hospital ward to admit visitors.

It was, but apparently in this particular patient's case an exception would be made as he had requested that only family and friends, their names to be referred to him first, be admitted. No one, so far, had come and I got the impression that the nursing staff felt sorry for him. The answer came back straight away and after having had my identity checked – I had expected this and had my passport with me – by the armed minder on duty in the corridor that led to the private room, possibly part of an isolation wing, I went in.

Still host to drips and monitoring devices Kennedy looked worse, if anything, than when we had found him, the bruising on his haggard face awful to see and now visible because he had been cleaned up. The only positive difference was the ironic smile on his face.

'There, and I thought I'd be safe with that proviso,' he croaked.

I pulled up a chair and sat down. 'You could have refused me entry,' I pointed out, nevertheless experiencing a pang of pity for him.

'Just don't talk about the job, there's a good girl.' He coughed raspingly and took a sip of water.

'There might be a rather long silence then as the only other thing we have in common is James.'

'Oh, I wasn't expecting him to be along,' Kennedy said roughly.

'No, he can't because right now he's on duty at SOCA's HQ while everyone's co-ordinating a sting operation to grab Lazlo Ivers.'

'You have been busy,' he said sarcastically.

'I hope we don't have a bad case of sour grapes here.'

He gave me a wide, mirthless grin. 'One of the big bosses going out in a blaze of glory. Only it was a real fire and the great man got himself banged up in a shit-house instead.'

I nodded. 'After surviving a savage beating and severe dehydration by being as tough as nails.'

'You could have had that put on my headstone,' he jeered, only to set himself coughing again.

'You're just like him, you know,' I shot back. 'James, I mean. You've got the same brand of what Patrick calls real buggerence.'

He gave me a sour look.

'Do you know about Sydney Hellier being arrested?' I asked, damned if I was just going to sit there in an awkward silence.

'The weird bloke who started the preservation society for the old cinema? No.'

'He was the one who lit the match. Which is ironic when you think about it. I take it he really did want to save the place originally.'

'He was easily persuaded it was a lost cause though. Just a couple of hundred pounds under his nose worked like a charm.' He chuckled. 'A man of cast-iron principles.'

'Several thousand pounds were found under the floor in his bedroom.'

'Ivers must have been giving him so much a week to keep an eye on the cinema and run errands for him.'

'Were you one of the men who first went with Ivers to see him?'

'Yes, I was. You have to go everywhere, to get as much evidence against them as you possibly can.'

'Tell me about Ivers.'

'What do you want to know except for the fact that he's raving mad, and bad, bad, bad?'

This, I saw, was right from the heart, it had to be for a boiled-in-the-wool Scotsman to show that much emotion. I told him about the scarecrows and how my comments to Patrick about my nightmare must have been picked up by the mikes at Slaterfords.

'That's how he works. He spreads fear. The way he walks when he's on a job, the way he talks. It's not just to disguise himself: it's to terrorize any witnesses. They have night-mares too, he's coming to get them. They refuse to testify against him.'

Baldly, I asked,'Why didn't you get your own initials carved on you?'

Kennedy did not even blink. 'Because I broke free and killed one of his filthy henchmen when he'd just got started. Ivers panicked and thought he might run out of time and breathing minders. That made it worth it, seeing the fear in the bastard's eyes.'

I touched a hand that was free from medical hardware. 'Sorry.'

'Don't apologize,' he muttered.

'Do you know if Lazlo Ivers is his real name?'

'He bragged to me – when he had thrown me in that bloody john to die – that he had any number of stolen iden-tities but that was the one on his gas bills.'

'So why are SOCA still struggling to arrest him?'

'Are they?'

I sat back in my seat and gazed at him. 'F9 are still behaving like clams then. Surely inter-departmental rivalry isn't as bad as that?'

Slowly, he shook his head.

'There's something you're not telling me.'

There was a hint of a smile. 'Do I have to tell you anything?'

'Patrick's life might depend on it and right now I reckon you owe him a favour, that's all,' I responded stonily.

'I'd already guessed that someone like that would have several aliaises. But I didn't believe him,' Kennedy said after a silence. It was manifest that he was very tired and probably in pain.

'What, didn't believe who he said he was?'

'No. He said it with a leer on his face – a bigger one than usual.'

'Please tell me what he said.'

'It's a complete load of havers.'

'But what did he *say*?'

'He said he was a cop, and somehow I took that at face value; that he occasionally impersonates a policeman. Criminals quite often do.'

I think I swore. 'Patrick's at a stake-out at Hellier's place waiting for him to turn up with the wages for setting fire to the cinema.'

'Ivers won't turn up in person, he'll send someone else and spend no more than the price of a bullet.'

'But, don't you see? He might arrive in police uniform and no one'll turn a hair!' I rummaged in my bag for my mobile, could not immediately find it and turned the whole thing upside down on the bed.

'I see you're well prepared,' Kennedy observed dryly, eyeing the Smith and Wesson thus tumbled on to the bed cover.

I grabbed the phone and then threw the gun back in with everything else.

'I hope you're permitted to carry that, Mrs Gillard.'

'Yes, Michael Greenway told me to make sure I had it with me at all times,' I said, pushing buttons. 'And, actually, it's Langley – Miss.'

He tut-tutted. 'Professional women get so annoyed when you call them by their married name.'

Halfway through dialling Patrick's number I slapped shut the phone.

'Has he ever told you how wonderful you look when you're angry?' Kennedy asked lightly.

'OK, so what *will* Ivers do?' I countered in a whisper, trying not to be thunderstruck by what he had just said. Perhaps it was the medication he was on.

'He'll come here.' When I did not respond, just stared at him, he went on, 'I'm afraid we're ahead of you on this one. Someone has slipped the fact that I'm still alive to one of his contacts. I'm definitely unfinished business and it's only a matter of time.'

'You're not all that well protected – not with just one armed copper.'

'I ken there's more than one but I'm not happy about it for another reason – this is a very public place. They should have chosen more carefully.'

'He might have smelled a rat if it had been somewhere more out of the way.' I opened my phone again and then paused. 'This is your case. Is it all right if I warn Patrick anyway?'

'Please do.'

But his phone was switched off, which, suddenly remembering his telling me not to call him was to be expected. I then rang Greenway and again there was only a messaging service.

'Keeping radio silence,' Kennedy commented.

'Can I get you anything?' I asked.

'You could shoot me and put me out of my misery.'

'I always ignore men's negative statements. Are you really going to retire?'

'I am. This is my last job.'

'You'll be able to go and see Lord Muirshire.'

'I imagined him to be dead by now – he's quite a bit older than me.'

'Not a chance. After his wife died he married Kimberley Devlin, the opera singer. It was he who told us you were a man of integrity. The pair of you will have a lot of catching up to do.'

'I could do with a cup of tea,' Kennedy said after a thoughtful pause. 'And, if you'd be so kind, a bite of something to go with it.'

There was the same armed policeman on duty, standing now and diligently gazing down the corridor in the direction of the entrance to the wing. At least I assumed it was the same man for, besides body armour he was wearing a helmet with the visor down. He turned when he heard me coming and I explained my errand.

'Get me a cuppa too?' he wheedled. 'Milk and one sugar?'
I told him I would, adding, 'Don't drop your guard.'

I passed a room that might be used as a decontamination area and went out into a long, straight corridor that eventually led to the main entrance. There was no one around. Kennedy was being kept in virtual isolation then.

I paused, reading direction signs, of which there seemed to be dozens pointing to a myriad of departments. None mentioned a café. I would have to go all the way back to where there were a few shops, including a coffee bar.

About ten minutes later I had completed my errand, having added a packet of mints for me and a London evening newspaper for the patient. News of the cinema fire was all over the front page together with a report of how firefighters had rescued three people from the roof of the building.

I stopped in surprise when I saw that the policeman had been replaced by another and who, when I first saw him was walking slowly away from me in the direction of Robert Kennedy's room. He was extremely tall and, even in his body armour, looked pole-thin.

Quickly, I went into the side room and put everything I was carrying but the Smith and Wesson on to a table. Then I ran, as silently as possible.

The corridor was empty now but I could detect voices, or more correctly I discovered when I got closer, a voice, a hissy, high-pitched voice. It seemed to be delivering a diatribe and was getting angrier and louder.

With the helmet on he did not hear my approach. I registered that the Heckler and Koch was pointing uncompromisingly in Robert Kennedy's direction, aimed and fired at the hands holding it at the same time diving to the floor by the bed. There was a roar of rage, the loud clatter of metal and there he was, standing right there looking down at me, the weapon not in sight. He rushed at me.

This time I got him in the body armour and he went over backwards from the force of the shot. But it was not enough to stop him and he picked himself up and again came at me, as relentless as the scarecrow coming through the window in my nightmare, a figure whose small but piercing eyes were staring at me through the visor. Then, before I could react, a boot had shot out and kicked the gun from my hand. All this had happened in seconds.

The weapon skittered along the polished tiles and we both went for it. I got to it first, having the advange of already being on the floor. His hands came at me, clawing, but I managed to evade them and tossed the gun on to the bed. I did not see what happened next as I was trying to avoid being kicked but heard it fire and the tinkle of breaking glass.

Feet pounded away down the corridor. He had got away.

'Where are they?' Kennedy was shouting. 'Where are the wondrous members of the armed support unit who were supposed to be watching our backs?' He coughed agonizingly and then gasped, 'Ingrid, are you all right, girl? I can't see you. For God's sake say something.'

A foot had caught me in the side, a deliberate vicious kick. I got to my feet, unable to speak just then, and thumped a hand down on the red emergency button on the bedside locker.

'Are you hurt?' Kennedy asked, placing the gun down on the bed.

'Just . . . winded,' I wheezed.

Various nursing staff arrived at the run then and got very annoyed with Kennedy for having detached one of his drip lines. Someone went away to try to discover what had happened to the protection team. Someone else stood tut-tutting at all the noise and disturbance.

I sat on the visitors' chair, shaking, ignored, the police-issue Heckler and Koch, it's firing mechanism smashed, beneath it. Then, when I felt I could move again I rang Greenway's number. He still was not answering.

Moments later a hunking copper wearing body armour but carrying his helmet under his arm strode into the room.

'Cummings,' he announced. 'Sergeant Cummings. What's gone on here?'

Before I could open my mouth Kennedy told him and I discovered, endeavouring to hide a smile, that like his son, he swore in Gaelic. So Cummings got the gist of what had happened without the trimmings, as it were. It transpired that the officer who had been on duty when I arrived was missing. They were looking for him. The rest of his team had received a visit – they had been on standby in a laundry room on the floor below – from a uniformed inspector, very tall and thin with a rather strange voice, who had sent them off to the hospital canteen for a break, saying he would hold the fort for them and remain in radio contact with the man on duty outside Kennedy's room. There was no sign of him either.

'Are you here *now* though?' I asked Cummings in a break in the conversation. 'I mean, is it all right if I leave? This senior F9 operative no longer has to rely for his personal safety on the wife of someone who works for SOCA?'

I did not wait for his reply, the auspices for which were not promising as when I left the room he still had his mouth wide open.

I had gone to the hospital by taxi and now hailed another, asking to be taken to the next road to Poplar Road, Walthamsden, where Sydney Hellier lived.

'That's Elm Street and it's a long road, luv,' said the taxi driver. 'D'you want the pub?'

I replied no, not really, but it would do. On second thoughts, a stiff tot of whisky would go down a real treat right now.

The Plate Layers' Arms was one of those Victorian pubs that appeared to have missed being modernised, or even painted, for half a century. Some of last year's Christmas lights were still twinkling sadly outside, the rest of the bulbs having failed, together with a couple of sorry-looking tubs containing last summer's bedding plants, dead as Marley's ghost.

I paid off the taxi and paused on the doorstep, seriously considering dropping in for a small bracer. I needed something to combat the continuing shakes and a fervent desire to burst into tears. You have low blood sugar, I told myself severely. What you really need is a hot, sweet drink, not alcohol. I went in, reasoning that they might serve coffee.

Why had I come back here? In truth I could not be bothered to delve deeply into my reasons, I was too tired. Just
the maverick investigator still at work perhaps.

It was quite late now, the clock above the bar that faced
me when I entered registering ten-fifteen, six minutes slow
according to my watch. The place was almost deserted, a
couple sitting at a table near a window, two or three men
playing darts towards the rear, no one behind the bar. The
sound of voices was coming through an archway where the
counter extended into another room. I went through a door
into the adjoining bar. It was just about full of men, some
in smart suits with designer smirks on their faces, others
obviously of lesser standing; the drivers, the pickaxe handle
wielders, the knife and gun carriers.

A mobsters' convention, no less.

'Get her!' a beanpole of a man squawked, jumping to his
feet. 'A thousand quid to the man that does! No, *two!*'

To a cacophony of upturned tables and spilled drinks
those in the room poured towards me.

It is very bad practice to chase horses when they refuse
to be caught in a field. They just go faster and learn the wrong
lessons. But I had once taken George by surprise when he
had been going through a slightly awkward phase shortly
after we got him by belting after him and grabbing him
around the neck with both arms. A gentleman to the last
he had succumbed to the head collar immediately. I had
been surprised by my own turn of speed and put it to good
use now, fleeing the building with at least twenty of them
after me. For the first hundred yards or so adrenalin gave
me feet with wings.

Unfit couch pototoes that most of them were, they were
getting closer. Panting wildly now I reached the end of the
road and turned left, expecting to be shot in the back at
every stride. Surely, surely, there was a police presence of
some kind around here? Or had some tall, thin uniformed
inspector turned up and told them all to go and have a
break, have a Kit-Kat?

It had been raining and the pavement was slippery
from moisture and the greasy detritus from the remains of

take-aways. I slipped and almost fell. The nearest man chasing me was now only a matter of yards behind, his breath rasping in his throat. Then, judging by the sounds, he skated on one of the discarded chips and crashed into a litter bin.

I turned left again into Poplar Road not able to recognize anything. My legs were on fire and someone else was catching up with me. I realized then that I was at the opposite end of Poplar Road to that which Patrick and I had parked when I had first called on Sydney Hellier, the house numbers I was passing now in the low twenties: Hellier's was one hundred and five. Looking at front doors, which fronted directly on to the pavement here, for numbers I almost went head-on into a lamppost.

Feet still thumped behind me. Then, seconds later, a hand seized the back of my jacket. Somehow grabbing the gun from the pocket, I shrugged it off, my bag going with it, and ran on. House number thirty-three.

Lungs agony, legs numbed now, I ran on. House number fifty-seven sort of floated past. I felt like I was stationary while the houses bobbed by me in a strange procession. A man on a bike was there too. He gave me a sideways look and almost rode into a parked car.

House number sixty-nine: big numbers painted black on a white plastic door.

A car was coming up behind me. It drew level.

'Goin' somewhere, darlin'?' hissed a voice.

I paused long enough to put one bullet into the tyre nearest to me and another into the bonnet right where it lived that resulted in a jet of steam emanating from under the wings and then tore on.

Where were all the bloody cops? I inwardly raged.

At house number ninety-one my legs gave way. I dragged myself into the doorway and sat with my back to it, my hands grasping the Smith and Wesson supported on my raised knees. I had one shot left: spare ammunition was in my jacket pocket.

Ye gods, the price on my head had ensured they were all still in pursuit, give or take a heart attack or two. Four more were just getting out of the car, that tall, thin figure in the lead, and a hairy, tubby little man who waddled as he walked at his side. This was going to be a bit like the Alamo.

Silly of me not to have thought that the sound of firing would not have roused someone. Three someones actually, who burst out of a doorway several houses away.

'Armed police!' Greenway's voice roared. 'You're all under arrest! Put down any weapons or we'll fire!'

Those of the cohorts who had only hard cash on their minds slithered to a standstill and then turned tail. It did them no good; their escape was now blocked by police vehicles. Several more, sirens howling, sped down from the other end of the road and braked to a standstill, their crews piling out.

I saw, almost inconsequentially, that Lazlo Ivers was approaching and had a gun in his hand. It was pointing directly at me. It suddenly ceased to point at me and I have never been able to remember pulling the trigger.

At some stage in the general chaos that followed I heard Greenway call above the wail of ambulance and police sirens, 'So who the bloody hell were they after then?'

Someone came over and looked down at me and I was too weak even to smile.

'It's a woman, sir.' And, alarmed he continued, 'She's armed!'

'It's not . . . loaded any more,' I panted, but of course no one heard me.

Greenway came closer. 'Did she fire that shot that got Ivers just now?'

I wasn't sure.

'Don't know, sir. She isn't moving – might be hurt.'

'Get the medics to see to her, now. I'll deal with the gun.' He walked up.

I found the energy to place the revolver down on the pavement. He crouched down to see me better.

'You're a very brave man,' I whispered.

'But . . . but you're at the hospital!' he blurted out.

'No, I'm here,' I said. 'They were having an AGM in the Plate Layers' Arms.'

'Are you hurt?'

'I don't think so.'

He lifted me up, steadied me and the rest of the threesome, Patrick and James Carrick strolled up to see what was going on. For several seconds nobody spoke.

'Ingrid, will you marry me again?' Patrick said in a faraway voice.

Nineteen

While it is not illegal for even crooks to congregate in a public house – and the police had no evidence that anyone present would have broken his journey on the way home hoping to put a bullet into Sydney Hellier – nearly all those arrogant or stupid enough to have gathered in such numbers there that night were urgently wanted to help with various enquiries. It transpired that the short, fat man in the car with Ivers was Ernie O'Malley who had grown his hair long, and a beard, presumably hoping it would disguise him sufficiently to enable him to enjoy a short period out of hiding in order to attend what became known in police circles as 'the annual company dinner'.

'I just literally stumbled upon them,' I said to Patrick afterwards. Neither of us had asked about the aftermath of the hospital disaster, a too-sensitive subject by far. I do not suppose that James Carrick was making any kind of issue about it either. I think we were all leaving it up to Robert Kennedy to raise every kind of hell.

James had gone straight off to the hospital when all he was expected to do at Poplar Road had been completed. I knew that he would contact us eventually but right now his reunion with his father was a matter for strict privacy.

Michael Greenway was delighted with me for several reasons, but mostly for snatching the prize, or rather prizes, from right under F9's nose. I very much doubted that this would make any difference to Patrick's decision as to whether to stay with SOCA or not. He did not say so but I knew he was annoyed at having gone bald and brown for next to nothing.

*   *   *

Two months later, the brown having faded to a light tan – or that might have been as a result of having been out in the sun a lot while on leave – and his hair now at the very-short stage, we travelled on a short-notice visit to Hinton Littlemoor. It was term-time so the children were not with us. They were still happily chattering about their recent stay at the rectory; moving scarecrows, policemen who let them try on their helmets and told them stories when they were not on guard outside. I was greatly relieved that there were no bad memories or nightmares and Vicky had quickly realized that daddy might look different but still sounded the same and gave her even better rides on his shoulders around the garden. I think we have another horsewoman in the making.

Sufficient progress had been made with investigations into Lazlo Ivers – who was recovering from the bullet wound to the shoulder – and his cronies to ensure that most of them were still behind bars awaiting trial for various offences. Ivers' DNA had been discovered at Cliff Morley's flat, Exhibit A being the partially eaten Mars bar. More damning as far as Ivers was concerned was the discovery of sundry weapons, including an antique silver 'ritual' knife hidden beneath the floor of a garage at his rather smart semi-detached house in Wimbledon. This had traces of dried blood in the engraved haft, Morley's and Madderly Ritter's DNA having so far been identified therein.

Some of the others at the 'AGM', as I preferred to call it, were senior members of other gangs throughout the West Country and they had subsequently been parcelled out to various forces who were, one hoped, grilling them medium-rare in order to learn about their friends. Some of the names were, in anagram form, contained in the information on the CD ROMs on which Miss Dean had been working. Michael Greenway was continuing to put her analytical mind to further good use on a part-time basis.

'That's better!' Elspeth exclaimed when we walked through the front door of the rectory, her gaze on her son. 'I mean, I'm not a racist or anything but you do need your children to stay roughly the way they were born.'

'So how's the job?' John asked a little later when we were having drinks before dinner. 'Are you going to carry on with it?' He was addressing Patrick as neither he nor Elspeth are aware of my deep involvement, although I am sure the latter has more than a suspicion. She never mentions it.

'For the foreseeable future,' his son answered. 'I simply can't keep chopping and changing.'

'Perhaps this is one of the last times we'll all sit around the dining-room table,' John said sadly.

'Surely not!' I protested.

'It's too big to fit into one of those little bungalows the diocese want us to live in down the road. We'll have to sell it together with a lot of the other furniture – unless you can use it.'

Elspeth said, 'We've decided to carry on in the village for a while. The news has got out, goodness knows how, and people are really upset and have been begging John not to retire yet. So we'll stay until he really feels he can't go on.' She frowned. 'At least it's not right next door. I think I should hate that – being able to see people doing horrible things to my garden.'

'It's going on the market next month,' John told us.

'No, it isn't,' Patrick said. 'The place has already been sold by private treaty.'

'Oh!' Elspeth gasped. 'How do you know?'

'I've been in contact with the Church Commissioners.'

'When do we have to move out?'

'You don't. I'm buying it. That's what we've come to tell you.'

Whereupon his mother burst into tears.

'But how can you possibly afford to?' she asked when she had calmed down her delight a little. 'That's if you don't mind my asking.'

'Our house is up for sale and I did a bit of successful wrangling about this one. After all, they won't have to fund a new rectory for a while. And, as you're well aware, there's a dreadful shortage of clergy in the diocese.'

'You're all going to move here! But there are only three bedrooms and a box room!' Elspeth exclaimed.

'And a stable and large garage we don't really need that could be converted into accommodation for you and Dad with another couple of bedrooms over the top. There's room for a conservatory that could double as a sitting room and the present kitchen could be extended into that disused coal shed to give an area where the children could have their computer and do their homework. Ingrid and I and the children will have to live in a rented house while the work's being done.' He grinned at me. 'And Ingrid'll write a load more books to pay for it all.'

'We have money saved up,' Elspeth said. 'Not nearly enough to buy this house, of course, but we can help with the cost of the extensions.'

'That's to fund your retirement home on Sark.'

'We're not going. We've just sold the building plot. It would have been too far away and we would have hardly ever seen you or our friends.' She beamed. 'Perhaps we could stay and live here with you.'

We saved the other piece of news until last. The matter of the question mark.

That's what we called him: Mark.